# The Traveler's
# BEST SELLER

# The Traveler's
# Best Seller
*Rick Incorvia*

©Copyright 2018 by Rick Incorvia

Title ID: 8681544
ISBN-13: 978-1721819607

Published by Affinity Marketing &
Communications, Inc., Palm Harbor, FL, USA

# The Traveler's Best Seller

*Rick Incorvia*

# Chapter 1 – The Diagnosis

I scanned the packed stadium. First I took in the seats in front of me. Everyone was on their feet, clapping and waving their hands. Then I scanned across the expansive nose bleed section. I had to shield my eyes from the bright stage lights. I hadn't done a thing yet. Not a word, just walked out on stage. But there they were, twenty-five thousand people on their feet, looking at me, waiting for me to tell my story. After all, who can say they rode side by side in battle with George Washington, or played for kings and queens alongside Wolfgang Amadeus Mozart. My stories grew larger with every travel. The students loved my new passion for history. The faculty thought I was out of my mind. The FBI knew I was in over my head.

This whole thing was like a wild roller coaster ride. In my wildest dreams I couldn't have imagined the turn of events that brought me here. It actually did start out as a dream. The kind of dream that wakes you up. And I don't mean just from sleeping, I mean the kind of dream that wakes you up spiritually.

After all, I'm just the history teacher at a moderately-sized high school outside of Cleveland, Ohio. I never imagined people would want to hear my story, and certainly never expected to change the world for future generations. I certainly never imagined that I'd end up in a history book.

It wasn't always like this. I used to hate waking up, knowing I had to go to that school. It was a crappy job. At a crappy school. The kids were rotten, spoiled, self-centered brats who didn't give a damn about me. They were cell-phone zombies. There were the usual bullies and popular kids who were way too cool to care about other students, let alone my last-period history class. There were the kids who sat in the back trying not to be noticed, the kids who sat up front trying to be noticed, and everything in between. The bored looks on their faces were enough to suck the life out of me. I was trying to teach history to kids who weren't even mentally present. Most of them couldn't name the vice president, let alone the past presidents or other people of historical significance who'd brought us to where we are today. I don't want to try to describe every type of kid. That's not what this book is about. But I will say, after my diagnosis, I was able to see things in these kids that had once eluded me.

Today, I could look into Corrine's eyes and see the hurt. It pained her to be here. But she was only here physically. Her mind was a million miles away. I'll never forget the way she flinched when one of the guys sitting next to her raised his hand to answer a question. I imagined an abusive father or an alcoholic mother. Her clothes were old and out of style. She had an oversized, tattered jean jacket that she wore every day. Probably to mask that she wore the same clothes almost every day. Her hair, a dirty blond that was rarely washed and never got trimmed. She kept to herself, books held close to her body, eyes always looking at the floor or at her desk.

Jim Atson sat three rows back and always seemed to be taking notes. However, every time I got close to him, he would turn his paper over as if the page was full and he had to start on the other side. I fell for it the first few times, but every time I walked by? I don't think so.

Then there was William Smith. Billy was tall and strong and mean—the kind of guy who does mean things to the person unfortunate enough to be sitting in front of him. He recently signed his name with a permanent marker on the back of Theresa's white blouse. Those who were unfortunate enough to witness his abuse often chuckled out of fear that he would retaliate and make them his next victims.

Today, I'm sad for Billy. What kind of family turns out a kid this malicious? His reputation at school is awful, but the stories I've heard about his home life are frightening. At the age of twelve, he started the fire that killed his parents and little sister. He was playing with matches in the attic and jumped to safety when the fire got out of control. He broke both his legs on the jump. The rest of the family wasn't as lucky.

Then there's Dean and Gina, and Andrea for that matter. They pay attention. But I can tell it's out of pity or some form of respect that's been engrained by an adult figure. I can almost hear these kids willing me to be more interesting, wishing I had better control of my class, and wondering why I don't send Bully Billy to the principal's office when he disrupts the class for the third time.

I'm an average Joe, five feet, eight inches tall, five-nine if I stand up straight. I guess you would say I'm skinny. My light brown hair is thinning on top. I spend too much time using a little hand-held mirror to look at the top of my head. I've been a bit depressed since the divorce. Lately, I have to push myself out the door. I have a second-period class, a fourth-period class and a seventh-period class. I get a lot of down time, but that's by design. It's not worth driving home between classes, so I hang out in my empty classroom grading papers. That way I don't have to take work home. Sometimes I hang out in the teachers' lounge, reading.

It was the last period on a Friday and the kids were especially sluggish, ready for the weekend. But today was different for me and somehow the kids knew. I was quieter. I didn't look past the kids today to drone on about the war of 1812 while scratching chalk on the blackboard. Today I couldn't pretend that I didn't care about their lack of interest. Today I saw them. I imagined them years from now. They knew I was looking into their souls. I would randomly lock on someone's eyes, and unlike how it had always been before, my gaze stuck with them, to the point of discomfort.

Corinne looked especially sad today. Her hair was just a little greasier than usual, and her head hung just a bit lower than yesterday. I think I was staring at her for a moment or two before she looked up and we locked eyes. Her head slowly rose up as the hunch in her back straightened. She was empty. I could feel it. My heart ached at her loneliness. She blinked twice but never strayed from my robotic stare. I tried to deliver an encouraging smile, but I'm pretty sure I delivered pity.

I silently scanned the room noticing each individual's body language. I smiled sadly at Dean and Gina who were anxiously waiting for me to explain this weirdness. One student after another would silently pull me to them as if a magnetic force was at work. A silent exchange of emotions would change our relationship forever.

The silence slowly caught the interest of the other students. One at a time they looked up to see what all the non-commotion was about.

I just didn't have words. My mind raced as I imagined these young adults as little children, and then as grown men and women. I felt as if they knew exactly what I was seeing. There was an eerie silence in the class. Everyone knew this was a weird moment that would be talked about after class.

When I looked at Billy, a darkness fell over me. He was lightly tapping the metal tip of his pencil on the edge of his desk. When he caught my gaze, he realized that his tapping was the only noise in the room. He stared back at me for a moment and then quickly took in the class staring at the both of us. He was awkwardly reclined in his undersized desk-chair combo. A single bird could be heard chirping through the second-floor classroom's opened windows. My imagination ran wild as my stare burned a hole into him. A single tear ran down my face. In my imagined life scenario, Billy would die at the age of twenty-two: a drug deal gone bad. He could see that the usual fear in my eyes had been replaced by sadness. His lip quivered unexpectedly for just a moment, and he did a quick preventive swipe across his eye with his sleeve. He sat up in his seat and forced a deep sniff to thwart the snot that accompanies sadness.

That Friday, I dismissed class ten minutes early and promised that things were going to change. "I will care more. I will try to make class more interesting. I will try to teach you things that will change your lives for the better." My voice was quivering so I waved my hand dismissively. "Get out of here."

The nineteen kids in that class knew something had changed. They couldn't put a finger on it, but something was definitely different.

What those nineteen kids didn't know was that I had just received a Stage 4 lung cancer diagnosis. I had been told, "Get your life in order."

I was halfway home before I realized I hadn't turned on the radio, and my left blinker was still clicking loudly from my merge onto the highway ten minutes ago. Typically I liked the distraction of the radio, but today, I had plenty of distraction without it. The movie of my students played over and over in my head. The words the doctor said to me played over and over: "Get your life in order." What did that mean? Was there some kind of death checklist? The driver behind me gave a gentle double-tap on his horn, letting me know the light had turned green. When I got home, I parked the car in one of the open condo parking spots, glad I didn't have an actual garage for fear that I might take the coward's way out and close the door with the car running. I sat in the car for a long time not sure if I was speaking or thinking out loud. "Get your life in order."

I tapped in my four-digit door code and entered my first-floor condo. The silence smacked me in the face. I am a creature of habit. I ran through my routine. I hung my keys on the hook and placed my worn leather briefcase snug against the wall near the door. Any moment now, my long-haired orange and white cat would emerge from the series of boxes I'd configured into an elaborate cat house. Baxter would be stretching and flexing his paws as if to show off his long claws before tucking them away in preparation of my ritual: scoop and squeeze, hug and kiss before filling his food bowl. It was the only way to get him to leave me alone while I cooked. I'm not sure when pushing microwave buttons became "cooking" in my world. Today I questioned every routine. As I pried open the tiny box labeled "Healthy Choice Meal," I got sick to my stomach. For all I knew, the last few years of microwave food might have been the reason for the cancer diagnosis. I didn't know, and the doctor either didn't know or wasn't telling me. When Leanne left me, I'd fallen into a funk. I quit going out; I stopped cooking. Hell, I had groceries delivered right to the house. Going to work was more than enough human interaction for me. I dumped the frozen meal into the garbage, promising myself that I would take the garbage out to the community dumpster before it started to stink. I figured that gave me a day—maybe two if I stayed out of the kitchen.

I loosened my boring brown tie and studied it for a moment. It was next to go into the trash. I was in a mood. I peeled off my clothes and kicked them into a corner. I roamed the condo in my underwear, taking in the photos on the wall, the furniture, the fixtures, wondering why I'd picked them. The litter box needed cleaning but I couldn't stomach it. I went into my spare bedroom, now my home office, and stepped onto the scale. I had lost two more pounds. I thought about tossing the scale into the garbage along with my dinner and my tie. I grabbed my laptop and brought it to the kitchen table. I put on a pot of coffee and typed in my log-in. The end-of-life diagnosis weighed in on me like a ton of bricks.

I slowly typed in four words.

E n d  o f  l i f e  i n s p i r a t i o n

Death, dying, end-of-life hospice, inspirational poems. End-of-life stages, end-of-life planning, end-of-life issues, end-of-life signs, end of life. End of life. I laid my finger hard onto the scroll down button and watched as entry after entry scrolled down the page like long movie credits in fast motion. When I got to the bottom there was a new button to push. It simply said, "NEXT 2,786,545 results." I pushed next to see page two results and again watched as the long page scrolled on forever to the very bottom. I did the same for page three and page four, my eyes not even focused on the words. The very last entry on page four caught my attention. It said, "In Your Dreams."

When I clicked on the link I saw a picture of Einstein and big headlines: "If you could meet anyone in the world from the past, who would you visit?" To a history teacher with a death sentence, this might as well have been crack or heroin. The site went on to talk about technology meeting history. The premise was that historical information, personality profiles and basic human interaction tendencies could be gathered about a person from the past to create a virtual replica of that person. You could meet Einstein and have a conversation with him. The technology would allow interaction, much like computer simulation games. The site spoke of top-of-the-line virtual reality body gear. The interaction was touted as being as real as it gets.

I wanted to know more, but the home page wouldn't scroll down. The site was frozen. A part of me laughed that a place touting such state-of-the-art technology couldn't even get its website to work. And let's not even discuss their ranking. So while waiting out the lag, I looked around the part of the page I could see. At the top of the screen were a few tabs.

"Our Story - Absinthe - Dreams - Contact us"

I clicked the first button. Nothing. I clicked on "Absinthe." Again nothing. I skipped over to "Contact us" and clicked. The tab darkened and began to redirect.

A page full of words flashed on the screen for a few seconds and then crashed. I tried it a second time. It crashed again. I was ready the third time and as soon as the site opened I took a screenshot. Moments later, the site once again crashed, but I had captured at least page one.

I pasted it into a document so I could read it.

"This is much more than dreaming. This is unconscious reality. You can meet Edward Jenner, the father of immunology; you can talk to Wolfgang Amadeus Mozart about his childhood, about music, about his father. You can have lunch with the great philosopher Immanuel Kant or discuss the problems of the late 1700s with George Washington. We have over 60 historical profiles for you to choose from."

The last few lines of the captured page spoke about absinthe.

"When a small amount of absinthe is mixed with our classified proprietary blend, you are taken to your destination. You become a time traveler. This is the time machine you never thought possible in your lifetime."

I wanted to know more but the site seemed to have been hacked, or was under some kind of cyber-attack. Maybe it was a government shutdown for all I knew. I looked back at the tab marked Absinthe. It wouldn't open, but I certainly could look it up elsewhere online.

I learned that absinthe was used in ancient times to remedy miscellaneous ills. It was well known and referenced in literature as a bitter-tasting plant that induced streams of consciousness. In the late 1800s, it was embraced as a drink by poets, artists and other creative, bohemian types. It was banned in the early 1900s because of its extreme side effects, which included hallucinations and disorientation. Absinthe has recently had a modern revival and it's no longer illegal in many countries.

I looked back at the last few words on the screenshot I'd saved. "This is the time machine you never thought possible in your lifetime." The words "in your lifetime" struck a chord.

I looked for a phone number, an address. Nowhere. I scoured the Internet for more information about businesses that use absinthe. I tried all sorts of key words: time travel, meet Einstein, In Your Dreams. I was led to one strange site after another but none of them related to this so-called place of time travel. I poured myself a second cup of coffee. In desperation, I retyped into the search bubble every word from the page that I'd caught in my screenshot.

A page popped up, labeled *Top 10 Most Compelling Pieces of Evidence That Time Travel is Real.* The link referenced The Montauk Project, John Titor, the Hadron Collider and even the Nicolas Cage theory. I was ready to leave the ridiculous site when the words "In Your Dreams" caught my attention again. At the end of this top-ten list, after the words "In Your Dreams" was a link. I stared at it for a long time. I placed the cursor over the link. Again, I hesitated.

When I finally found the courage to withstand more disappointment, I clicked. A long redirect finally opened to a blank page. I slumped in my chair and then sighed deeply. I closed my eyes and rested back on the now uncomfortable kitchen chair. When I opened my eyes, there it was. The same site I'd found nearly an hour earlier. There was Einstein smiling at me. "If you could meet anyone in the world from the past, who would you visit?" This didn't look like a legitimate webpage. It had the same first landing page as the original but no links, no additional tabs, no other pages. After one paragraph with familiar language about historical information, personality profiles and basic human interaction tendencies being gathered on a person from the past to create a virtual replica of that person, the page seemed to end abruptly. Except for a final sentence: "Call Ann for additional information. Time Travel." But no number. Anger pulsated through my tired and aching bones. Another goddamn dead end.

I re-read the paragraph three more times, wondering how someone could expect you to call them without giving you a number. Everything about this stupid site pissed me off. Everything about this site also intrigued me. As a history teacher, I had a hundred questions for Mozart. Two hundred for George Washington.

I read the closing words one last time. "Call Ann for additional information. Time Travel." Maybe the number was in the word "Time Travel." It had the right number of letters. I began to scratch digits onto the white envelope next to my keyboard. T-8 i-4 m-6 e-3. The number began to form: 846-387-2835. "Time travel." I laughed at myself for thinking it was possible—as I prepared to dial.

The phone rang endlessly, ten, maybe twelve times. I was about to hang up when someone picked up the phone. After a long moment of silence on both ends, a timid female voice whispered as if she didn't want to wake the person next to her. "Hello." I was silent for a moment and the woman softly hung up. I looked at my phone, trying to put a face to the voice that had spoken that one word.

I dialed again. The phone rang fourteen times before it was answered. This time I said "Hello?" There was no response, but I knew someone was listening. "Please don't hang up. I have been trying to find you for a long time."

After another moment of silence, the soft voice asked, "How did you get this number?"

"From the Internet... End of life... I'm dying." I unexpectedly put it all out there in one chopped-up sentence.

"Why would you call me?" The soft voice tried to hide that she already knew why I called. With every moment it became clearer that this was not a business that was on the up and up. As a man who always followed the rules, I was surprised that I just didn't give a damn if this was illegal or immoral—or even dangerous. I was dying. I had been so busy doing all the right things; I hadn't made time to live before I died.

I said one more word. "Please." It was just one word. But it was one word from a dying man. A final word, a wish spoken with desperation, in a barely audible voice.

Finally, she replied. "How long do you have?"

I let the question sink in. She was only the second person I'd shared my news with. I imagined that I would answer this question a hundred times in the months to follow. "Four months, maybe five, I'm told." I took a deep breath and continued. "Stage 4 cancer." And then I began to ramble. "I'm a history teacher. I have questions for Einstein. I want to have lunch with George Washington. I want to have passionate, insightful stories to teach my students about history."

The soft female voice carried a hint of Asian descent. "Where are you calling from?"

I quickly offered up, "Cleveland." She responded enthusiastically. "Oh, you're actually pretty close to us. How is your strength?" I had been feeling especially tired every day for the last few months, but I'd thought it was depression. I would come home, eat and go right to bed. "Why do you ask? How strong do I have to be to dream?"

She was quiet for a long time. I worried that I might have crossed a line by mentioning dreaming. "It is a two-hour drive to my office. Are you sure you're up for it? People are often very tired after a session."

I responded quickly. "This is very important to me. If I'm too tired after a session, I can get a hotel room."

Again... a long silence. "How do I know you are legit?" she said, this time sounding just a bit gangster.

# Chapter 2 – Caution to the Wind

I stopped at the bank at 9:05 the next morning to pull out the $8,000 she charged for the adventure. Hell, if it was a rip off scam, I would die with a little less money in the bank. The address she gave me was supposed to be right across from Stark State College of Technology, just under two hours from my place.

The drive was very different from yesterday's drive home from the school. I think I felt hope. The drive went quickly. I looked at people at red lights tapping away on their cell phones. A couple of days ago, this would have pissed me off. Today? I just smiled sadly. I wondered which ones would live to be wise, old patriarchs or matriarchs of their families and which ones wouldn't survive the car ride to their destinations. As I got farther south, traffic lights and buildings were replaced with rolling fields, wildflowers and dilapidated wooden farm houses. I imagined those houses captured in a photograph, painted and hanging in an art gallery. As I closed in on the address, small clusters of rural businesses were separated by long stretches of overgrown fields. The equivalent of a Wal-Mart for farmers displayed tractors, fencing, riding mowers and stacks of livestock feed. On my left, another wild field of brilliant purple and yellow flowers caught my attention. I was ahead of schedule. I cut sharply across the left lane, prompting a long blast from an oncoming eighteen-wheeler. I smiled to myself, thinking, "Bite me! What are you going to do, kill me a few months ahead of schedule?" I skidded to an abrupt stop on the gravelly dirt berm and slammed the car into park. The trucker gave me a long, parting double salute from his horn as he sped along his way.

I opened the door of my Honda Accord. Just like me, my car is conservative and getting pretty old. I remember the day I bought the car, twelve years ago. The salesman said, "These cars last forever." Who would have known that it would outlive me?

I left the door open and ventured into the wildflower field. The stalks were a good five feet tall. They seemed to go on forever. I was in awe of Mother Nature. I put my arms out and walked deeper into the field, letting the tops of the flowers skim across the underside of my outstretched arms. The sun beat down on my face, at first forcing me to close my eyes. Then I realized this was a blessing. I took step after step, deep into that wilderness, without opening my eyes. The sounds were like a mystical orchestra. The smells like nothing I'd ever encountered. The sun finally tucked behind a cloud, and I opened my eyes. I took a few more steps and the endless flowers opened up into a clearing. I froze. Eight deer were staring at me as if I were some kind of demon. Their legs stiffened, tails went up. Most of them were lying down but ready to react. I pretended not to see them and slowly sat down at the edge of the field. I closed my eyes, hoping to become one with them. I opened my eyes about a minute later to the sound of a big deer snorting in disapproval of the doe that was inching her way up to me. I pretended to close my eyes again but peeked through blurry eyelashes. Another loud snort popped my eyes wide open, startling the doe just as she was about to sniff my face. She bounced backwards like a startled cat, and the herd erupted into a loud stampede. Hooves pounded the ground all around me as the confused gang stomped around trying to decide which way to run. Thirty seconds later the noise was replaced by silence. My heart was the loudest noise in the field, and I fell back with both hands on my chest. I stared at the brilliant sun for just a moment longer than I should have. I finally closed my eyes and laid in the silence as one insect after another found the courage to start adding its instrument back into the orchestra.

I was tired. I wanted to sleep. But twenty minutes from now I was supposed to meet Ann. I stood awkwardly, wishing I had something to hold on to while I worked out the kinks in my equilibrium. A rush of panic flooded my body when it occurred to me that I'd left eight thousand dollars under the front seat, the car door open and the keys in the ignition.

When I got back to the car, I found an occupant rummaging through it. A fat raccoon was attempting to drag off my small thermal-lined lunch bag. I'd packed an overnight bag and a few snacks just in case I would be too tired to drive back. I tried to scare off the raccoon, but he sloppily hissed at me, the straps of my lunchbox still in his mouth. I didn't really care. I wasn't hungry anyway. I smiled as he dragged my lunch off into the wildflowers. I wanted to stay and watch him figure out how to unzip the bag, but it was time to go.

When I got to the address, my heart sank. It was an abandoned gas station. I turned the car off and slumped back into my seat. Why would someone play such a cruel joke on a dying man? I bounced my forehead off the steering wheel three times. Then I felt it: the eyes on me, watching my every move. I sat up straight and looked around for another vehicle. I got out of the car and walked around, looking. Where were those eyes? I felt them. She was watching me, and I knew it. This definitely was an illegal operation and she had to make sure I was legit. I was on stage; I had to look like a dying man and not a cop or whoever else might want to stop her from fulfilling my dreams. I walked up to the dirty gas station windows and swiped away a four-inch swath of dirt. I cupped my hands and pushed my face to the window to see if I could see inside. As expected, it was dark and empty. I turned dramatically and let my body slide down the glass wall, cupping my hands over my face as if to sob. I bounced my shoulders just enough for the sob effect, all the while peeking through my fingers. I sat for two long minutes before starting to doubt my intuition. Had I just imagined being watched? As I made my way back to the car, I heard my phone ringing where I'd left it on the passenger-side seat. I spun around one last time trying to locate the person that I know for certain was watching me. I spotted it: the front half of a black car, across the street almost a hundred yards south of me. It was tucked between two buildings. I nodded my head and smiled gently towards the car, as I opened the door of mine.

"Hello," I said, in an awkward position, knees on the driver's seat and right hand holding the headrest of the passenger seat.

"I'm sorry, I had to make sure it was you," that familiar voice said, just above a whisper.

"What now?" I whispered back as if someone might hear me in this deserted, remote location.

"Follow me." The black car's headlights flashed twice, and the car jerked forward. As it got closer, she slowed and flashed her lights one more time. I started up my old Accord and quickly forced the shifter into drive. The car jolted forward, almost stalling. I made a sharp U-turn and stepped on the gas to catch up to the sedan, which I could now recognize as a late-model Oldsmobile. I still couldn't see her through the car's tinted windows. I didn't want to spook her, so I stayed back a few car lengths more than my usual. About half a mile down the road, we made a right turn and then a left into a small plaza, typical of Ohio strip-malls in 2008, all overgrown foliage and what looked like a ghost town. It was a three-tenant building but the two end units were boarded up. The middle unit had a small sign next to the door that said Ann Tranz Dental. I saw it right away. If you switched the names, you could read it as Tranz Ann Dental. Transcendental. I don't know; maybe it didn't mean anything.

Her window came down just enough for a hand to motion for me to park right in front of her storefront. She backed up into the spot next to me so that we were face to face. I lowered my window and we officially met for the first time. A petite woman of Asian descent, she smiled and introduced herself simply as Ann. I introduced myself as "the history teacher." I felt it said more about me than a name could. "OK, History Teacher, we need to take care of business first." I reached under my seat, pulled out my discreetly wrapped bundle of money and extended it to her. "I'm going to need your driver's license as well." That made me suspicious and I gave her a skeptical look. She remained firm, flicking her fingers, indicating for me to hurry up. What the hell. What do I have to lose? I obliged, and she tucked the paper bag and my license under her front seat. She proceeded to get out of the car.

She was even shorter than I'd thought from first sight. "Come with me," she said in her wispy voice.

She fiddled with a handful of keys before unlocking the door. Once inside, she locked the door behind us. That's when I saw the man come from around the side of the building and get into her car. He screeched out of the parking lot.

Now I looked sadly at Ann, wondering, "Is this some kind of hoax? Are you really taking advantage of a dying man?"

She answered my unspoken question in her monotone. "He is going to count and secure your money. As long as he calls me with good news in the next five minutes, everything will go as planned." Behind a waiting room was a hall. Ann led me past three rooms with dental chairs and the usual paraphernalia. She stopped at a door marked "Private Staff Only." She punched in a numeric code and looked at her watch before entering what looked like a storage room for supplies. I tried to take in as much as I could. There was a sink with cupboards above, and a side wall with folding doors like you might see hiding a washer and dryer in an apartment. She looked at her watch again and opened the folding doors. Nothing there but a six-foot-wide wall of shelves holding dental products. She hesitated, nervously checking her watch again. I tried to make sense of this as I took in some of the products, oddly looking like they were on display in this private room. There was a whole shelf of something called Septocaine. Another shelf held boxes of Activa Bioactive Restorative and another product labeled Aquaprene. I noticed two boxes of Pentron syringes and some kind of refill packs. I tilted my head to read the instructions but was interrupted by the old-school ringtone on Ann's phone. "OK. Good... Yes, we are ready to enter." She tucked the phone back into her rear pants pocket and slipped on a long white surgical jacket. "Excuse me,

Mr. History Teacher, it's time." She motioned for me to step away from the shelves. She pulled some kind of a hidden lever inside the shelving and I heard a click. The doors slowly parted and opened just a bit, as if spring-loaded. Ann pushed the doors the rest of the way open, exposing a well-kept secret lab. It had been carefully disguised to look like a boarded-up rental space under construction.

Inside were two men wearing surgical masks. The first briefly acknowledged me with a nod. The second kept his eyes locked on a monitor the size of a small home theater. He must have gotten the beep he was looking for and began typing away. Three smaller monitors lit up directly in front of him. The first showed a diagram of a human head dissected into sections, each one meticulously labeled and color-coded. A few more taps on the keyboard and different parts of the brain lit up. He seemed happy with his progress and moved on to the middle monitor. This one seemed to track heart rate and blood pressure. On the third monitor, two words flashed softly at the top of the screen: "Cranial stimulators." The man looked at Ann and spoke through his mask. "Stage one is ready."

# Chapter 3 – Maiden Voyage

He caught me by surprise. "Ready for what? What is stage one?"

Ann must have seen the panic in my eyes. "Sorry." She explained, "Stage one is simple questions and answers. We find out more about you. We find out who you want to meet and what you hope to get out of your visit. We also want to make sure you are healthy enough to travel."

My heart was pounding erratically. Ann was telling me to relax and that she needed to take my vitals. She wrapped a blood pressure thingy around my arm and began to pump it up. For the first time, it was apparent that I was either about to take the trip of a lifetime or, more likely, about to be taken for $8,000 and put to sleep forever, here in the middle of nowhere. Then it occurred to me: if I am about to be put to sleep, it will save me from the final stages of cancer. I may as well go all in. Ann's voice faded back in. "Are you allergic to phenobarbital?"

I quickly answered "No," remembering I'd had phenobarbital years ago during a minor surgery. "In the event that we would decide to give you phenobarbital, you could experience the following side effects." She began listing side effects.

"Dizziness, drowsiness, excitation, aggression, confusion, loss of balance or coordination..." By the third side effect, I was no longer listening; instead, I'd gotten lost in my own head. The more fuss they went through before putting me under, the more I started to believe I was actually going to meet my historical heroes. She poked and prodded at me for another fifteen minutes and then slid a laptop in front of me. "Please answer the following multiple-choice questions by circling your most likely answer and crossing out your least likely answer. Then answer the twenty-four questions with one or two-sentence answers, saying the first thing that comes to your mind. This will be the only time you will have to answer these behavioral questions. They will help us understand how you like to be interacted with. It helps us choose settings and a program that will best fit your comfort zone."

I think she was waiting for a response from me, but I was speechless.

"When you come back for future travels, we can just get right into the jump," she went on. I was in la la land. I just kept waiting for whatever was next. "Let me know when you are finished with the assessment," she concluded.

The three of them met in front of the three monitors and pointed and mumbled short, inaudible phrases obviously not meant for my ears. Forty long minutes later I was finished with my behavioral assessment.

"OK, Mr. History Teacher, it's time to choose your adventure."

"Tim Peregrine," I finally acknowledged. I thought it best she knew my name at this stage. She smiled, as friendly as could be. "I know, Mr. Peregrine. We ran your plates, your personal records and your medical files. We know all about you. Don't you worry; you're going to love this adventure. You are a perfect candidate." She gave me a minute to let all that sink in. "Now, take all the time you need and decide who you want to visit from the booklet in front of you."

I scanned the pages, getting more excited with each new name I read.

Edward Jenner was considered the father of immunology and a major influence on medical advancements. During his time, smallpox was ravaging the population. Jenner developed the vaccine that would hold the bugs at bay; he set a whole new path by which vaccination would revolutionize medicine, ultimately leading to the eradication of smallpox worldwide.

Next on the list was one of my favorites, Wolfgang Amadeus Mozart.

Mozart was one of the most popular musicians in world history. He was the very definition of a child savant and made huge leaps and bounds in classical music. He was an eccentric character and a celebrity of his time. His impact upon music, one of the great threads of any cultural fabric, is almost incalculable.

I scrolled past the philosopher Immanuel Kant and the mathematician Leonhard Euler to get to George Washington, our first president.

The Eighteenth Century was marked by two major events, one of them being the French Revolution. The other, of course, was the American Revolution of the late 1770's that separated the United States from the British Empire. George Washington was the man who commanded the American forces against the British army. America's significance grew out of the

Revolutionary War, and Washington was the man who, first and foremost, founded this nation. Our nation, which would become the greatest superpower the world has ever seen.

This had to be the starting point of my journey. I looked up at Ann and said the words: "George Washington."

She escorted me to what might as well have been an alien spaceship. I was seated and strapped into some kind of a hi-tech gamer's cockpit. There were light-emitting diodes, speakers, dials and monitors everywhere. I could see my heart rate in the top corner of one of the screens, 135 and climbing. "Just relax, Mr. Peregrine. This is going to be most pleasant."

I looked up at Ann. "Am I supposed to be able to fly this thing?"

For the first time, I heard Ann laugh. "No, Mr. Peregrine, this is how we monitor your reactions to the simulations. We can also control the temperature; we can make it night and day or rain or shine. This will seem very..." she hesitated to get my attention and repeated herself, "very real. We will monitor you every step of the journey and if we ever feel you are overstimulated, you will hear one of our voices reminding you that you are in fact sitting right here, safe and sound. As long as we can keep your vitals at a safe level... the simulation will continue."

She began to place peel-and-stick electrodes on various locations on my body including one on each temple. "I'm going to shave a small patch of your chest hair to attach this monitor and clip these sensors onto a couple of your fingers."

"Sqveeze, please." The assistant's accent told me he was probably Russian as he placed a spongy dog toy in my hand. He swabbed the bulging vein in my arm and looked me right in the eyes as he said, muffled through his surgical mask, "You're gonna love dis." He expertly penetrated my vein and attached an IV. Ann nodded to the assistant, and he gave a syringe two flicks of his finger. He smiled proudly as he released whatever it was into my bloodstream.

Ann worked some fairly heavy virtual reality goggles onto my head, turning the room black. I remember thinking they were too heavy and would pull my head forward. But as she reclined my seat, the weight of the goggles gently eased my head back into the comfortable cushiony seat. "Just relax, Mr. Peregrine. Think about what you're going to say to George Washington." I felt a tingle in my left arm and began to get dizzy.

I remember hearing the other man's voice for the first time. "Starting the program."

The last words I remember hearing were from Ann. "OK, Mr. History Teacher, time for the teacher to become the student." She eased padded headphones over my ears and the room silenced.

When my awareness came back, I was on a bumpy ride, hearing the clippety-clop of horse hooves. The smell of horse and wood and hay lit up my senses. It was real! I was going to see George Washington!

Cautiously, I opened my eyes. I was the only passenger in a bouncing carriage. I looked down to take in the fabric I was seated on, as it felt like velvet to the touch. Brown wood trim, expertly crafted and sanded, decorated the door, and the small window on each side of the carriage. The weather was chilly, and a hint of fog filled the morning air. I could hear birds, but the predominant noise came from the carriage's wheels along the rough ground and the horse's hoof beats. As we slowed down, I slid over to the window to take in the rolling green grass. That's when I saw Mount Vernon, George Washington's mansion, in all its glory. Tall trees adorned both sides of the huge white house, which had a red roof and black shutters. A massive dirt driveway went from the road to the main entrance, circling a football-field-sized area as green as could be. There had to be twenty windows on the front of the house and three entrances. The roof was nicely pitched with two towering chimneys. In the center of the roof was an eight-sided cupola.

When the carriage turned right onto the circular driveway, I had to scoot over to the left window to see the house. That's when I saw him: a tall man with gray hair, chopping wood. I watched him split two pieces before setting the head of the ax on the ground. He pulled a white handkerchief out of his back pocket and wiped his forehead and the back of his neck. He leaned heavily on the handle of the ax to aid him in a stretch to regain the tall posture that George Washington was known for. Spotting the coach, he let the ax fall to the ground and began to straighten his clothes.

This puzzled me at first. George Washington chopping his own wood? By the front door of his mansion? I started to think about that old story about the cherry tree and little George. I always tell my students that story is completely bogus. But as the coach circled and I lost sight of George through the tiny opening, I forgot all that. I slid back to the other side to take in the residence. Big, stout block after block formed the face of the house and nearly a dozen upstairs windows with tic-tac-toe wooden dividers supported small panes of glass, making up the four-by-four-foot windows. I had to stick my head out to see the eight-sided tower on the rooftop. Each side had the same tic-tac-toe window design, but these windows were at least eight feet tall. From that tower room, you would be able to see friend or foe coming from quite a distance. And from any direction.

The horses stopped abruptly and George Washington himself surprised me as he reached into the carriage to unlatch the door. Odd that he wouldn't have a servant—a slave—to do this for him. Just like he ought to have somebody else chopping his wood...

"Good day, traveler. I have been expecting you." As I stepped out of the van—I mean carriage—I noticed that my recent aches and pains were gone. I felt healthy and quite vibrant. I was greeted with a strong handshake and an odd opening line. "By law, I must let you know that you have not actually traveled in time. You are safe and sound in the year 2017." Not the greeting I expected. I hoped it would be the last time I was reminded.

"Come in and meet the missus! We have a very busy day. We can talk along the way. Are you a strong rider?" I nodded my head "Yes," hoping the program would oblige. I knew George Washington was an expert rider, one of the best in his day. I had ridden when I was young, but only a few times, and always remembered having a healthy respect for a horse's size and power, wondering if I could manage it. "Good. I have a strong steed for you," he said with a nod.

He escorted me to the house's central entrance. As he lifted the clunky latch, and the thick wooden door swung open, the smell of meat, butter and musty air filled my nostrils.

The initial room was quite grand. Huge paintings hung in the few spots between the many windows. A twelve-person table setting was perfectly arranged, with white table cloths, dishes and glassware. Silverware was tightly wrapped in white linen napkins. Wooden chairs with checkered upholstery on the seats were lined up perfectly. We walked right past this table, thank goodness. We walked past room after room full of expertly crafted furniture. It looked fairly simple but solid, as if George had built it himself. An armchair with a soft round cushion was pulled up to a desk with at least 10 drawers. I think it was his office. I wanted to stop and open every drawer and inspect every quill pen, every note, every inkwell. He walked by way too fast on his way to a comfy room off the kitchen. Servants were toiling in the kitchen; the smell of meat and bread hung in the air.

"My manner of living is plain," he started out. "I hope you are not put out by it. We have tea or coffee, sliced tongue and fresh bread." When I didn't speak, he continued. "We can offer you buttered eggs if tongue is not to your liking. The butter was made fresh this morning." His proper diction amused me.

"Tongue, please," I said with a smirk.

Mr. Washington continued. "Breakfast is quite relaxed here. Those who expect more will be disappointed."

Soft steps could be heard on the wooden floor. A handsome middle-aged woman entered with one of the kitchen servants. This must be Mrs. Washington! The servant carried a tray of hot bread and an assortment of dishes, saucers and silverware. "Ahh, Martha, this is Mr. Peregrine from almost 250 years into the future. He'll be joining us for the day."

"Good day, Mr. Peregrine. Would you like coffee or tea with your toast and tongue?" The servant behind her waited patiently for my response.

Martha had her hair covered with a white bonnet-like cap with a frilly trim. Her garb was a mix between a fancy robe and a casual dress with an exaggerated ruffled collar. As the kitchen servant placed the tray of fresh bread on the table, Martha delicately shook my hand. The servant wore a long skirt with a white apron from the waist down. Her puffy white bonnet looked like it hid a large head of hair. The white sleeves, tight on her dark arms, ended just below her elbows. She smiled and curtsied ever so slightly, awkwardly tugging at her apron.

"Coffee, please." I finally muttered. The smell of fresh bread had me lifting my nose towards the ceiling to take it all in. Rolls about the size of a New York bagel sat in the middle of the dark wooden table alongside a plate of thinly sliced tongue that was feathered like a hand of cards. Martha extended a kitchen knife to George, but he gave her the "talk to the hand" sign and looked right at me. "No need for the formalities, Martha. Mr. Peregrine and I are going to get to know each other quite well today." He grabbed two of the oversized rolls with the biggest hand I'd ever seen and placed one on my plate. He tore his in half and laid one of the halves back onto his plate. He knew I was watching. He dipped it in a saucer of butter, stabbed two pieces of the thinly sliced tongue and draped it over the bread. He leaned over his plate and took a huge bite of his quickly assembled "breakfast sandwich." I tried to remember what I knew about the Earl of Sandwich and his invention. Would that idea have gotten to America this quickly? But I forgot all about this as George slid the saucer of butter between us and silently tilted his head to give me the official "Let's eat" signal. He dipped a second time and motioned for Martha to join us. "Come, come," He said through a mouthful of bread and tongue.

"Nonsense, George. You know I don't eat tongue and bread; certainly not in the morning."

George motioned again for her to join us. "Martha prefers hoe cakes. Much like your pancakes but made with corn instead of wheat. She likes them with melted butter and honey."

"George knows that I ate my breakfast hours ago. When he gets into one of his moods to chop wood, I don't know how long he'll be out there." I smiled and nodded, wishing I had more to say. I was awestruck. I was eating toast and tongue with George and Martha Washington. I caught Martha glance George's way, perhaps just a bit put off by his breakfast manners. I had to force myself to remember that this is all virtual reality. An awkward silence filled the room as George double dipped the other half of his roll. Could the Father of our Country's table manners be a programming error? "I don't know where George's manners are this morning. We usually say grace before meals." That was reassuring. At least Martha had been programmed to act like a proper eighteenth-century hostess.

"Yes, yes, my apologies." George wiped his hands on the beige cloth in his lap, closed his eyes and extended his hands to the both of us. That was a familiar and reassuring gesture, I thought. But was it authentic?

"Oh Lord, with humble hearts we pray thy blessing this day and that at this table we are blessed. That thou will come to share the yield thy bounty given to farm and field. Thank you, God for all that grows; thank you for these friends of mine. Amen."

Martha and I chimed in with our "Amen." "So, Mr. Peregrine—"

"Please, call me Tim."

Martha nodded in approval and continued. "Please tell us, Tim, how different is your future?"

"Much different in many ways. Still the same in other ways, Mrs. Washington." I looked back towards George and began to ramble excitedly. "The Constitution that you signed in 1787 is still shrined in Washington, D.C., which is still the capital, and there are now fifty United States."

George straightened up and leaned back in his chair, blinking with confusion. "Fifty?... Where did they put them all?"

I smiled and continued. "The Constitution has been amended twenty-seven times but it's still the working Constitution."

George refocused on his meal, his last bite squeezed between his buttery thumb and finger.

"And we are the strongest nation in the world!" I stopped talking and dipped my toast and tongue. I let it drip onto my plate. George seemed to be trying to figure out the layout of fifty states. I continued as if teaching one of my classes. "The horse and buggy only exists in remote locations because of the invention of the automobile."

George looked over at Martha and then back at me. "Tell me of this automobile."

I tore off a bite of the dripping bread and spoke with a bit of a muffle. "A century from now, a man named Henry Ford will begin to mass-produce a motorized coach. He will sell over ten thousand in his first year! Today..." I hesitated and clarified, "Today, meaning 250 years from now, these vehicles can drive themselves to a predetermined location, without a driver."

George backed up to a full upright position. "How is this possible?"

I ignored his question and continued. "There is more. The post office is nearly obsolete because every man, woman and child old enough to read carries a hand-held device, about the size of a wallet." I wished I hadn't been required to leave behind all my high-tech devices. But a good teacher can make a point using an analogy. I pulled out my wallet and flipped it open like an old flip phone. "You can immediately talk to anyone, anywhere in the world by pushing their personal numerical code." I pretended to tap in a number.

"Nonsense. This is talk of another planet. Martha, are you hearing this?" I could see George's mind running a mile a minute trying to imagine the uses of such an invention. "What about letters?" He began fidgeting in his chair. "Do people still write letters?"

I smiled a sad smile. George had written hundreds of letters over his years, many that changed the course of time and some simply to loved ones. "Yes, Mr. Washington, some people still write letters. And all your hand-written letters have been saved and are archived for all to read. Your letters to generals, to Congress, your pleas for more troops, more supplies, more food, more clothes." George's mouth tightened, and his thumb and forefinger massaged his lips. Perhaps he was reflecting on the hardships of his military life; for whatever reason, the room was suddenly silent. I wondered if I had shared too much, too fast. Martha politely excused herself, obviously uncomfortable. She nodded to her servant to help her clear the table.

George gave his mouth one last wipe and firmly stood. His chair slid back and nearly tipped when one of the legs got snagged in a groove, no doubt worn into the floor by George himself over many years of breakfast. "Let us get on with our day. The farm isn't going to run itself."

I took the last big bite of my bread and tongue sandwich, wishing I hadn't said quite so much. The napkin fell from my lap to the floor as I stood. I bent to pick it up, once again noting the painless flexibility that had been given to me in the traveler's form.

George sat on a wooden stool by the door, silently changing to his riding boots. The shirt and shoes that I'd been wearing moments ago were replaced by boots that laced up over my calves. I took in my new ruffled white shirt and the thin leather coat that hung almost to my knees. I was feeling very 1700's, sporting white ruffles that poked out of both jacket sleeves.

I could tell George was lost somewhere between the past and the future. Selfishly, I decided not to say more about the future. I'd come here to talk about the past. I asked him if he minded if we talked about some of the famous battles he'd fought in, but by a non-response, he silently dismissed my comment.

As we headed for the stables, George suddenly stopped dead in his tracks. "Instant communication." He was lost in thought for a moment, then continued, "to anyone, anywhere, at the push of a button." I nodded, realizing how this must seem like a fairy tale to George, and disappointed that for our generation, it's simply taken for granted.

We continued into the stable. I wanted to stop and touch everything, but George was now stepping with authority. We walked past a single-axle cart with big wagon wheels. Two rake-like features were mounted behind the cart. I think it was a homemade gang plow. I imagined that it might be used to pull vegetables from the vine. A big tree stump had a hand-made ax stuck into it, and a long, bent rod of some kind lying next to it. We were walking past what I thought was an empty stall when a huge, all black horse's head popped up, startling me, its eyes wide. George ignored the horse and walked past two more empty stalls. He announced himself to a muscular all-white horse, which greeted him with a stately nod. As I watched Mr. Washington interact with his horse, he pointed to a tall, three-legged stool just outside the stall across from him. "That's your saddle. You'll be riding Amory." On cue, the proud horse shook her head like a supermodel fluffing her hair for a commercial. She was huge! I was immediately intimidated. "Talk to her," he said. He spent a brief moment acknowledging his own horse. Its name, "Nelson," was carved into the door of the stall. I positioned myself so I could watch George, careful to saddle up my horse just like he did. He grabbed the twist of the saddle, stepped into the stirrup and whipped his long body over his horse. Nelson did all the adjusting as if Mr. Washington had mounted him 10,000 times. I mimicked his every move and mounted my shiny light brown horse. She adjusted to my sloppy mount and proudly raised her head, shaking her mane. "She's beautiful," I said, adjusting my ass into the saddle, hoping she would respect me as her rider.

"She ought to be," he responded, the pride obvious in his voice. "She's a Narragansett Pacer."

I was familiar with the Narragansett Pacer. It was, I announced, "The same horse Paul Revere rode on his famous midnight run." I was trying, childishly, to impress George.

He looked at me, one hand holding the reins of his horse. "You know Paul Revere, too?"

I just smiled.

George made a clicking sound with his tongue and cheek; his horse reared and sprang into action. My horse didn't wait for a sound from me. In fact, she didn't wait for anything. She followed the majestic duo in front of us, now melded together like the metaphorical Centaur creature: half man, half horse.

I was in full gallop, following George Washington. We galloped down a well-traveled dirt path at the rear of the property, right alongside the Potomac River. His horse was strong and wide, kicking up the dry earth as he maneuvered around tree roots and jumped small ravines. Amory mimicked every move. My eyes were wide open, tears making tracks towards my ears from the wind in my face. I dared not take a hand from the reins to wipe for fear I would fall off. I watched as George and his horse ducked to avoid a low branch; I followed suit. When I lifted my head, I saw George pulling away in a grassy clearing. I gave my horse a nudge from my heels and my best yell: "Yaa!" The steady beating of hooves on the ground gave me such an amazing rush. I felt more alive than I had in a long time. I leaned forward and challenged my horse to catch up. We were at full gallop when George and his horse veered left and went airborne to clear a wooden fence. I second-guessed myself for a split second and then bore down on the reins and closed my eyes. My horse didn't hesitate, even for a moment. Amory was going over the fence with or without me. She sprang into the air... and there was silence. No hooves pounding, no sound at all, as if time stood still. I opened my eyes and saw George pulling his reins back and to his left. His horse lowered his huge hindquarters and skidded to stop while turning, so George could watch my landing. My horse's front legs touched down and I felt myself ready to fly over her head. Then her hindquarters dropped and she skidded to a stop, making me look like a pro.

"You're quite the rider, Mr. Peregrine." He said this with a smile unfamiliar to people who have only seen paintings of George in battle or in formal poses. Our horses fidgeted and puffed heavily. George made another clicking noise, and Nelson began to walk. Amory followed behind until I gave her a little boot pressure, asking her to pick it up a bit so I could ride alongside George.

"There's water up ahead. We'll let the horses drink and I will show you my favorite thinking tree." He gave

Nelson two long strokes down his now sweating neck and patted him gently a half a dozen times on his right shoulder. As we rode, George made brief small talk about the fresh fish Martha would have prepared for our dinner tonight. I couldn't help wondering what time that would be, having heard about George's strong work ethic. "And what about lunch?" I thought to myself. He didn't even mention lunch. We stopped at a thin run of water. I assumed it was a runoff from the Potomac or possibly a creek that flowed into the river. When the horses had their fill, George did his clicking noise and both horses snapped to attention.

We walked them up a grassy incline. They kept their heads down, navigating the challenging terrain. When I was confident that the horses had the tricky footing under control, I looked up. I saw the huge tree that no doubt was the "thinking tree."

I was so impressed with George's "oneness" with his horse. I could also tell he was used to traveling long distances with very little conversation. When we finally reached the shade of the huge oak, he gracefully dismounted. I followed suit. Two heavily frayed ropes were loosely tied to one of the thick bottom branches, with three of four feet dangling free. George looped one of them through his lead and expertly tied off his horse like a cowboy would rope a calf. I went with a square knot, hoping it would go unnoticed. "Watch me," George said as he untied my rope. He held up the dangling rope from the tree and slipped it through the lead like he was threading a needle. He exaggerated his next three moves and I nodded my head, pretending "I got it."

He inhaled deeply and slowly blew the breath back out of his stately nose. "This is my love," he said, scanning the horizon, "farming Mount Vernon." He motioned for me to come closer and then pointed with a long arm. "To your far right is the River Farm." His extended arm moved counterclockwise as he called out his other farms. "Muddy Hole Farm straight ahead, Dogue Run Farm to the left, Union Farm still farther left, and we are standing on Mansion Farm." From up here, all those farms looked like ant farms. The day's work was already under way with busy, dot-sized workers hustling about. I asked him how many acres he owned. He squeezed out a grin. "I'm not at liberty to say, but it stretches over three miles inland, and fronts the Potomac River and Dogue Creek for over eight miles." I already knew from history books that he had 7,400 acres.

From where we were, I could see the Potomac River, the little Hunting Creek and even a glimpse of Dogue Creek. His holdings went on for as far as the eye could see. I wanted to take the conversation to famous battles and his presidency, but I could tell he wasn't ready.

Mr. Washington was a brilliant land speculator, an enterprise that grew out of his early career as a land surveyor. When I asked him how he got started, he finally began to open up. He began by telling me how his father passed away when he was only eleven years old and that he was forced to grow up fast under his mother's strict rules. By the age of seventeen he was Culpeper County's official surveyor. And by the age of twenty, before he met Martha, he served in the Virginia militia with the rank of major. George was modest in describing the French and Indian War and his own accomplishments. But in his early 20s, he had been considered a giant of his time. He was six feet three inches tall and 235 pounds, with a strong physique and perfect posture. He already had quite a

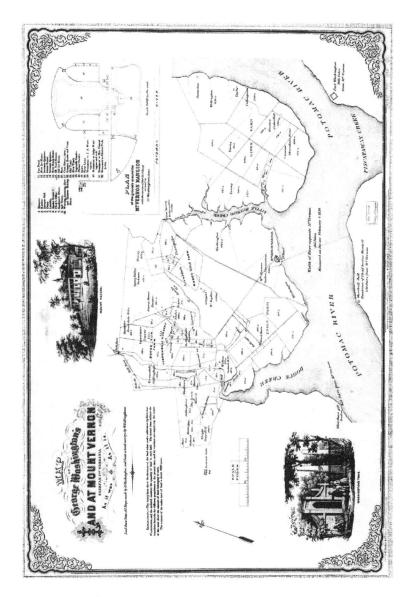

Map of George Washington's land at Mount Vernon

*By Gillingham, W.; Washington, George [Public domain],
via Wikimedia Commons*

reputation for both a willingness and the ability to fight. From the age of twenty-three to twenty-six, he commanded the Virginia forces protecting the frontier from Indians.

By the age of 43, he was getting more involved in politics, and on June 15, 1775, he was elected commander of the new American army. As George told the stories of his painful army years, each battle was tied to the names of friends and "good men" who didn't survive the ordeal.

In 1776 his army out-maneuvered the British army, forcing them out of Boston. But, of the battles that would follow, nine out of the next ten were disastrous. As bad as they were, the rough winters proved to be the toughest enemy of all. Too often, British surprise attacks would force the tired and hungry American army to fight or retreat with only the clothes on their backs; sometimes without shoes. Stories are told of the British following their bloody footprints in the snow. The important victory at Monmouth, New Jersey in 1778 gave the poorly trained army the hope to fight on.

At this point, George stopped talking and stared at the ground, shaking his head. "Our own government was slow. Thousands died over the winter of 1779 waiting for food, clothes or shelter. Typically, soldiers had a six-month or one-year term. When their term was up, they were very reluctant to re-enlist since they hadn't received the pay they had been promised." He seemed lost back in the day and then looked back at me, forcing a sad smile.

Once the war was won, George desperately tried to stay out of politics. He wanted nothing more than to farm his Mount Vernon property. The long war had drained his finances; his many acres had become dilapidated, badly in need of direction and dollars. Much to his dismay, in 1789 he was inaugurated as president of the United States, after being unanimously elected at the age of fifty-seven. George would go on to serve a second term but absolutely refused to do a third term.

His stories were filled with bigger names than a Hollywood movie: the likes of Benjamin Franklin, Thomas Jefferson and John Adams. Even Daniel Boone made it into one of his stories.

The George I was speaking to under the thinking tree was a 66-year-old man. He had no idea that his last day would be December 14, 1799, at the age of 67.

It became obvious that we were not tending the land today. Today would be spent here at this tree, telling and listening to stories. I wondered how many times he had told Martha he was working the land but instead was pacing here at his thinking tree. We talked a bit more about his farm and the estate, but I wanted to talk about December 25th, 1776—and the awful winter of 1777 at Valley Forge. George grew visibly uneasy just thinking about it.

There were two crates stacked behind the huge trunk of the big tree. George grabbed them, one in each hand and plopped them side by side, maybe four feet apart. He was staring out over his acreage, still standing. We shared an awkward silence. "Mr. Washington, I have to tell you that you are still considered the father of our nation. Your every battle has been reenacted, every letter published. There are hundreds of monuments dedicated to you, all over the United States. There is even a sixty-foot tall bust of you and three future presidents carved into a place in the West called Mount Rushmore. Please pardon me for being a bit star-struck, but you are truly still a hero, 250 years later."

George turned and looked down at my five-foot-nine-inch frame. "I rejoice knowing the Americans have sustained freedom, even prospered. The theory was sound. The ground work was tedious." He hesitated, "Many good men died." More silence.

"What do you want to know?" His voice sounded like he was surrendering, finally. He sat on the crate with a slight groan.

"George, I want to know if the stories are accurate. I want to start with 1776, Christmas, at twilight. The battle for Trenton, New Jersey.

George leaned forward to pick up a random stick and flicked it forward, and then a handful of grass from the already sparse, hard ground. "Are you sure you want to go there?" The voice came from George, but somehow the words sounded more like a warning from a programmer.

I blinked twice, but on the third blink I couldn't open my eyes. The sounds were different. Loud, and getting louder. Finally, I managed to open my eyes. I was surrounded by infantrymen... Wait! I am an infantryman. George's war voice bellowed. "Men, I want sixty rounds of ammunition in every backpack, a blanket and three days' rations. No more, no less. Now shoulder your muskets and head to the western bank." It was cold and wet and windy. The riding clothes that I had on were now worn and tattered and filthy. A soldier tossed me a ragged shirt. "Slip it over your head, like a scarf. It will keep your neck warm."

Even before I pulled the shirt over my head, I could smell the death. This was a shirt from a dead man. I shook the thought from my mind and closed the flap of my backpack, having stuffed my poor excuse for a blanket over my sixty rounds. Men were tossing their backpacks over their shoulders and splashing past me over the half-frozen, half-slush, rutted ground. Off in the distance, hundreds of horses pounded the ground with anxious hooves. Cavalry men tightened their saddles and double checked their pistols. We were on the western bank of the Delaware River, near McConkey's Ferry in Bucks County, Pennsylvania. I knew from history that many of the Continental Army's soldiers had already gone home, but those who remained were hardened and seasoned, firmly believing in their commanding officer, George Washington. To these men, Washington had become more than a commanding officer; he had become a father figure. I noticed that my fellow soldiers were barely dressed. Shoes were often little more than rags tied around weathered feet. I saw a soldier without shoes. In the dead of winter.

Most of these men had served their time; their enlistment period was quickly coming to an end. They hoped three more weeks would come and go without another battle. They had farms and families and businesses back home. They were under-equipped, underpaid, underfed and had every right to think about going home. But home to what, should the revolution fail? As long as they were here, under George's command, they would fight when called upon. If Washington believed in them enough to cross this ice-choked river with men, horses and tons of weaponry, it was because he had a plan. George always had a plan. Admittedly, his plans were often complicated and risky. A hundred things could go wrong that would foil any plan. But George knew that to sit idle was also a death sentence. In three weeks, it was likely that he would lose a good chunk of his men, and the long odds of winning this revolution would grow only longer. George Washington had a way of reminding his men what was at stake. If he was ready to die for the cause, then by God... they were ready to die, too.

I could hear the splashing of boots and bellowed orders: "To the boats!"

I was kneeling on the ground with a ragged pack clenched tightly in my cold, numb hands. "Shit," I said aloud. "I'm in the goddamn war." I was scared, yet honored to be here. I had the advantage of history and knew it would get bad, really bad, but the battle would be ours. The plan was to surprise William Howe's fierce Hessian army before dawn. We had to surprise them. It was our only chance.

I followed at least a dozen men onto one of the flatboats and immediately ended up on my ass. A skinny, dirty, weathered arm reached out, partly uncovered by the undersized jacket the man wore. "Steady, lad," he said. I detected a veteran's self-confidence in his voice. I quickly composed myself and the same skinny arms handed me an oar. "Let's pull for it, gentlemen." Three boats ahead of us were already in trouble; the overstuffed craft took on icy water. Our pitiful little fleet rattled around like flies in a bathtub full of ice cubes. Soldiers doing duty as oarsmen alternated pushing chunks of ice away and rowing towards the other side when we could fit them into the water unencumbered. One of the men sat on the tip of the boat with his two legs hanging over like the front legs of a spider, attempting to move the giant slabs of ice left and right. As if this weren't enough, the cold wind turned into a blinding snow storm. "Pull, men! You need to put your backs into it, or we'll be swept down river."

The crossing was even worse than I'd anticipated from all I'd read about it. All the craft miraculously survived the crossing but one of the men had already been badly injured. He was trying to keep the heavy cannons from toppling off the makeshift floating transports, overfilled with tens of thousands of pounds of iron.

By the time we got to the other side, I was ready to drop. Even in the traveler's form, my arms were burned out from rowing, and I worried that my face and feet were already frostbitten. A profound sense of gratitude came over me as I realized our forefathers were such bad-asses! I wanted another chance to tell my students what I now knew. As we huddled on the New Jersey bank, George rode up out of nowhere to address his frozen, weary troops. He knew we needed something to keep us moving forward. He nodded as a signal for one of his aides to address us. From the first words he spoke in his booming voice, I knew I was hearing Thomas Paine. As he repeated his famous words, his horse eagerly reared on its hind legs.

"These are the times that try men's souls. The Summer Soldier and the Sunshine Patriot will, in this crisis, shrink from the service of their country. But he that stands it now, deserves the love and thanks of man and woman. Tyranny, like hell, is not easily conquered, yet we have this consolation with us that the harder the conflict, the more glorious the triumph." When he had finished, his final words echoing across the ranks, only silence remained. The soldiers' icy breath filled the air.

Finally, Washington broke the silence. "All right, men," he said, his voice firm with resolve. "It's time to go."

Suddenly the scene changed. Instead of shivering in a frozen field, I was standing in the corner of a comfortable dining room, with a cheery fire blazing on the hearth. I realized I was seeing the results of some brilliant programming. Whoever created this virtual world had taken me from the banks of the Delaware to the town of Mount Holly, New Jersey. It was only eight miles away, but a whole world of difference.

At the table in front of me, the British Colonel von Donop savored his Christmas dinner. He ate the finest meats, vegetables and fruits, served on a lace tablecloth. He was being attended to by a very gracious and ever so accommodating and beautiful young widow who had shown an interest in him. All the other local women had fled; the look on the colonel's face told me he couldn't believe his good luck.

"Ahhhh, the fortunes of war," he said in a braggart's voice.

"Colonel von Donop?" inquired an eager young German adjutant. I knew from my studies that his name was Captain Cohan Ewald. "Might we be leaving soon for Bordentown? We have been here since Monday." His tone betrayed his weariness at his colonel's obvious desire for down time. Bordentown was his command's next stop. It was close enough to support Col. Ralls' troops in Trenton, should any difficulties arise.

But von Donop was not ready to go just yet. "Don't vorry, Captain," he barked, then softened his tone as he turned to his newfound companion. She was ever so slyly glancing back at him. "Colonel Ralls will be fine for one more night. Just look at the veather out there." Once more, von Donop cast his glance toward his smiling hostess. "Don't you agree, my dear?"

She smiled in a way I would not have described as sincere and handed him another brandy. The name of the woman who entertained—or you might say distracted—von Donop that Christmas night is not really known for sure, but the story that locals told is that it was Betsy Ross. Yeah. That Betsy Ross.

Suddenly I was back in the snowy darkness, shivering. But I didn't recognize the spot. It wasn't where I'd been last; an officer I hadn't seen before was standing on the riverbank, cursing up a storm.

It was early the morning of December 26, 1776, and I was standing on the Delaware's west bank, eight miles downstream from Washington's troops. The angry officer was an American general, James Ewing.

His seven hundred troops were to coordinate an attack with Washington. But the falls at Trenton had created a massive ice jam. Pockets of water flowed through only sporadically. Here, the Delaware was too frozen to cross by boat and not frozen enough to march seven hundred men across. Many attempts were made... all failed. If George Washington were to secure victory, it would be without General Ewing's reinforcements.

Then, suddenly came another change of scene. I found myself silently congratulating Ann's programmers on how well they'd designed the simulation. It was still the morning of December, and still on the western bank of the Delaware, but now at a place called Neshaminy's Ferry. The general here, John Cadwalader, was also attempting to cross the river to aid Washington. The same ice that blocked General Ewing's troops farther north had Cadwalader pinned down, too. He had been assigned to cross at Dunks Ferry, across the river from Burlington, New Jersey. But his boats could hardly be put into the water there, let alone be rowed or pulled to the opposite shore. He had moved north to Neshaminy's Ferry in a second attempt, but it was the same story here. Slabs of ice the size of his boats, as hard and sharp as bayonets, filled the river. With his second heartfelt attempt ending in failure, the general had no choice but to send his tired and frozen men marching back to camp. There they couldn't do anything but pray for George Washington and his troops, who would be expecting, but not getting, help from the two generals.

Finally, I found myself back to stay with that main army, the only American force that had managed to get across the river. Troubles continued to mount for Washington and his men. The weather took a turn for the worse. Sleeting wind alternating with rain and snow made the trip unbearable. And yet we bore it. This was the worst weather his troops had ever seen, and they had already faced one grim winter that claimed men without a single shot from a rifle or the sting of a bayonet. For the weary Continental soldiers, every step was a challenge. By now, we were already four hours behind schedule.

The road had run upward from the river, a good two-hundred-foot change in elevation. Portions of that incline were sharply pitched, which made the work of Henry Knox's burly gunners nearly impossible. As if that wasn't enough, they still had to get the heavy artillery across Jacobs Creek. Despite the name, Jacobs Creek was no ordinary stream. The steep ravine required Knox's men to lash their longest drag ropes to trees and winch their cannons down, and then drag them back up the perilous opposite slopes. The gun carriages and their big wheels were made of wood; every jolt made the weapons less stable and more vulnerable to breakdown. Without wheels, a cannon may as well be an anchor.

Washington rode alongside his men, offering encouragement and direction, all the while aware that we were losing our only advantage, darkness. He had to push us, faster, faster, and faster still. "Press on, boys. Press on," he would shout. He could not risk any more delay. I got to witness the legendary horse story through my stink-filled scarf/shirt, which was now pulled up over my nose. My ears were frozen, my hair wet and frozen, my feet numb, my bones aching. I paused briefly, again, in awe of the simulation program, and in spite of my discomfort, thankful that I had the joy of experiencing it in this way.

Galloping on icy ground, George's horse skidded to a stop just ahead of me. Bucking and panicked, the beast lost its footing and fell to its front knees, threatening to toss General Washington and possibly crush him under its weight. Washington panicked not for a second. Dropping his reins, he grabbed the horse's mane with his powerful hands, pulling with all his strength as if trying to right a sailboat about to surrender to a gust of wind. Miraculously, he pulled the animal itself upward, steadying it enough to keep it—and him—from tumbling to the earth. "Was that real?" yelled one of the youngest soldiers. "Am I dreaming?"

"No lad," said the soldier standing next to me. "I saw it too. We all did, and this I know: nothing can stop George Washington from reaching Trenton this day. I just hope we make it with him."

Perhaps that anonymous soldier was wrong. Perhaps there was still something that could stop Washington from reaching Trenton. Soon after steadying his horse, the general halted his men and gave them the practiced command to ready themselves for an attack.

"Hello," came the call. "Don't shoot. We're Virginians."

Washington held his fist up, silently telling his troops to hold back, but stay on the ready. "What are you doing here?" Washington demanded.

"One of those damnable Hessians' spies sneaked across the river yesterday and killed one of our boys, so we had to even the score. We just came from Trenton. Gave 'em a little taste of their own medicine. I reckon we got two or three of 'em." Washington's face didn't betray him, but I knew his heart must have sunk at this news. The element of surprise he had plotted so carefully had vanished. His own men—at least men fighting for the same cause—had blown everything. He must have been silently fuming. He was visibly tired, his left eye twitching. All was lost. Or so it seemed.

"What now, General?"

Washington looked over his troops, momentarily relaxed after their brief rush to prepare for battle. "We have come this far, Hamilton," Washington answered his young aide. "If we go forward we may very well lose our lives. The element of surprise is gone. The chance of arriving before the sun rises is evaporating by the second. But if we march these men back to the river after all this, we will surely lose our army. Captain Hamilton, we have no choice. We go forward."

I wanted to warn him that General Ewing and Cadwalader's troops were unable to cross the river; his reinforcements would be no-shows. But I feared that by telling him this I might change history. Not meaning to, I took this moment to remember once again that this was a simulation.

We marched on with a little less confidence. From the little they said, the men around me were contemplating their last brave moments, wondering if they would ever see home, wife, children or family members again. I wished at that moment that I had a speech of my own to replace the fear and doubt in their eyes with resolve.

The morning of December 26th, 1776, on the outskirts of Trenton, the sun had risen at 7:20 a.m. but George Washington wasn't there. He had failed yet again. He wouldn't arrive until after nine. From where I stood, just behind him, I could see him staring toward the town in the distance, or at least where the town should have been. We couldn't see anything. Another storm had commenced, and it was historic. The sleet and snow that filled the air were completely blinding and deadened all sound except for the hissing wind. And that seemed to be the break that Washington needed. Also to his advantage was his awareness of the lay of the land. He knew the town was there. The Hessians inside the town, on the other hand, had no idea that American muskets, bayonets and cannons were steadily advancing on them. George Washington's prayers had not failed him. All Hessians had gone indoors, convinced that no one in their right mind would be looking for a fight in this weather. With the benefit of well-researched hindsight, I could tell what George was thinking. He knew this storm was a gift. What he didn't know was that a spy had infiltrated his headquarters and the Hessians were well aware of his plans to attack during this holy season. When those foolish Virginians had shot up their town and taken off, Colonel Ralls and his men had made the only reasonable assumption. That had been the rebel attack. I was also privileged to know what was going through the enemy commander's mind, too. "What wretched fools these soldiers were," Ralls had laughed. Afterward he was to write, "It was hardly an attack worthy of my attention."

Washington's troops got to within fifty yards before a young Hessian officer spotted them. His name was Lieutenant Veto Holt. "Define... or else," he shouted. Moments later as it became clear that his force was under attack, we could hear him warning anyone within earshot, "The enemy! Turn out!"

American cannon fire boomed overhead, tearing up everything in its path. Colonel Ralls was sleeping off a late night of brandy and fun with his new lady friend. From where I was, the sound of thousands of our troops yelling as they charged the surprised Hessians was deafening. It had to have awakened Ralls, even from his hangover. Washington's troops were getting off ten shots to the Hessians' one; the startled mercenaries scrambled to organize without their commander. We were in a full charge now. Bullets slammed into soldiers, knocking them off their feet. Some would stay down, reddening the snow; others got back up and fought as best they could. I took a rifle butt to the face and lost my footing. The large Hessian who'd hit me thrust his bayonet at my face to finish me off. I turned my head and pushed the blade aside. It stuck hard into the frozen dirt and we began to wrestle. I pushed his grunting face away with my left hand and swung my right elbow across his mouth. That took two of his teeth and gashed his upper lip. His eyes widened, as he stabbed down at me with a dirty six-inch blade that seemed to appear from nowhere. I caught his wrist when the knife's point was two inches from my chest. My arm began to shake as he leaned his heavy frame onto the knife. I squealed as the first two inches slowly penetrated my thin excuse of a jacket and then pierced my chest cavity. Bloody saliva dripped from the Hessian's mouth and sprayed as he taunted me. "Your heart rate is too high," he whispered eerily. This was getting too real.

The lab tech was warning me to calm down or he would have to stop the simulation. I bucked the Hessian off, sending him onto his back. I scrambled to my feet and yanked the wobbling musket out of the frozen ground. I thrust the dirty bayonet through his defending left hand, stapling it to his heart. As his eyes went gray, so did my vision. I fell to the ground, my jacket sporting a growing wet, red stain. I lay on the ground, the battle raging all around me. Musket fire whizzed past me, soldiers fought all around me, and cannon blasts frightened me, but also kept me awake.

The bloody battle favored Washington and his men, but not without loss and injury. George almost lost his second cousin, Captain William Washington and Lieutenant James Monroe—our future fifth president—as they bravely fought to recapture a battery of cannon that had been temporarily lost to the Hessians. The battle see-sawed back and forth, with the Americans the eventual victors. This godawful battle is remembered as one of the great victories for America. Many, many other battles did not and would not go our way. Liberty and freedom were still far from secure, but this battle gave America hope.

As I lay on the frozen turf bleeding out, my eyes closed. I could hear the battle rage on, men grunting after the sound of a rifle butt striking a head or gut. Men fell all around me. As things quieted down, I surrendered to death. I couldn't open my eyes. Now my hearing seemed to be failing. I became aware of one of the soldiers shaking me and then a firm slap to my face. When my eyes opened, I could see that George Washington himself was trying to wake me up. I instinctively felt my jacket and checked my hand for blood. There was none.

I was still under the thinking tree. I had fallen off my crate and gone into a convulsion. The techs told me through George's voice that they were going to have to end the simulation; they explained that they needed me to stabilize for my return. George sat me back up on the crate. I put my hand to my sweating forehead and placed my elbow on my knee for support. I felt George's big hand pat my back. "And now you know," he said. I rested a second elbow on the other knee and covered my face with my hands. I thought I felt George pulling at my hands, but it was Ann removing the heavy goggles from my face.

A gentle voice whispered. "Hey, you.... Welcome back... You OK?"

# Chapter 4 – The New Me

Monday couldn't come fast enough.

I couldn't wait for my first class to start. I showed up in a white George Washington wig, tied in a 1776 man bun. I sat, stately I hoped, at my desk with a tiny bottle containing a dark liquid meant to look like ink for my quill pen. Strictly for showmanship, I dipped the feather and pretended to write as the students filed in. I could feel their eyes on me as they entered the room, trying to figure out if I was a substitute or a lunatic. They settled into their seats without the usual whiny coaxing, probably out of sheer curiosity. When everyone was seated, I looked up and over the room. I stood with my hands locked behind my back, my body erect. I paced the room for an uncomfortable twenty seconds, wondering how to start. My heart pounded... with life. All eyes followed.

I finally spoke, louder than usual. "We all know George Washington was the first president of the United States, but there is more to him than that bullshit story about cutting down a cherry tree." I paced to the far side of the room where a student was trying to conceal that she was texting. When she glanced up at me, I shook my head, once left and once right ever so slightly, indicating my disapproval. She immediately complied, jamming her phone into her purse. Eyes continued to follow me. I cleared my throat and spoke slowly. "I had the privilege of spending the weekend with George Washington." I could see the students eyeing me up and then looking at one another as if to say, "How lame." I was undeterred. "George Washington was six feet three inches tall and 235 pounds." I hesitated, taking in three or four of the students' gazes. "That was a giant back in 1776. He was so fearless in battle that his soldiers thought he was protected by the hand of God." I continued, emphasizing key words and regularly pausing for effect. "In one battle, he fought through a hailstorm of bullets, returning with two bullet holes in his coat, and one in his hat. He had two horses shot out from under him and seemed to repel bullets like two opposing magnets that push away from one another." I described my ride in the horse-drawn carriage around his dirt driveway and told them how I had been star struck when Washington opened the carriage door. I started to say, "Imagine meeting..." Then I froze, as every name I thought of was sure to emphasize that I didn't know who kids idolized these days. I repeated myself, "Imagine meeting..." and I played it safe. "The person you most admire... You can pick someone dead or alive."

I let silence reign for as long as I could, hoping they would silently come to a conclusion regarding their idol. As I went on, I described my tongue and toast breakfast and heard a few groans of disgust. "What? It's not like they had toaster strudel two-packs in sealed plastic, like you do now." The class chuckled. I was encouraged. I described my exhilarating ride on one of Washington's horses. I held my hand out to show them how tall the horse was. I simulated a step into the horse's stirrup and exaggerated the mount, throwing my right leg over the horse. I stopped talking and rode my imaginary horse. I ducked and leaned as I maneuvered over the terrain, eyes wild with concentration. I remembered every rut, branch and stream. When I got to the part where we were galloping at full speed, I was lost in the moment. I finally spoke.

"When I saw George leap over that four-foot fence like a Centaur..." I hesitated. I swallowed exaggeratedly. "I panicked for just a moment... but my horse didn't flinch. Her hooves were pounding at full speed, kicking up the clay earth." I was pounding out the sound of a galloping horse on my desk. "And then everything went silent."

I closed my eyes, clenched my jaw and gripped my imaginary rein. I forgot I was in front of my class and silently floated over the fence in slow motion, reliving that magic moment. My fists clenched the reins, my forearms tight. I leaned forward as if I was going head over heels. At the last moment, I reared back and skidded to a stop. I took two deep breaths and lifted my head. I relaxed my grip on the reins and put my arms over my head like I'd just kicked the game-winning field goal. I opened my eyes. "Nailed it!"

The class roared with laughter. My class. Roared with laughter. My class was listening to me. And enjoying it!

As I took them back to 1776, Christmas, twilight—the battle for Trenton, New Jersey—I boomed my best George Washington voice. "'Men, I want 60 rounds of ammunition in every backpack, a blanket and 3 days' worth of rations. No more, no less. Now shoulder your muskets and head to the western bank.'" I went back to my own voice and continued telling the story, but now from my point of view. "It was cold and wet and windy. My clothes were worn and tattered and filthy. The ragged old shirt that was wrapped around my neck and mouth for warmth stank of death. Taking clothes and shoes from the dead was necessary for survival." I reached below my white button-up shirt and lifted the neckline of my t-shirt up and over my nose to further simulate what I was describing. I closed my eyes and eased the t-shirt just below my nose. I used my forefinger to block my nostrils from the imaginary smell. I used my remaining three fingers to cover my mouth. The seconds ticked away, and the students waited for my eyes to open. I lifted my chin toward the ceiling, letting the now stretched undergarment slide back to my neck.

I continued in a softer, more emotional voice, my head moving back and forth in disgust. "The winter was brutal." I could see the students' eyes widening. Even the guys in the back of the class sat up to hear better as I lowered my voice even more. "I shook away the thought of the dead man's clothing and folded the flap of my backpack after I stuffed my poor excuse for a blanket over my sixty rounds." I mimicked every movement that I described. "Men were whipping their backpacks over their shoulders and splashing past me on the half frozen, rutted ground. I stood up, struggling to lift my heavy pack with my numb and clumsy fingers. Hundreds of horses were stomping excitedly off in the distance." My voice quickened and grew steadily louder. "Cavalry men tightened their saddles and double checked their pistols. I was on the western bank of the Delaware River, near McConkey's Ferry in Bucks County, Pennsylvania." I reminded them that McConkey's Ferry was a real place, and this was a real story, and that it took place "only a few hours away from right here."

As my story continued, the students began to ask questions. In my class! Students were interested and participating! When I got to the crossing of the Delaware, I spoke as if I were George Washington. "I know it's cold. I know you're tired. But we must cross this ice-choked river with all our forces." I switched back to my voice. "In one of the worst storms, in one of the worst winters, in recent history." I went on to explain, "The mission was to surprise William Howe's fierce Hessian army at dawn."

These German soldiers for hire were part of an army that was the cream of Britain's fighting crop. General Washington's rag-tag men stood proud, ready to die. With faces stung and reddened by the fierce weather, they comforted each other with nods of firm intent. These battle-weary New Englanders, Southerners, Pennsylvanians, New Yorkers and Jerseymen bonded together for a common goal." I raised my voice. "'Liberty or death' was spoken with a proud posture; rifles were pounded together like shot glasses, toasting." I walked to the back of the room, all eyes following. I stopped in front of Dean, slammed my palms on his desk, and yelled, "Liberty or death!" The class jumped. I continued, louder and faster. "The anxious men checked and rechecked their supplies. Gunners checked to make sure they had packed enough shot, powder and fuses for the cannons."

The room was silent, waiting on my every word. I spoke much quieter now. "A journey across this half-frozen river was a crazy idea that would take hours. Hours that they didn't have. The schedule was tight and had to be precise to prepare for and pull off the attack before daylight, since surprise was their only advantage. Every minute lost could cost a life. Every hour lost could lose the battle. This battle seemed to have the fate of the Revolution at stake." I glanced at the clock on the classroom's rear wall. The bell was about to ring, and I took the opportunity to bellow, much too loud for a classroom setting, slamming my hands on one of the empty desks. "Victory or death!"

Once again, the students were startled. Some held their hearts. Some laughed nervously. "That was the extent of their choices."

The bell rang and two of the guys in the back took turns pounding their desks and chanting, "Victory or death!" The room was abuzz with laughter and chatter.

When the last student left the classroom, I plopped onto my chair and peeled back the white wig. I was drained. I was glad I had only two more classes today. I spent the next period alone in my classroom. I wrote the names of a few of my favorite George Washington books on the chalk board. I had no intention of giving them as homework or mandatory reading. It was time to treat these students as adults. If they were interested, they would enquire.

As the next students entered the classroom, I was writing one of George Washington's famous quotes on the board. "If the freedom of speech is taken away, then dumb and silent, we may be led, like sheep to the slaughter." I took them on a similar journey to what I'd done with my previous class. I described my meal with George and Martha and told them how and when George accumulated his acreage. When I brought them to the bloody battle for Trenton, I was in full story mode, like a dad telling a scary story to his kids at a campfire. "We struggled to get the cannons down and then back up the steep embankments of Jacob's Creek. Soldiers were tired and frost-bitten, many with little more than rags wrapped around their wet and frozen feet."

As I described the approach to battle, "blinding snow tearing at our faces," tears began to flow down my face and my voice choked. I couldn't stop the tears.

I didn't try. I relived the moment when we witnessed George Washington yank his horse's mane to keep them both from falling. I explained how he kept his troops moving, even as they fell to the ground to rest or quit. I bellowed in George's voice, "'Rouse that man!'" I quoted him yelling through the storm from atop his white horse: "'To rest now is to die!'" I wanted to make sure the students knew this had been no parade march.

"The battle favored George Washington and his men, but not without loss." I peeled off the wig and plopped into one of the empty desks. Staring forward, I swallowed hard, wiped away the tears streaming from one eye and continued. "George nearly lost his second cousin, Captain William Washington. Lieutenant James Monroe was wounded as he bravely fought to capture the cannons that were tearing their men apart. Does anyone know what became of Lieutenant James Monroe?" The more I got lost in the story, the more they listened.

One of the students yelled, "He became our next president!"

I was impressed. I nodded to Mark. "Close. He became our fifth president." I wondered what had taken me so long to figure out how to communicate with these students. I shook off the distraction and then I continued. "The battle see-sawed back and forth, with the Americans the eventual victors... this time." I was telling the same stories, but this time, with more confidence and passion. I relived the final moments of a soldier's life as if it were me. "The powder in our guns was too wet to fire so we fought with our muskets as clubs." I surprised one of the students with a simulated stabbing motion to her gut, and then a rifle butt to the jaw of the guy in the seat in front of her as he turned around to follow my story. "That's when it happened!"

I seemed to modify the story just a bit each time I told it. I simulated a blow to my face with the butt of a musket. "I blacked out just long enough to bounce off the frozen ground." I fell to the classroom floor. "A wild, screaming man with a Viking red beard was positioning his musket for a final bayonet stab to my heart." I held up my forearms and tucked my legs as if preparing to fend off an enemy. "I'll never forget the yell he let out as he thrust thc wcapon downward. I used my right forearm to redirect the blade from my chest to the frozen ground. My arm was gashed from here to here!" I lifted my arm to show the class the meaty side of my forearm. "He tugged at his musket, but the bayonet was stuck in the frozen ground. He pounced on me and got in two pretty good punches before I landed a good, strong elbow to his jaw. I heard his jaw break and saw him spit out two teeth. My blood and his were now mixed."

The classroom was utterly still. Every eye was on me; half the students' mouths hung open, enthralled with my story. I pressed on.

"His left forearm was pressed against my neck, cutting off my circulation. The pressure to my neck eased up momentarily as he reached for something from his boot. I tried to get to it first, but the bayonet had gone through the shoulder of my coat, pinning my left side to the frozen ground. A dirty six-inch blade appeared, and this wide-eyed enemy once again went for my heart. I caught his wrist, slowing the knife. Our eyes locked. Two strangers who had never met before, trying to kill one another for God and country. I felt the blade penetrate my sad excuse for clothing.

Somehow, I got my second hand to his wrist a moment before he did. My arms began to shake as he lowered his chest onto the knife's handle. His bloody spit spattered my face as he huffed and puffed. I could feel the blade pierce my chest. His ice-crusted beard touched my chin and his bloody saliva flowed onto my face as he yelled, trying to summon more power from his muscles. The blade slowly deepened, sliding neatly between two of my ribs. I summoned everything I had to buck him off me. I tore loose from the bayonet and stood. We both went for the musket. He stumbled. I steadied myself and forced the bayonet out of the frozen ground. My choices: die... or kill. He crab-crawled backwards too tired to stand. I stabbed through his defensive hand, pinning it to his heart. I felt the long bayonet pass entirely through his soft body, missing the ribs, and once again stick into the hard earth. I stumbled backwards and fell to the ground, the dirty knife still embedded in my chest." I acted this out, stumbling backwards between two desks as if I was clutching the bloody knife. The students were on the edges of their seats.

I was back at Trenton. I continued from the floor.

"I lay on the frozen turf bleeding out." I closed my eyes. "I could hear the battle rage on. I remember hearing the grunts of other soldiers as they fell all around me. As things quieted down, I surrendered to death. I couldn't open my eyes and all the noise eventually faded. That morning, I died for my country." I was silent for a moment, then opened my eyes and sat up. "The battle was considered an American victory."

I stopped talking and just sat on the floor for a while. The class remained silent. When I finally stood, I readjusted the white wig back over my messed-up hair and returned to my desk. "Let me tell you, the British Empire was pissed off." The students chuckled on cue, breaking the silence. "And we lost a lot of the battles to follow. We lost a lot of men. Some died by bullets or cannons. Some in hand-to-hand combat, some froze to death. And a lot died from starvation and disease." The bell rang but the class remained seated. I think they wanted more. Maybe they were waiting for me to tell them it was OK to leave. That was a first.

When the room emptied, I once again closed the door. I was tired. I began to erase the map of Washington's land holdings, since it told the story best if it was drawn while I explained the timeline of his acquisitions. I hesitated half way through and turned to look at the empty chairs. I smiled, thinking back to the faces that had gazed at me like children being told a scary bedtime story. My smile turned to sadness as I remembered my diagnosis. Why had I waited so long to live with passion? I finished erasing the chalk board and sat down. I adjusted a few items on my desk and laid my head down to rest. I had two hours until my final class and badly needed a nap. I slept, white wig on my head, for nearly the whole two hours. I was awoken by a student mistakenly walking into the room. I'm sure I scared him when he saw my dead-looking body slumped over my desk. My head popped up when he bumped a chair. "What are you doing here?" I snapped, without really meaning to, my wig all disheveled.

"Is this room 301?" the hapless student stammered.

I blinked, adjusted my wig and tucked in a few wild strands of white hair that had come loose from the hair tie. "No." I pointed to the ceiling. "One more floor."

In my final class of the day, I took my students to George's thinking tree, describing Washington's property as if I were standing there. I drew on the chalk board like a mad genius excitedly explaining his new discovery. "He inherited this and this!" I stated as I circled two areas. "And he acquired this when he married Martha. And this is the property that he purchased over the years."

For the third time that day, I went back to 1776, Christmas, twilight. The battle for Trenton, one of my favorites. My stories came faster, easier and with even more animation. I slipped in and out of character quickly, not caring that I acted as if I'd really traveled to 1776, not caring if they thought I was losing my mind. I rowed across a river with frozen fingers, the boat playing bumper cars with ice floes, and then I marched them across Jacobs Creek. And again, I fought to my death in Trenton. I occasionally caught one student looking at another as if to say, "Who is this guy?" or "I had no idea Mr. Peregrine had it in him." It was obvious I had stumbled onto the right formula: passion without care that someone might judge you for being you.

Going back to 1776 to visit George Washington might not be these kids' dream journey, but it was inspiring to see their interest in my ecstasy. I finished with my now-patented closing lines. "Every minute lost could cost a life. Every hour lost could lose the battle. A third of the army was leaving in two weeks. They had served their agreed enlistment time. This battle had the fate of the Revolution at stake. Victory or death!" I yelled. "That was the extent of their choices." I had timed my "Victory or death" yell perfectly. The bell rang, and students gathered up their books.

One of the guys in the back pounded his chest. "Victory!"

Another started the chant "USA, USA..." It caught on and continued into the hallway, creating a bit of a ruckus. As the last few students funneled out the door, greasy-haired Corrine timidly smiled at me. "Victory, Mr. Peregrine... Major victory!" I smiled a sad but grateful smile and mouthed the words, "'Thank you."

I closed the door behind her, letting myself smile one more time as the last muffled chant of "USA" faded away down the corridor. I held the door shut and rested my head against it. I almost fell asleep leaning against the door. The bell for the next period classes sounded and I lifted my head. I locked the door and turned to face the front of the room.

I sat in the farthest row back in the seat closest to the door. Billy's seat. I rested my elbow on the desk and propped my head onto my palm. It felt heavy to me as I stared at the chalkboard. My latest drawing was the attack plan of the famous battle for Yorktown.

My stomach rumbled. I hadn't eaten since breakfast when I'd had a bagel with a wedge of store-bought ham. That had been at 5:30 a.m. I'd pretended it was fresh-baked bread and tongue. I nodded off twice before forcing myself to stand up. I decided to grab a cup of old, cold coffee from the teachers' lounge before making my trip home.

Mr. Hingels, an English teacher, greeted me as I walked into the lounge. "Well, if isn't George

Washington." He finished pouring a cup of coffee from a new, full, fresh pot.

Mrs. Nescie, the biology teacher, appeared when the refrigerator door closed. "Man, you had the brats all riled up today, George."

Mr. Hingels held up the pot of coffee. I acknowledged him, and he poured me a cup and handed me two packets of sugar. I took the coffee but refused the sugar. "What? You're off the sugar?"

Mrs. Nescie gave him a stare that lasted a moment too long and I knew that Principal Bailey had shared my diagnosis with the staff.

"Oh, sorry... Yeah, I'm trying to cut back too."

We shared an awkward moment of silence and then Mrs. Nescie spoke up. "Are you getting treatment?" She gave me the appropriate sad eyes and I smiled awkwardly.

"Yes," I said, just above a whisper. "It started today. In second period."

The rest of the week was magical. We discussed one famous general after another. The students' eager faces encouraged me to act out scenes. I was General Horatio Gates, a former British officer who led the Americans to victory at Saratoga. Gates would have lost that battle if not for the enterprise and initiative of Benedict Arnold, from whom he stole the credit and the glory. Thus contributing mightily to Arnold's disgruntlement and eventual treason. Gates' actual military ability was demonstrated some years later, when he totally bungled things at Camden, South Carolina.

I was Baron von Steuben, a former Prussian officer who joined the American army at Valley Forge. Von Steuben became the drill-master for the American troops, teaching them how to march and maneuver in ranks, as well as how to effectively use their bayonets. We covered General Thomas Conway, leader of a plot to force Washington to resign as commander in chief. And, of course, we talked about Benedict Arnold. "You see," I explained with a finger in the air. "Washington had enemies on the American side as well. Things happen, alliances change, when people put their personal agenda in front of the good of the people as a whole. That's when the treachery begins."

# Chapter 5
# The Angels Themselves Were Moved

When Friday came, I was already packed and ready to make the two-hour drive to see Ann. I had called her on Tuesday to let her know I would be coming back. I must have sounded like a child who had just returned from Disneyland. Our appointment was for nine Saturday morning. This time I was more prepared. There was no anxiety wondering if I was going to be robbed or murdered. I had my hotel booked; I had my journal with me. I had started writing in it every day between classes and when I got home. I wish there was a way to record my travels like a movie, so I could relive them again and again. I asked Ann if she was able to record my travels. She laughed but didn't answer the question. I guess not.

Ann and I often struggled to communicate. Her guard was always up. I constantly had to assure her that our interactions were our secret.

I told her I was already the buzz of the school with my new passion for teaching. That made her nervous. Though reluctant to ask questions, people were always nice to me now that the word was out about my cancer. Last Wednesday, in the teachers' lounge, Mr. Shipsan, the Spanish teacher said to me, "I have to ask. How do you do it?"

"Do what?" I responded.

"Where are you getting your passion? Is it the diagnosis?"

One of the other teachers who was pretending not to be listening looked up.

I took a deep breath and smiled. I noticed I was nodding slightly in acknowledgement. "I had a dream." I hesitated, realizing how much that sounded like Martin Luther King. "I had a dream that was so real..." I hesitated again. "I saw the potential me. The me that I could be. A more confident man, actually teaching kids who actually found me interesting. In the dream, I quit giving a damn whether I might make a fool of myself." Just like in the classroom, I was on a roll. I continued. "I liked that version of me."

Heads were nodding.

"Have you ever heard that cowboy song, 'Live Like You're Dying'?"

Heads continued bobbing up and down in acknowledgement, but they remained silent.

"It's true; it's amazing." I started to tear up, which made a powerful moment awkward and weak.

Mr. Shipsan offered an awkward fist bump that turned into an even more awkward man bump/hug of some kind.

Mrs. Bregala saved the moment. "Leave that man alone, you weirdo." She grabbed his arm and pushed him away like he had leprosy. "C'mere," she said, pulling me in for a full hug. "God bless you. You are a beautiful man." She put her hands on my shoulders and held me at arm's length so she could look me in the eyes. "You work your magic with these kids and let God work his magic on you."

I asked Principal Bailey for Thursday and Friday off to better prepare for my next travel. I was hooked. I couldn't stop thinking about the next adventure. I needed time to reflect, regroup, and plan more visits with Ann. I told him I just wasn't feeling well. He obliged, no questions asked.

I made it to Ann's phony dental office at 8:45 that Saturday morning. She greeted me with a smile through the door glass. She struggled a bit with the key. It reluctantly gave in after a valiant fight. She twisted, and the heavy-duty tumblers clunked. "You're early." She waved her familiar four finger motion. "C'mon." She raised her hand to shade her eyes from the rising sun, then took a peek left and right before locking the door behind me. She wasn't shy about asking for her money.

Once I got inside the secret office, Ann's Russian assistant greeted me enthusiastically. "Hey, it's da traveler!" Vlad—short for Vladimir— was shaking some kind of yellowish serum in a corked test tube. He placed it in a homemade test tube holder, nothing more than a foam block with holes drilled into it. He eased the tube into the foam beside six others, making sure the liquid line was hidden below the foam. As he walked the foam block over to the refrigerator, he addressed me again. "Vere are ve taking you today?"

I was struggling with the decision like a kid in a candy store. Two days ago, I'd wanted to visit Thomas Edison and Alexander Graham Bell. Before that, it had been the Wright brothers, Davy Crockett and even Walt Disney.

When the time came to make the decision, I said, "Mozart. Wolfgang Amadeus Mozart." I felt the urge to bow as I said his name. I had really gotten into his symphonies and sonatas over the last few years, but most recently while writing at home. I had to turn to music and writing when I found myself yelling at the television, especially during the commercials. The never-ending commercials. I recently had a tantrum during a commercial about some new drug for restless leg syndrome. The numerous side effects were listed quietly, over the soothing sound of beautiful music and the distraction of happy people dancing and petting puppies. The narrator spoke of one awful side effect after another with a disturbingly pleasurable tone. I'd pulled the plug on the TV that night and asked Alexa to play me some nice, relaxing music. She'd suggested Mozart. I was glad to have my old friend back in my life.

It was magical. I downloaded a book about Mozart. I was drawn into his colorful world. His father, Leopold, fervently developed his two young children, Anna and Wolfgang, to be amazing musicians at a very young age. They traveled by horse and carriage from Salzburg to Munich, Vienna, Brussels, Paris, London, Prague, Rome, Naples and Venice to perform for royalty. Even at the age of six, Wolfgang was quite the character, charming kings and queens, princes and princesses.

Ann Tranz smiled. "That's one of my favorite travels." I found it comforting to know that Ann had actually gone on the simulations, or so she said. Vladimir was prepping me for the IV while Ann hooked me up to a heart monitor. She looked over to her other assistant—his name was Andrew, I'd learned—who was adjusting the height of his plush leather chair. "He's going to Salzburg to meet the Mozarts."

Andrew smiled through his mask. "Ahhh. I have two different Mozart adventures! Would you like to meet the child prodigy?" He held up his hand indicating the height of a small child. "Or Mozart in the later years when he became obsessed with the opera?"

"Which one do you recommend?" I asked, struggling to make eye contact as Ann and Vlad stuck monitors to various spots on my body.

"They are both excellent simulations," Andrew bragged.

Ann interrupted. "Do the child prodigy. It's a happier travel."

As Vlad prepared to add the elixir to my IV, Ann eased the hair off my forehead and slipped the virtual reality goggles into place. I heard a hum and felt the chair recline. Ann seemed preoccupied with reading the ever-changing stats. She finally gave Vlad the one-word approval: "Ready."

He, in turn, addressed Andrew. "You got dat ting downloaded yet?" I could hear Vlad flick the plastic barrel of the syringe.

"Ready to travel," came the response from Andrew.

"OK, cowboy, time to go," Vlad said. "See you ven you get back." I felt the now familiar cold rush in my veins. Either Ann or Vlad slipped the big puffy headphones over my ears. The dark room now went silent as well, but my mind was racing.

* * *

I heard a faint tinkling from what sounded like a piano's higher register, but with the sort of twangy sound you'd never get from a piano. As the music began its crescendo, and chords were mixed quicker and stronger, I half expected to be in the front row of a Mozart concert. When my simulated eyes came alive, I was in a small parlor listening to a very young Wolfgang Mozart practice on the family harpsichord. The house was dark and musty; it smelled of thick, damp cloth, if that makes sense. Two candles helped light the otherwise dim room. A thick, handmade cloth covered a table where a tight-lipped, pale man sat. His long fingers clutched the bow of a violin that he was using as a conductor's baton. "Oh, my God! It's Leopold Mozart." Books and sheets of music were spread out on the big wooden table. The cloth covered the top, like a bedspread, but exposed the table's thick and well-decorated legs. Leopold looked my way and nodded, indicating his pleasure with how well little Wolfgang was playing. That's when I noticed that I was wearing a puffy, ruffled blue dress with a scarf of sorts tied like a belt. My arms were dainty and pale. My feet were tiny, and laced up in a half-shoe, half-sandal that didn't even reach the floor. It took me a while to figure out that I was Wolfgang's older sister, Maria Anna. In fact, I wasn't sure of it until Leopold pointed at me with his makeshift conductor's baton.

"Very well. Nana, you try it." He tapped his stick on a sheet music holder and lifted his chin.

I was dumbfounded. "Me?" Nana must be what they call me, I thought. Either way, I was sure I couldn't do what he had asked.

He scrunched his eyebrows angrily and called my name again. "Nana! Enough of this daydreaming. We are going to practice until we get this right."

Wolfgang couldn't have been more than six years old. He moved to the edge of the beautiful instrument, much like a piano in appearance. He tinkled the last two ivories on the keyboard, causing his father to wave him off dismissively.

"It's your sister's turn, Wolfgang. Come here and sit down next to me."

Defiantly, Wolfgang again twiddled the two notes and remained standing next to the harpsichord. "Want me to show you, Nana?"

I instinctively felt sibling rivalry building. I told him, "Go sit down." In a teenage girl's voice. I took my seat on the poorly padded bench and took in the beautiful instrument. To me it looked like an antique, but of course to the Mozart family it was probably the latest model. It had two rows of keys, like steps leading up to the open lid, which was propped up with a wooden rod. The exposed strings that went from short to long formed the look of a grand, horizontal harp. Two skinny legs held the instrument's smaller rear end. Two stout legs stabilized the heavy keyboard end. Between the legs were two pedals. I placed a foot delicately onto each pedal and tapped a single note with a finger from my right hand.

Wolfgang made a fart noise, blowing air onto his pale, fleshy arm, laughing rather hysterically.

Leopold pointed a stern finger, ordering him, "Come here."

Wolfgang straightened up and put his hands in his pockets but remained beside the beautiful instrument.

"Nana, let's go! We don't have all day." Leopold pointed his bow at the keys. How I knew where to start I'll never know. I put my hands to the keys and closed my eyes. Only the sound of my heart was audible. What if I can't play? An angry voice bellowed. "Anna!" I let my fingers go and to my surprise, they made beautiful music. I watched as a young girl's hands made absolutely beautiful music. I could play with my eyes closed. In fact, I preferred it. I didn't have to think about the keys; I felt them. It was like I'd practiced this tune a thousand times. When I finished, Leopold said, "Nicely done, Nana." I looked at my little brother and stuck out my tongue. I laughed out loud. I had just stuck my tongue out at Wolfgang Amadeus Mozart.

Father—that seemed more natural than to think of him as "Leopold"—insisted we take a bow holding hands, even if the bow was just to him. "We practice our music and our manners. We are Mozarts," he said. His pride had a snobbish edge, I thought.

I found it easy to get into the role of jealous sister Nana, having had a bratty little brother of my own. I found Wolfgang to be positively annoying yet absolutely adorable. As I already knew from what I'd read, I would be his closest friend, having spent so much time with him under our father's watchful eye. We would always travel together, sometimes for years at a time. That included a lot of time together riding in bumpy carriages or on a ferry boat. It wasn't unusual for us to travel for a week or longer to take up temporary residence as we waited for finicky royalty to fit us into their schedules. Wolfi was often sick by the time we got to our destination. Father said he was "susceptible."

Leopold often had him play through his illness, as he was very driven by money. He was very aware that Wolfgang was of most value as a child prodigy and often lied about his age. His tiny stature made the lies easy to believe. Even as a full-grown adult, he was barely five feet, three inches tall.

Somewhere along a carriage trip across France, I became Nana Mozart. I was no longer Mr. Peregrine in Nana's body. What little was left of the school teacher from Cleveland was somewhere between Salzburg, Austria and Cleveland, Ohio, separated by the Atlantic Ocean and over two hundred years. This latest trip, which included a voyage across the Channel, was to play for the King and Queen of England in Buckingham Palace. On the long ride, Wolfi mimicked a dog that was following us, yapping and snapping at the horses.

I poked him in the side. "Stop."

He retaliated and accidently kicked Papa.

"Enough! We are almost there. Behave yourselves." I was immediately still, but Wolfi was not. He dropped something on the floor of the carriage. While he was retrieving it, I felt a tugging. He had untied the ribbons on my shoes. I was going to tell on him as Papa was looking over his glasses at me with angry eyes. "What's going on?"

Wolfi's eyes met mine and with his devilish and irresistibly playful smile, he motioned for me to shhhhhh.

I smiled back. "Nothing, Papa." I would get back at Wolfi later without angering father.

"Who's going to be there, Papa?" Wolfi asked as he wiggled his way back into the seat. I leaned over to retie my shoes... in double knots.

"King George III and Queen Charlotte," Mama offered. "I hear they are quite talented. The king plays

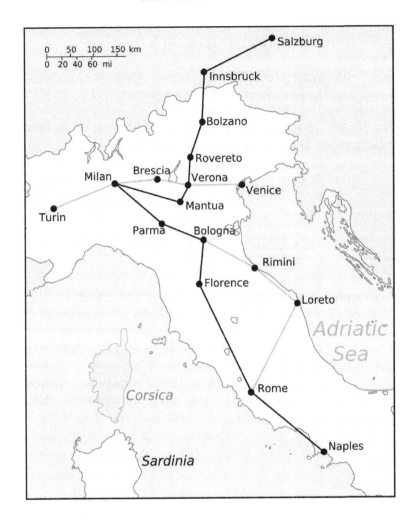

Mozart's travels in Italy

By Self-made by Jappalang [Public domain], via Wikimedia Commons

the violin and the flute, and the queen can sing and is quite talented on the harpsichord."

Papa snickered. "We've heard that before." He smiled at the children and Mama continued.

"They could be talented. Not all nobility exaggerates their gifts."

Papa retorted, "Too many do." He continued, "Wolfi, if they do play, I don't want you correcting them or telling them where they blundered. Just applaud."

Wolfi was kicking his heels against the base of the seat. "It's not my fault that–"

Papa interrupted. "Enough," he continued, sternly. "I mean it, Wolfi." The kicking got harder and Mama placed a hand on his leg. "Please, Wolfi, the kicking." Papa had told us on the way that the King had bought Buckingham house for his Queen a few years earlier to give them a home near St. James Palace, where most of the royal functions were held. Father warned us that it wasn't going to be like performing for the Austrian royals at the Hall of Mirrors at Schloss Schönbrunn, and was actually quite modest compared to the magnificence of Versailles.

Still, when the carriage pulled off the road in front of an eighty-foot-tall mansion with fifty-foot pillars, grand doors and spectacular window frames, I was a child in awe. It looked like a hotel for the rich and famous. A footman came to the door in a silly red outfit and a funny little red hat. He held out a hand to Mama. "Ma'am." He aided us onto the step he had set on the ground below the carriage door.

"We're here," Papa said, stating the obvious. "Now make me proud, children." I was overwhelmed immediately. My hands were clammy and my legs wobbly. Maybe it was from the long ride. I wish we had a day to settle, or at least an hour. But, alas, we were already later than expected and the royals were awaiting our arrival. Wide hallways led to sweeping staircases and massive rooms, and yet, it seemed homey. My neck hurt from looking up at the grand details of the ceilings. Enormous paintings, detailed with lavish golden frames, lined the walls. The decorative work was like nothing I'd seen in my limited life. I had a moment, a brief moment, where I remembered who I was. I wanted to forget. I had to focus.

A crowd stood waiting for us to join them. We received such a warm welcome. As we walked through the house, people smiled and bowed to us as if our very presence gave them pleasure. I put my arm around Wolfi's shoulders, claiming him as my brother. Everyone seemed especially charmed by this and we received ahhhh's and awwww's as we passed by. We were led to a great hall where we were met by a stately man and woman, likely in their twenties. "Welcome, welcome," the man said with a smile. He took Wolfi's violin case from Papa and set it aside, so both could take turns shaking Papa's hand and then Mama's. The man turned to Wolfi and me, leaning in uncomfortably close as adults so often do. "So, these are the talented children." He made me uncomfortable as he eyed us up and down. "Are you ready to play for us?"

I politely responded, "Yes, sir."

Then Wolfi chimed in with a squeaky voice, "We're here to play for the king and queen!" The man stood erect and laughed. The other people standing around joined in but looked nervous. Then the man took our hands and led us through the crowd, toward the front of the enormous room where a beautifully carved clavier stood on its huge clawfoot legs. It looked like it had been polished a hundred times, it was so shiny. I glanced back at Mama and Papa. They had just exchanged a comment with each other but smiled encouragingly. Still, something was wrong. Papa seemed unsettled.

"Here you are," the man said, sweeping his hand toward an elegant, well-padded bench in front of the clavier. Then he turned to Wolfi. "Will you play violin while your sister accompanies?"

Wolfi backed up his head and stared at the man. "I can't."

The man put his hands to his hips and gave an inquiring lift to his eyebrows as he looked over at our parents.

"You took my violin," Wolfi said.

The man smiled. "Indeed I did." He patted Wolfi on the head and repeated, "Indeed I did." He turned to his right and clapped his hands. "The boy's instrument." A servant hustled towards the back of the room. During all this commotion, I noticed the woman taking a seat at the front of the room in one of two grand chairs placed side by side.

I pulled in a breath. "No, it couldn't be."

The servant returned and handed the instrument to the man, offering a bow of his head. "Your Majesty." I looked at Papa; he nodded, silently affirming. The young couple were the king and queen of all of England. It wasn't just their hospitable demeanor that had fooled us; they weren't dressed as sumptuously as other royalty we'd met. The dress I was wearing, and Mama's, too, were fancier than the attire of either the king or the queen. When I was getting situated at the keyboard, I was distracted by this discovery and failed to listen to the last instructions the king gave us. I panicked, looking to Papa for a hint.

His eyes widened. He knew the look. Everyone was now seated and looking at us, ready to hear our wonderful music. But I didn't even know what we were to play or who was to start first. Had the king given a direction that I had missed? Wolfi readied his violin under his chin, his bow arm in place. He was ready for me to start, but what piece? We usually started with me playing alone on the clavier, but because the king had asked for both of us to play... Wolfi had a very serious look and nodded at me once, then twice. Finally, he whispered "Vivaldi."

"Ahhhh, the sonata in G minor." I glanced at Papa, whose eyes were wide as pies, and I began. I saw him let out the breath he was holding and noticed that he squeezed Mama's hand. I decided to look only at Wolfi. It took me two full phrases to rid myself of the butterflies in my stomach.

Yet, once those butterflies were gone, the music took over, and it didn't matter who was in the room or where they were. The world only consisted of me and a child savant, my brother Wolfgang Mozart. "Oh, the sound." When I closed my eyes, I felt it weaving its way between us, wrapping around my torso like the embrace of God, giving me comfort and lifting me to places divine. My fingers were no longer connected to my hands. Wolfi's excellence inspired me. Our mortal bodies were taken over by a magical force. The music was just notes on paper until we released it for all to hear. Then suddenly, my hands were still. The combined notes of violin and clavier hung in the air for a moment and then faded.

Applause broke through the stillness. I opened my eyes for an instant, and was surprised to see that we were not alone. I put a hand to my cheek and found tears. Wolfi looked back at me, and seemed pleased and only a bit surprised to see my tears. He understood the power of the music.

The king rose. "Bravissimo!" He clapped as he walked towards us. But when he saw me up close, he was startled. "Oh, my dear Mistress Mozart, tears?" He pulled out a lace-trimmed handkerchief and dabbed at my cheek. For my ears alone he said, "The angels themselves were moved, my dear." He pressed the handkerchief into my palm, and I knew it would be a prized keepsake. Not of worth for itself, but for the moment it brought to mind.

In truth, the rest of the concert was a blur. I played well and did all that was expected of me but for some reason, never recaptured the magic and the glory of that first piece. Even later, during the carriage ride to our inn, I pondered the words the king had said to me: "The angels themselves were moved." Even Papa's endless chatter at being paid the equivalent of 264 florins didn't touch my mood. Too often, for him, it was all about the money.

Mama reached across the carriage and put her hand on mine. "Nana, are you ill?"

Papa stopped counting his money. "You're not getting sick, are you? We've been asked back to play again."

I shook my head. I was far from ill.

Wolfi poked me and mimicked throwing up.

"No," I said. I was just trying to relive the glorious moments. "I'm fine."

Papa finally voiced his approval. "You did very well. Tonight was a great success! Nowhere have we experienced such a warm welcome. The audience was not like those at Versailles who often treat our performances as an interruption of their true goal for the evening, their inane conversation. Tonight, the lords and ladies were attentive. And I could tell their interest spurred you to play your best." He leaned forward and put a hand onto each of our knees. "I am very proud of you children."

On any other night, I would have bathed in his praise. But, tonight, I could only pretend to be pleased. For there was a sorrow in my heart that pushed back against the elation. I knew this journey would end. What if I never felt this again?

Mama picked up on my mixed emotions and put her arm around me. "Come here, Nana." She eased my head to her chest and gently adjusted and brushed my hair with her fingers. She knew just how to calm me. I let my eyes close and fell into a deep sleep.

I woke to the sound of Vladimir's voice. "Time to vaky-vaky, cowboy." I must say, I was disappointed to be back, but even more saddened to be me again. But, I must admit, I was elated with the travel. With my headphones off, I was able to hear the familiar sound of Andrew clicking away on his keyboard. As Vlad removed the heavy goggles, I adjusted my eyes to the ambient lighting of the twenty-first century.

"How long have I been under?"

Vlad looked at Andrew as if this was a question that only he could, or should answer.

"How long do you think you were under?"

I was in deep thought.

Andrew smiled pridefully as he addressed Vlad. "How long would you say we've been here at Mr. Peregrine's side?"

Vlad looked at his watch. "It's been six hours and fifteen minutes."

Andrew smiled, unable to control his cocky grin. "How long did it feel like you were traveling with Leopold and Wolfgang Mozart?"

Admittedly, I was impressed, but the smile ran from his face when I simply responded, "Don't forget about Mama."

# Chapter 6 – Mozart in Cleveland

On my way home, I called Principal Bailey to consult with him on some special needs for the coming school week. I wanted our best sound system set up in my classroom.

"So." He hesitated. "Where did you go this weekend?"

My strange answers were now expected. I'm not sure what he really thought whcn I told him I had spent the summer in Salzburg with the Mozart family. Maybe he thought I was losing my mind. Maybe he thought I was taking hallucinogens. What he did know was that his school was coming alive and even one of our local news channels wanted to meet Mr. Peregrine, "The Traveler", a name I had been given by fellow teachers, after my George Washington story-telling antics. He was happy to oblige and personally called the audio-visual teacher. He asked if she could get volunteers from her class to come in on a Sunday evening to set up my classroom. One of the students offered his personal over-the-top home sound system.

And so one Sunday night, the school came alive with strange music and way too many versions of "Testing, one, two, check, check." Six students, Mrs. Ouida and the principal pitched in to help me make the preparations. When the sound system was all set up, one of the students cranked up Falco's "Rock Me Amadeus" and the group broke out in a nerdy head bopping dance. When the song finished, I insisted that they play something very different. It was a newly downloaded performance of the Sonata for Two Pianos in D major, a much quieter number. I wanted to refocus the group on the remaining tasks. I asked the students to use a roll of brown craft paper from the art department to block the light out of all the windows of my classroom. Three hours later, when worried parents began to ring their kids' cell phones, it was time to wrap up and send the students home.

When I got home, I fussed with my now tattered George Washington wig. With a little attention, I was sure I could make it look like something Mozart might wear while conducting a concert. I had a red velvety robe that had been hanging in my closet for fifteen years. Holding it up against my body made me smile. I proceeded to cut it as cleanly as I could to the lines of a conductor's suit jacket, eighteenth-century style. I put on my best white shirt and slipped the customized bathrobe over it. I scanned the back of the closet for a frilly white neck scarf I remembered my ex-wife had left behind. I tucked it around my collar and then tied it into a Windsor knot, just like I'd done to my boring neckties for the last twenty-two years. I slipped on my wig and posed in front of the bathroom mirror. I held my chin up high and picked up a toothbrush, pretending it was a conductor's baton. I wasn't Leopold or Wolfgang, but I did look pretty good. Next, I pulled out a white plastic hanger. So far, my closet hadn't let me down. I broke off the long straight bottom piece and swished it a few times, as if conducting, to see if it would suffice. It was nearly one o'clock in the morning and my body was aching. I needed sleep.

The next morning, I met my history students just inside the classroom door. The brown paper on the windows and the strangeness of my getup stopped them, one at a time. As they looked me up and down, wondering what new nonsense I had planned for the day, I held out a wicker basket. In a terrible Salzburgian accent I said, "Your cell phone please. You'll get it back after today's surprise test." Early students were reluctant to give up their phones but as the basket filled, it became obvious that it was mandatory.

Two of the AV students and Mrs. Ouida were planted around the room in strategic places, ready to assist.

My students sat attentively, their eyes full of questions. Why the outfit? Why the covers on the windows? Why the additional staff?

I tapped my white plastic baton on my desk and the students knew their questions were about to be answered. "Today's test will count for half your semester grade," I lied.

That generated a murmured chorus of groans.

I tapped my plastic hanger piece again. "Silence!" I said in a tone I'd learned from Leopold Mozart. "You will spend this class in silence." I waited for a reaction. The reaction I got was silence. I continued. "In one minute, the room will darken. Interruptions of any kind will not be tolerated. You will be treated to music by one of the best composers of our time. Wolfgang. Amadeus. Mozart." I said his name and then took a bow as if I had just finished a concert. "You only need listen today. Feel free to put your head down. I don't care if you sleep." I hesitated again. "But be sure that interacting with anyone while the lights are out will not be tolerated. Is this clear?" Heads nodded but the silence remained. "I want you to let the music in." I put my baton down and clenched my fists to my chest. "I want you to feel the music." I nodded to the student manning the lights. The room went dark. Completely dark. And the violin of Wolfgang Amadeus Mozart began to sing.

In the darkness, I found myself mimicking Wolfgang's movements. First his bow arm, then the arm holding the neck of the violin. As I pictured him, my arm began to sway, first left and then right, on long string pulls. I wished I had night vision glasses to see how each of the students was reacting. The sound system was outstanding. When Nana joined in on the harpsichord, it was easy to imagine that you were sitting right between them. The music brought me back to Salzburg with a playful little boy who turned into a serious professional, almost a miniature adult, once the music started. I pictured his smile and half expected that, when the lights came back on, my shoelaces would be untied.

During soft violin concertos or the gentle beginning of a harpsichord crescendo, I could hear a little shuffling or an occasional cough or throat clearing. Otherwise, the room was filled with only the music of the late 1700s. When the Vivaldi piece began to play, I laid my hands on my desk and began to mime the keyboard part. I was surprised how much of the finger movements I still remembered. Suddenly I was in Buckingham Palace and the tears began to flow right on cue. When the final combined notes of the violin and the clavier faded, I was expecting applause. Instead, the lights came on per my earlier instructions. I had hoped to catch the students off guard. I'd imagined some of them swaying to the heavenly melodies in the dark, perhaps others acting as if they were the maestro himself, unifying the performers, setting the tempo and listening critically to control the music's interpretation and pacing. Instead, I was the one caught by surprise. I pulled my hands from my imaginary desk keyboard and, for a second time, wiped away my tears.

Not everyone was as moved as I was. Some slept. Others blinked and yawned and stretched to prepare for whatever I had planned next. Alex, who sat in the second to last row, near the windows, put both hands to his eyes to quickly wipe away tears and then wiped his palms on his pants. Quiet little Corinne caught my attention next. She sat in the rear of the classroom, in the end row closest to the door. She too wiped away tears but only with one hand. The other hand was trying to conceal a wetness between her legs. She noticed that I'd noticed and gave me the agreed "closed fist, baby finger up" classroom sign for "May I go to the restroom?" I gave her a nod and called the students' attention to the blackboard. Whatever had been going on in the darkness was her business. However, I must admit I was glad she, too, had been moved. I didn't expect her to come back to class so I continued with the lesson. She and I would have to discuss the assignment in private.

"Well, did you enjoy that?"

The students looked at each other for social cues.

"Don't be silly! I have been acting like a fool for weeks now trying to make this class more entertaining."

Still the class was silent.

"Maybe I should go back to the old Mr. Peregrine, scratching away on the blackboard."

The silence was broken by Madison, one of my few students who willingly participated. "I loved it." All eyes went to Madison.

"What was it about the music that you loved?"

She tucked her long black hair behind her left ear and put her hand to her heart. "It made me feel."

I smiled and nodded. "Yes, me too, Madison. Would you be willing to share more about what you felt?"

She gathered the rest of her hair forming it into a momentary ponytail and then let it drop down her back. "At first, it was like I was walking through a garden. No, not a garden." She corrected herself. "More like a field of wildflowers. I imagined picking all different flowers until I had so many, I could barely hold them in one hand." She held her left hand in front of her as if she had a bundle of flowers. "Then, I walked to a giant gate where I met an angel. I handed the flowers to her. I didn't say anything, but she knew I wanted her to give them to my sister." Tears flowed down her face as she showed how she'd handed off the flowers.

I let the room remain quiet as the students respectfully acknowledged her feelings—and braveness in sharing them. "This is what music can do, if you let it. It makes you feel. It doesn't have to be Mozart or Beethoven. It can be hip-hop or jazz or even Metallica." I paced the room looking for the next brave soul.

Alex spoke up next. "I thought it was awesome!" He waited for me to address him.

I held out a hand letting him know he had the floor and that I was hoping for elaboration.

"I liked the heavy violin parts. I imagined my father and me building a house in fast motion. When the music slowed down, we rested."

I nodded, grateful for his sharing.

And the next student shared... and the next. As I began to learn about these students, one at a time, I loosened up even more. We were learning to trust one another. We were getting to know one another.

When the class was over, students left the room conversing with one another about the music, the class, and their feelings.

Mrs. Ouida came up behind me and whispered, "Wow, what did I just witness? That's how learning was meant to happen."

I took in a deep breath and let it out as slowly as I could. "Yeah, that felt good."

I noticed her watching me closely, though, as I shook my head. "What's wrong?"

I looked over my shoulder at her. "I forgot to tell them their homework assignment." Another deep breath... and a full release. "Aw, screw the homework."

When Mrs. Ouida shared the outcome of the musical team effort with the other teachers, my audience grew. First, Mrs. Bregala joined the group since she didn't have a fourth period class. By my third class, seventh period, two other teachers and

Principal Bailey were in attendance. With all the faculty reinforcements, my request for silence was not a problem. With so many teachers in the room, getting the students to share took a bit more effort, but every class ended with real energy and momentum.

But my health was steadily failing.

Because I had so little stamina, I requested Tuesday and Thursday classes only, but promised they would be well thought out and entertaining for as long as I could manage to keep working. Mr. Bailey not only agreed "off the record" to this schedule but insisted that we hold my Tuesday classes in the auditorium, so that all the students could attend. I shot down the idea when he first presented it. Then I thought about why I'd become a teacher. I wanted to teach each new generation about the people from the past, who had dared to make a difference. Now more than ever, I felt the need to teach young people that things were quite different two thousand years ago, two hundred years ago; even twenty years ago. As important as it is to know who we are, it is more important to know why we are the person we have become.

By the end of the week, the school had received dozens of calls from parents. Some were concerned about Mr. Peregrine's health; others were elated about the recent interest their child had shown and shared at home. A news crew showed up on Thursday, asking if they could talk to me between classes. During the interview, they asked about my diagnosis and if it was the reason for my recent theatrics. The reporter asked, "Is it true that you think you've actually gone back in time to visit George Washington and Mozart?"

I thought about what Ann would say if she saw this report. "Don't be silly. I'm just trying to make learning a bit more entertaining."

# Chapter 7
## What's it Gonna be, Cowboy?

Friday night, when the news crew told me their station planned to air the story, I was pacing the bedroom with nervous anticipation. I worried that I may have jeopardized any future travels. The interview, as edited, turned out to be fairly brief. They cut out the question from the reporter and only quoted me as saying, "I just want to make learning a bit more entertaining." I decided right then: no more interviews.

My backpack had been packed since Wednesday. When my 6:30 alarm went off Saturday morning, I was already in the shower and had to quickly rinse the shampoo from my hair so I could shut off the buzzer. I took baby steps across the tile floor so as not to slip. I'd planned to take a nice long shower but now that I was out, hair washed and body parts clean, I decided to spend a bit more time writing in my journal. I was still trying to decide who I wanted to visit. Thomas Edison and the Wright Brothers were both serious contenders but there were so many other people I wanted to meet.

This time Ann asked me to park at the gas station. She said she would pick me up. I'd waited there for fifteen long minutes before Vlad rolled up in a silver Chevy Malibu. He lowered the passenger window to tell me, "Cowboy... let's go." In my backpack, I had a change of clothes and yet another $8,000 in cash. Last Thursday, when I'd gone into the bank to pull out cash, the bank manager was called over. He said it was routine to ask when large cash withdrawals were made. I told him that I was buying cars at an auction. I think he bought it, not that it was any of his business.

Once we got inside the lab and Vlad had handled the money, Ann greeted me with a smile. She asked how I was feeling.

"Like I'm dying," I said with a shrug. Ann placed a hand on my shoulder, first as acknowledgement of my comment and then to direct me towards Vlad to start my preparation.

"How far back ve gonna go today, cowboy?" The question caught me by surprise.

"How far back can I go?"

Vlad stood in front of the fridge's open door and looked over to Andrew, twisting his neck to make sure Ann was out of earshot. "How far back you vant to go?" he whispered with a raised eyebrow.

"I don't know. Joan of Arc? Plato? King Arthur?"

Andrew locked his eyes on Vlad and very subtly shook his head.

"Vhat?" Vlad whispered. "He's a dying man. Give me break."

Andrew rolled his eyes in Ann's direction and I knew this was a discussion I should have privately, if ever given the opportunity. Andrew spent most of his time staring at a computer screen, tapping away at a high speed. I think the surgical mask was simply to hide his identity.

Ann approached, "OK, Mr. Peregrine, who are we visiting today?" She placed a spiral-bound booklet containing names and brief descriptions in front of me, much like a waitress delivering a menu.

"I'll take an order of Alexander Graham Bell and for dessert I'll have a Malt Disney."

Ann was preoccupied and silently scrunched her forehead, asking me to clarify or pick one.

My attempt at humor had been lost on her. Again, I felt like I was at a restaurant. "I haven't decided." I couldn't help myself; I made one last attempt to slow down the pace. "What are your specials today?"

Ann tilted her head and smiled ever so slightly. "OK, you look over the menu and I'll be back in a couple of minutes." She was playing along, reluctantly, I think.

I looked over at Vlad. He wrapped my arm in preparation for taking my blood pressure and tapped his finger on the booklet. "Stick to da book today. Ve vill talk."

I leafed through the booklet, this time just skimming the names. I already had my top three. However, on the last page, near the bottom, were three new names of interest. Julius Caesar, Mark Antony and Cleopatra. "I don't remember seeing these options last time."

Vlad flipped the booklet to the back cover. "Dis is an old booklet." He started to walk away with it and I stopped him.

"Wait. I would love to visit Cleopatra, Queen of the Nile. Can you take me back to just before she takes over as ruler of Egypt? Can you take me back to 50 BC?"

He looked over to Andrew who was holding his mask down to blow on a fresh cup of coffee. He clumsily sipped. He pushed up his heavy-framed glasses and responded to Vlad. "I don't even have those files loaded anymore." He set his coffee down and pushed his chair back, obviously considering the request. "I would have to start it mid-travel."

Vlad stared at him. "Dyin' guy over here... You download, yes?"

Andrew took a deep breath and slid his chair back. He glanced Ann's way. She was peeling a label and wrapping it around the skinny neck area of a glass lab flask. Andrew squinted a stink-eye at Vlad. Vlad in turn, winked at me with a smirk.

I addressed the two techs. "Why would these simulations have been removed? Was there an issue?"

Both men were quiet. Vlad finally spoke. "Minor glitch. Problem for us, not for you. We have made improvements since dis model."

Andrew opened three drawers before finding one full of black thumb drives. He sorted through them, reading tiny labels until he found what he was looking for. I felt the IV pinch and winced for just a moment. Andrew let out an "aha" through his mask, holding up the drive like he'd just found gold. "Cleopatra! This is still one of my favorites."

Ann approached the station. "What's it gonna be, cowboy?"

I looked to Vlad for help.

After an uncomfortable silence, he spoke up. "He vants to do Cleopatra."

Ann looked at Andrew with a hint of concern. He responded with a nod. "I got this."

I twisted my head to look Andrew straight in the eyes.

He repeated himself, louder. "I got this."

Vlad started spewing stats to Andrew. "Blood pressure ninety-five over seventy... Heart rate ninety-five... Make dat one-oh-two and climbing. It's time to relax, cowboy. It's time to add the magic serum."

I didn't like my nickname, but I kept my mouth shut.

As Vlad prepared to add the elixir to my IV, Ann eased the hair off my forehead and slipped the virtual reality goggles into place. I heard a hum and felt the chair recline. Ann seemed nervous.

"You got dat ting downloaded yet?" Vlad said as he flicked the syringe.

"Ready to travel," came the response from Andrew. "OK, cowboy, time to go. See you when you get back."

I felt the now familiar cold rush in my veins. Either Ann or Vlad slipped the big puffy headphones over my ears; with my goggles on, I couldn't tell who it was for sure. The room went silent, but my mind was bouncing around like a pinball machine.

I heard voices echo from a distance. I couldn't make out the conversation. When my simulated eyes came alive, I was standing outside the doorway of a magnificent palace bedroom. I immediately noticed my attire. My sandals were made of golden leather straps wrapped up and over my calves. The ankle portion was bejeweled, 31 B.C. style. I was wearing a heavy, odd smelling leather jacket of sorts, with sleeves nearly to my elbows. It was stitched in a crisscross manner, making it sword resistant, I presumed. I wore a thick leather kilt with a belt clasped at the waist. My kilt was made of two-inch leather strips flowing downward, one overlapping the next like a wooden shadow box fence. A rugged sword handle stared at me from its sheath.

I could hear two voices, just above a whisper. "I can't trust anyone but you and Puzo. They are plotting to kill him as we speak."

Instinctively, I unearthed my sword, wishing it came out of its sheath more quietly. I peeked an inquisitive eye into the doorway.

"Puzo! Is everything all right?" I was startled by the voice of a young woman. "Puzo, are you there?"

I stepped farther into the doorway, my sword clumsily drawn. Two women stood before me, Cleopatra and her maid, I presumed. I cleared my throat. I tried to clear my head and get into character. A wrong move in King Ptolemy's palace could quickly get you beheaded. "Yes, Princess, I thought I heard something."

A golden leopard with black spots that was lying on the floor next to Cleopatra tensed up and rose to all fours. The princess stared right through me. "Puzo, you know that sword makes Arrow nervous."

I froze for a moment too long as I figured it all out. I was the great Puzo of Sicily. I was familiar with his legacy! He had been enslaved by the Romans as a child and trained as a gladiator. He was fierce and proud and often compared to the more famous Spartacus. He'd been a gift to King Ptolemy, meant for amusement. Cleopatra bought his freedom before he was forced to fight. He was—I am—Cleopatra's most trusted guard.

"Puzo?" Cleopatra said, worry in her voice. "Are you all right?"

I nodded my head as majestically as I could at the two young ladies and gently sheathed my sword. Arrow relaxed, plopped to a sitting posture and looked at Cleopatra for any signs of further concern. Neva, her maid, continued working scented oil into the princess's hair adding beads and pearls along the way.

I went back to my post and admired my exquisite body. I must have been six foot two with 250 pounds of muscle. I flexed my entire upper body, noticing the bulges in my arms and the firmness of my midsection. I pounded on my stomach a few times, amazed at my new body's machine-like strength. I admired my enormous calf muscles. I listened to make sure Cleopatra and her maid were still deep in the bedroom, and then I checked. I had to. I reached right under my kilt and fondled my new gladiator package. I smiled proudly, wondering if Vlad, Andrew and Ann could see what I was doing.

I tried to recall all that I could about Cleopatra and her father, King Ptolemy XII. I believe he had three daughters old enough to be named ruler should he be assassinated. Cleopatra looked to be in her early teens, which would put her oldest sister Tryphaena in her early twenties and their middle sister Berenice in her late teens. Cleopatra was considerably younger than the others but by far the best suited to rule Alexandria. At least in her opinion. She also had a younger sister, Arsinoe, and two very young brothers, Ptolemy XIII and Ptolemy XIV. Cleopatra would not yet be queen.

Her oldest sister, Tryphaena would be very dangerous and quite aware that Cleopatra was her father's choice to succeed him as ruler. Cleopatra was aware that her sister was capable of murder, as she had ordered many a beheading to be carried out by her three faithful guards.

Berenice, the middle daughter, loved playing dress-up and bossing around her many servants, but she wasn't queen material. She never even ventured outside of the castle walls. The commoners scared her. They were dirty, smelly... and poor. Certainly not worthy of her attention. Cleopatra, on the other hand, was intrigued by the streets outside the castle walls and often sneaked out to mingle, dressed as one of them, to learn their thoughts and the many languages spoken in the cosmopolitan city.

I listened intently from just outside the arched stone doorway. Sound traveled well in the stone palace. Cleopatra was concerned. The king had been missing and hadn't been heard from for many days.

Cleopatra called me into the room. "Puzo, have your men heard nothing of my father?" I did not respond, and she stood dramatically, leaving Neva sitting on the bed with a hair brush in her hand. I saw Neva eye me up. She was tiny and thin, with olive skin and dark hair that hung onto her shoulders. Her simple garments complemented her figure. She managed to give me a smile with her big dark eyes without moving a muscle on her face. I watched Cleopatra pick up a small dagger and slip it into the hip portion of her garment. I couldn't help it; her outfit made me think of "I Dream of Jeannie."

"Puzo..." she hesitated. "It's time to find out the truth. Please post a guard at my door to watch over Neva and then escort me to Tryphaena's room." At the corridor's first turn, we were greeted by two steel-jawed guards standing at attention. They had heard our approach.

One spoke to me as if a trusted friend. "Shall I move to the princess's doorway, Puzo?" I nodded, and the guard trotted down the narrow stone hallway.

As we walked through the palace's endless corridors, I found myself in awe. I will never understand how these amazing structures were built without modern tools or electricity. Stone tablets the size of mattresses lined the walls. Iron braces somehow secured these huge slabs to the wall. Each one was covered in painted carvings and characters that I could not make out. Some resembled giant scrolls; others were chiseled drawings. The stone walls opened up to a fifty-foot vaulted space, all grand archways and painted ceilings and statues of man and beast, all adorned in gold. Stairs curving up from left and then back down on the right led up to a golden chair with carvings so intricate and grand that I could only assume King Ptolemy would sit there as he listened to his subjects before granting their wishes or sending them off for a beheading. On one side, a grand archway of heavily gilded stone was being guarded by two men, majestically dressed in much heavier garb than mine.

When I got close, the two guards came to life. Their eight-foot spears crossed, but not a word was spoken. Cleopatra looked at me with confusion. "Puzo, you know the rules." I did not know the rules, but it was clear that I was not getting past these two guards. One of them watched me as the other unlocked a strong wrought-iron gate behind him. As it swung open, I took in its detailed decorative finishes of golden vines and leaves. Cleopatra was about to disappear, and she glanced back at me with what I took to be just a hint of nervousness.

As she entered Tryphaena's luxurious room, I remained outside, doing my best to look like a demigod. The simulation was brilliant. When I was part of the story as Cleopatra's guard, I was in the story. However, I was also able to follow Cleopatra as a fly on the wall, so to speak. I could now see her even if I wasn't there with her. I could feel her fear, her joy, and her thoughts. For a moment, I was back in my gamer's chair, wondering what the challenge had been with this particular simulation. Why had they pulled it from the list? As far as I was concerned, it was brilliant and exhilarating.

I could see Tryphaena in her oversized bath. One of her servants bent over the side, massaging oil into her hair. Then, without warning, she stood up, exposing her perfect, naked upper body. "How dare you enter my room?" The stoical guard closest to her reacted to her tone and put his hand to the hilt of his sword.

Cleopatra knew to tread lightly, so she spoke softly. "Sister, when you are queen, I will bow to you." She lowered her eyes in respect and waited for her response. Tryphaena motioned for the guard to relax and then snapped wet fingers, sending one of the idle maids to bring Cleopatra a tray that sat on a marble bench. The servant held the tray towards Cleopatra, offering her a glass of wine and a bowl of figs, her eyes looking downward in a show of respect.

"Please, drink, my sister," Tryphaena said. She tilted her head nonchalantly, squeezing some of the oil from her long black hair back into the bath. "Why are you here?" Tryphaena snapped.

I knew from my reading that poison was a favorite tool of government during the Ptolemy dynasty. So I didn't doubt that Cleopatra feared her wine might be poisoned. Even so, she could not show that she did not trust her sister. She held up the glass as if to toast Tryphaena. I noticed her eyes darting over the glass and the blood-red liquid; she must have been looking for signs of powder or oil in the wine. She evidently saw no sign of either, because she delicately simulated sipping the wine. From where I stood, I could see the wine didn't actually touch her lips, but she made sure to flex her throat muscle as if swallowing.

The maid took a step back, and Tryphaena motioned for her to offer the bowl of figs. Cleopatra eyed up the bowl and delicately fingered the smallest one, careful to touch it only with a thumb and single fingertip. To me, the fruit looked unusually oily. When

Tryphaena closed her eyes to dip her hair back into the bath, Cleopatra placed the fig back in the bowl and wiped her fingers on her sleeve. The silent server girl, who had watched Cleopatra pretend to maneuver the fig in her mouth for a moment, then bowed her head in respect. When Tryphaena lifted her head out of the water and again squeezed the oil from her hair, Cleopatra finally asked the question she came to ask. "Where is father?"

"Father is gone. The fool. If he knows what's best for him, he will stay gone. Alexandria needs to be ruled fearlessly. Not by an old drunk who foolishly plays his flute while his guards and servants laugh behind his back."

Her words were harsh, but they were true. The princesses' father drank himself to sleep every night now. Often sleeping in his own vomit. But Tryphaena was not the best choice to rule in Ptolemy's place. She was rude, coarse, impolite, and out of touch with life beyond the palace walls.

Cleopatra, on the other hand, took me with her when she sneaked out dressed as a commoner. I would lurk a few yards away, dressed as a common street guard. By the age of 14, she'd learned to speak half a dozen languages. She loved to practice them as she mingled with the street vendors. Inside the palace walls, her friend and servant Neva always walked two steps behind her, anticipating her every whim. But on the days that they would enjoy the streets and Cleopatra dressed like a commoner, the two would walk side by side. On these days, Cleopatra left her jewelry and makeup inside the palace walls. Her father, the king, was hated by most. He taxed his people heavily and they felt he foolishly wasted the money they had worked so hard for. It was common knowledge that Cleopatra was his favorite; therefore, the streets could be a very dangerous place for her should her identity be revealed. At the same time, the commoners feared Tryphaena. They had witnessed her publicly beheading anyone who spoke ill of the kingdom or the crown. She had sent men and women to be locked up in dungeons where souls are often forgotten. Their crime was simply failing to refer to her as "Princess" or "Your Highness."

Cleopatra kept herself, and me, very busy. I was ordered to be always either at her side or at a calculated distance. One of her favorite outings was to visit the tomb of Alexander the Great. On it was inscribed a scripture telling of a messiah who would rise from the dead. Many thought Alexander was that messiah. By now, he had been dead, and in this cloudy, glass-covered casket for three hundred years. On one of these visits to the great conqueror's tomb, I listened as Cleopatra prayed out loud for her own safety and the safety of her father.

Later that day a train of camels was escorted into the palace yard. Cleopatra looked out her window, glad the stench of the camels didn't rise to the second story. The caravan brought gifts from Gilead and Arabia in trade for grain. Cleopatra loved the sound of the bells and bangles draped on the camels. It was probably much like an ice cream truck's jingle to a child in our time. The royal princesses always got to peruse the gifts first, choosing whatever they wanted for themselves. Tryphaena had established many years ago that as the oldest she would get first call on everything.

Sacks of spices were unloaded first. Curious fingers pinched at each pouch as each princess put a small pile of fragrant dust into her palm. After a quick sampling, the remaining powder was blown into the air to make room for the next. The courtyard quickly filled with the scents of cinnamon, cumin, coriander and frankincense.

Another container held precious items wrapped in parcels of silk so fine, they were almost transparent. Cleopatra watched as Tryphaena unwrapped bracelets and sashes, Persian slippers, silver mirrors and hair ornaments. Cleopatra reached for one of the bracelets and Tryphaena instantly pulled a dagger from her slipper. I had to stop myself from reaching for my sword; that would be grounds for a beheading. Cleopatra gently returned the bracelet to Tryphaena's discard pile.

When Tryphaena was finally bored with one satchel, she forced a smile, letting the younger princesses know it was their turn. Tryphaena moved onto the next satchel pulling straw off the top to expose hundreds of jars of scented oils and essences. She admired samples of almond and coconut oils, fine perfumes and balm of Gilead itself, a most treasured item.

Afterward, Cleopatra assigned me to spy on her sister. Tryphaena had organized a dozen slaves, followed by a dozen guards, to move her personal items into her father's plush quarters. It was as if she knew he wouldn't be coming back.

A rumor was circulating that a poisonous snake had purposely been let into King Ptolemy's sleeping quarters. His trusted bed servant had tried to corner and capture the deadly six-foot puff adder. The unsuccessful—and unlucky—servant was bitten and died a painful death moments later. It was thought to be an accident until two days later when the king's taster sipped his wine and went into convulsions. The king then disappeared with a few of his most trusted guards and has now been missing for seven days.

Tryphaena suddenly raised her voice to one of her guards. "How could this be? Are your men imbeciles?" She was pacing. The guard steadied himself for her next onslaught. "I want him dead!" The guard bowed his head and took three steps backwards before turning and briskly walking out of the room.

When I told Cleopatra what I had seen—what I had heard—she was devastated. "She is the one trying to kill father?" Cleopatra fiddled unconsciously with her thumb and forefinger and I knew she was thinking back to the oily figs. "She was going to kill me!" She pulled me in close enough to whisper. "She must not find out that I know." The beads in her dark hair danced on her shoulders. Her perfectly trimmed eyebrows and long lashes caught my eye. Her eyelids were powdered a soft blue and her eyes heavily outlined in black, making her blue eyes look like brilliant marbles. Cleopatra stared right past me and continued in a whisper. "I wonder how she found out that father is still alive." She was close enough that I couldn't help inhaling her fragrance. Her hair beads swayed like the doorway of a 1970s dorm room—I momentarily flashed back to my college years and my friend Sally's dorm room. "Find Neva," She said, a rare rattled tone in her voice. "You must dress like an Arab and be ready to follow us from a distance."

"Where are we going, Princess?" I asked.

She whispered. "Meet us at the library at dusk."

When Cleopatra and Neva arrived at Alexandria's grand library, both were dressed as commoners. Neva was always at Cleopatra's side, unless I performed that duty. And while even by the age of fourteen Cleopatra was always thinking, "How would a queen conduct herself?" tonight she looked and acted like any other streetwise resident of this teeming seaport.

Outside the library's doors we met Cleopatra's trusted friend, Olympus. He had news that King Ptolemy was expected to dock at the harbor in the middle of the night, only for a moment, to pick up supplies. And, hopefully, to pick up Cleopatra herself. Then he meant to head for Rome to ask Caesar to help him regain his crown and control of his kingdom.

That afternoon, Cleopatra, Neva and Olympus made their plan to get out of Alexandria.

When Cleopatra returned to the castle, she heard Tryphaena angrily spewing orders. "I don't care! Kill the beast." When she saw Cleopatra and me, she glared right through Cleopatra and shot me a look that surely meant, "and I'll kill you, too." Was I the beast she had just referred to? Her three guards unsheathed their swords and started towards us. I lowered my eyes for just long enough to locate my sword's hilt. That's when I noticed the trail of blood. I was outnumbered, but thanks to excellent programming, experienced enough to know they did not approach me as cautiously as one would approach a warrior the likes of Puzo if they were prepared to do battle. In fact, I believe, one of her guards rolled his eyes. I kept my hand on my handle as they jogged past me, their bronze ornaments clanking around their leathery kilts.

Finally, Cleopatra spoke. "Sister, what's wrong? Whose blood is this?"

My heart was pounding, and I can only assume that Cleopatra's was too, but she was so good at keeping her fear hidden.

"When I find that beast of yours, I will deliver his head to you on a platter." Tryphaena spun quickly, her long hair and gown swirling around her.

When she disappeared from the atrium, Cleopatra let out a breath of relief. I released the death grip on my sword. "Arrow must have attacked one of her guards. This is bad." We followed the bloody trail to Berenice's room, now thinking the worst. Had Arrow killed Berenice? Cleopatra stopped in the doorway. Her sister was lying face down on her bed. Blood was spattered on the wall and in the corner of the room. When we heard her sobs, we knew Arrow had killed her pet monkey, "Baboon." Relief filled Cleopatra's eyes but then she quickly forced the emotion of sympathy. "Sister," Cleopatra said with concern. "What happened?"

Berenice lifted her head and turned like a snake ready to strike. "That beast of yours killed Baboon. I left for only a moment to get him his favorite toy." Her eyes dropped to the blood on the floor, and her voice softened as she sat up on the bed. "I heard him squeal, but he does that sometimes when I leave the room." Cleopatra looked at me, and without a word I knew she wanted me to stand guard outside the door to give her a private moment with her sister. At least as private a moment as royalty gets. Someone is always listening... a guard, a maid or any other servant who kings and queens and even princesses deem to be loyal, deaf or too scared to repeat what they've heard.

One would think that danger would come from opposing kings and armies sent by rival monarchs. In reality, life within the palace walls was every bit as risky, especially with three sisters who are all looking to fill the recently vacated title of ruler. Berenice sat slumped on her bed. She was five years older than Cleopatra but still a child. A spoiled child at that.

"Did you have her do it on purpose?" Berenice said, in a voice so sad that it brought a rare tear to Cleopatra's eye.

She sat on the bed next to her older sister and brushed the dangling strands of beaded hair from Berenice's forehead, revealing black trails of mineral ash, smudged and running down her face. "Oh sister, I would never." She assured her in a soft, sincere voice. Cleopatra embraced her sister.

Berenice began to sob. "He backed Baboon into the corner. He was screaming and screaming. I yelled at Arrow." Berenice backed away to look at Cleopatra with wide eyes. "I even threw things at her. But it was like I wasn't even in the room."

Cleopatra tried to end the awful story with a soft "Shhhh, sister," beginning to rock her back and forth. Berenice wasn't finished. "Baboon tried to bounce off the wall and over Arrow, but that beast swatted him right out of the air and back to the wall." Cleopatra knew Arrow; no doubt her leopard had picked up the limp creature and given Berenice an apologetic look as she took her kill out to the garden to play with it.

It was incidents like this that Tryphaena would use to sway her palace alliances. Somehow, I was quite sure that by this time tomorrow, if not sooner,

Tryphaena would have Berenice in agreement with her proposition: "Cleopatra must be held accountable."

My mission now was simple: to make sure Cleopatra made it through the night. Olympus was plotting her escape and we awaited final details. I was told to be extra vigilant this night and to post four of my most trusted guards at the first bend in the corridor leading to Cleopatra's room. They would be our first, but not only, line of defense. As I set the guard, I could hear Cleopatra chatting with Neva about what to bring and what to leave behind.

Late into the night, a server boy was announced and escorted to the doorway by two guards. He was a small Ethiopian child, no more than eight years old. I instinctively pressed on his shoulders, forcing him to kneel. He bent over so low his head touched the stone floor. He started to cry, trembling with fear as Cleopatra approached. No doubt he had been trained that ill-received news could cost him his exposed head.

"Speak, servant." Cleopatra kept her royal stance and spoke in a firm voice.

When he lifted his quivering head, Cleopatra smiled slightly to assure the boy she meant him no harm. She waved for the two guards in the doorway to back off, so the boy would feel safe. He was clutching a tablet. He once again lowered his head as he extended his skinny arms, the tiny tablet in his outstretched hands. Cleopatra's eyes met mine and then returned to the tablet. I took it from the boy, inspecting for signs of powder or poisonous resins. I handed the tablet to Cleopatra and motioned for the two guards to escort the boy out.

Cleopatra walked the tablet to an oil lamp in the room's far corner. She broke the seal and untied the string. It was a message from her friend Olympus! He had news of King Ptolemy. The timing was perfect. The king planned to sneak into the harbor just before sunrise with his trusted advisers to rescue Cleopatra and sail for Rome. "Make haste, Cleopatra," the tablet read. "But beware, do not eat or drink this night. Friends of Tryphaena's have been hired to poison you."

The sun would be rising in a few hours. Neva and I stared at Cleopatra, waiting for her eyes to meet ours. She flipped an hourglass and whispered, "We leave at the last grain of sand."

I was instructed not to let anyone past the guards posted at the turn of the hallway. Neva and Cleopatra had packed two small but gloriously adorned crates. Cleopatra shared yesterday's stale bread to keep our hunger pains at bay. We anticipated an evening surprise from Tryphaena. A poisonous offering, perhaps a puff adder, a tray of laced figs or a peace offering in the form of poisoned wine. As night approached twilight, we prepared to disappear. We hid on one of the upper roof gardens inside a tangle of vines. From there, we could look down into the main courtyard. We saw Tryphaena and her guards pass an open hallway that led to Cleopatra's wing. No doubt she was searching for Cleopatra. My two trusted guards had already stealthily made their way to the harbor with the two royal crates. We remained perfectly still and silent. When we saw four of Tryphaena's guards prepare a small boat to row out to Cleopatra's garden palace, it was obvious that they were searching for her. She thanked me for advising her not to hide there; her favorite place to clear her head had been her first choice. Soon, the cover of darkness would be gone; we were ready to move towards the harbor. Neva and Cleopatra kept their eyes on Tryphaena while I watched for Olympus to wave a torch from the harbor. That signal would let us know the dethroned king's ship was docking and that the coast was clear. Tryphaena knew something was up. If we were to fail at our escape attempt, we would lose our heads. All of us.

After what seemed an endless wait, the distant glow of Olympus's torch told us to make haste. I rushed the princess and her faithful Neva to the docks, not sure if I should look for danger in front of me or behind. The king's spotters had seen Tryphaena's guards rowing out to Cleopatra's Garden Palace; that spooked his crew into an early cast-off. I leaped onto the moving boat, startling one of the king's guards. We both reached for our swords. "I have Cleopatra!" I shouted. With a deliberate nod, I slowly took my hand from the handle of my sword. When the guard nodded back, I reached for Cleopatra's outstretched hand and pulled her aboard. When she removed her hood, the guard smiled. He knew Cleopatra was King Ptolemy's favorite. I flicked my four fingers telling Neva to hurry up. The princess's maid reached past my hand and locked onto my wrist moments before the ship's stern distanced itself from the wharf.

The simulation was amazing. But much like a dream, a lot of it didn't make sense. I remember the tech saying a simulation is only supposed to last a max of six hours, but this felt like weeks. We spent ten days on the ship, encountered a horrible storm, and then outran an attempted pirate attack. Once clear of the danger, the helmsman ordered us to switch out the royal purple sails for white, so we looked more like common fishermen. I thought it silly, since common fishermen certainly didn't have twelve gold-tipped oars manned on each side of their ship. Maybe it would fool a pirate from a distance.

Maybe this older simulation was different. Maybe they'd left me there in that chair for the weekend. Maybe they can't wake me. Maybe they'll leave me here forever. Why should I care? This life was way better than my real life. I am the great Puzo, protector of soon-to-be Queen Cleopatra, ruler of Alexandria and all of Egypt! I can think of worse ways to live... or die.

I think it was back on day six when Neva and I met port side to vomit together during another rough storm. The ship bounced, and I reached for her arm to keep her from falling. Our eyes met. I'm sure we had a moment. As I loosened my grip on her arm, she grabbed my hand. Her hand was so tiny and soft. She looked at me with obvious desire. We stared at one another, using each other's bodies as additional support on the bouncing ship.

Then we heard Cleopatra's voice. "Neva, come down below." Cleopatra had noticed our moment. The king forbade any kind of flirtation among his courtiers. Cleopatra gave me a stern look and I bowed my head to silently acknowledge the rebuke and ask forgiveness. Neva went below to read to Cleopatra. I continued to purge my insides over the rail, glad I was not one of the rowers below battling the storm and enduring the whip. Neva read to Cleopatra faithfully twice a day, both to calm the princess's nerves and to educate her. They read stories about great kings and queens; they practiced Latin to prepare for communicating with the Romans. Today's story was

*Homer's Odyssey,* the adventures of Odysseus's voyage home after the Trojan War. It was one of Cleopatra's favorites. Later, when the storm had passed, Cleopatra met me at the bow of the boat and assured me that even the great Spartacus had been known to empty his stomach on trips to Rome. She seemed so much older than fourteen. She spoke nothing of my warm embrace with Neva.

The sound of the drum beat that kept time for the rowers continued hour after hour and day after day until it became a part of the background. An occasional snap of a whip could be heard indicating that one of the slaves had fallen asleep or lost time with the other oarsmen. Brief water breaks were allowed in shifts. The slaves were allowed to eat and sleep in the evening when the winds filled the sails enough to keep the ship moving forward.

The king made his appearances in the evenings, always with an overflowing cup of wine in his unsteady hands. Every evening, without fail, he had drunk himself stupid. When he pulled out his flute, Cleopatra would shake her head in embarrassment. "Why can't he act more like a king?" she would say to Neva or to me. I think he was nervous about coming face to face with Julius Caesar.

He had every right to be nervous. Caesar's armies plowed through provinces like locusts, destroying everything and anyone that got in their way. If he wanted Egypt, now was the time to take it. King Ptolemy and the future queen were coming to him like a moth to a flame. He could kill them or imprison them and sail to Alexandria with Rome's vast fleet carrying his massive armies. Tryphaena's sharp tongue and handful of guards couldn't save her once the Roman troops had trounced the terribly outnumbered Egyptian army. Egypt was full of gold and ivory but perhaps more importantly, flush with much-needed wheat to feed the ever-growing population—and its army.

On our last night on the ship, I dreamt that I was in Rome, in the arena. Two men of enormous size were cautiously approaching me. One was swinging a medieval-looking ball and chain over his head. The iron ball had spikes that would destroy any man hit by this miniature land mine. Number two was circling around behind me, hoping I was distracted by his partner's whirling ball of death. I let him think all my focus was on number one. As the whirling ball got closer, I could hear it whip the air every time its orbit got closest to me. Instinctively, I did an inventory of my weapons. I had my sword and shield, a dagger in my right boot, another at my hip. I wore a chain bracelet, triple wrapped around my wrist. I was a master with the short chain. I dramatically tossed my sword and shield to the ground and unclipped a simple clasp to let the two feet of chain dangle, its end still attached to my wrist. The tiny ball at the end of my chain paled in comparison to the monster that was doing revolutions around number one's head. But it armed me with a twenty-four-inch rabbit punch that came from nowhere and could be an effective choke collar.

Fighting is all about timing, and not advertising your moves. I acted as if I was timing my attack on number one. I knew this would draw in number two from behind. Out of the corner of my eye, I saw him raise his sword. I was waiting for that moment. As he swung for the kill, I backed into him, closing the gap and causing his swing to go beyond my body. I grabbed his arm and, using his momentum, threw him in the direction of the whirling flail. He took a mean hit to the leg. The spikes stuck hard into the bone of his upper thigh. Number one had to yank it out quickly before I attacked him. I eased out one of my daggers. I went with the one on my right hip. With number two writhing in pain, I could concentrate fully on the remaining barbarian. I had my dagger in my right hand and my twenty-four-inch ball and chain in my left. He started up his motion, eager to get full momentum again with his deadly ball. I couldn't let that happen. I exaggerated a motion as if throwing my dagger at him, causing him to flinch defensively. On the flail's next revolution, I dived and rolled at him as soon as the ball passed. I came up at his feet and sliced the tibial nerve of his dominant leg. This was a debilitating injury causing extreme pain and complete loss of function of that leg. The momentum of his rotating flail and the loss of use of his right leg sent him tumbling to the ground. For the first time, I was aware of the crowd cheering as I slammed my knee into his chest, knocking the wind out him. The crowd chanted as I eased the dagger to his throat. He was huffing and puffing, sweat dripped down his dirty forehead, making faint paths of cleaner skin. His eyes met mine and for the first time, I saw surrender in his eyes. "What are you waiting for? Kill me," he whispered. I hesitated. We didn't know each other, and we certainly didn't hate each other. We were simply sport for the bloodthirsty fans. I tightened my jaw and pretended to thrust my dagger deep into his neck. He winced in anticipation of pain. When he opened his eyes, I winked at him. He let out a big breath and closed his eyes. I'm not sure if he was grateful or disappointed.

I woke up in a cold sweat, each hand still grasping a weapon. As I regained my composure, I thought of

Vlad and Andrew. They had to be monitoring me. My heart rate must have been 200 beats a minute. Why have they not communicated with me? Was this to be my new life? Puzo the Great. I was so impressed with the simulation. I was dreaming while in a dream. I took a moment to inventory my weapons. Dagger at my side and in my boot. Chain on my left wrist, sword and shield at my bedside. I stood and stretched, and flexed my rock-hard upper body, again admiring the bulges in my arms.

We had been sailing for almost two weeks. As much as I admired my demigod body, I could no longer tolerate its rank odor. The sun was just coming up, rowers were getting chained onto their benches and preparing for the final day of rowing. The winds were calm. I took the moment to strip and dive into the chilly waters. I scrubbed my body parts with nothing more than water and my bare hands, but certainly it would be an improvement. The water was crystal clear. I could see the bottom. I took a deep breath, pushed my head down and legs up to dive. The sea was deeper than I thought. Much deeper. By the time I hit bottom I was nearly out of breath. I pushed hard off the bottom in a rush. When I hit the surface, I inhaled a large breath. Shaking my head, I wiped the excess water from my face and hair and began to breaststroke towards a rope ladder dangling from the hull. In the corner of my eye, I saw Neva. She had been watching me bathe. She was standing quietly, probably admiring the sunrise. I don't think she knew I saw her. I climbed aboard as if I didn't see her. She watched me dry off and dress back into my uniform. When I finished lacing up my boots, I looked across the deck and smiled. She quickly turned to face the sunrise. I wished I had let her have the moment without letting her know I'd seen her. She didn't look back. Quietly, I went below to get some breakfast.

# Chapter 8 – Dug in Like a Tick

This morning we were finally to arrive in Rome. King Ptolemy insisted we put the royal sails back up.

Ptolemy had strategically bought peace with Rome by offering 6,000 silver talents to Julius Caesar and Pompey. Ships now sailed regularly between Alexandria and Rome, trading everything from spices to weaponry. Pompey was Caesar's right-hand man. He was a vigorous soldier, often referred to as the bearded executioner. In just three months, he had almost rid the Mediterranean of pirates, taking 846 pirate ships out of commission. These pirates had been robbing the ships along their trading routes. The fearless Pompey had also captured Jerusalem a few years earlier, leaving Roman soldiers in charge of the new province of Judea. He was not a man to have as an enemy. Ptolemy and Cleopatra hoped he would honor their agreement, now two years old. The gold would be long since spent and the agreement easy to dishonor.

As the ship approached the harbor at Ostia, the seaport for Rome, Cleopatra approached her father. Ptolemy was looking at the quickly approaching land, his fingers drumming on the ship's rail and his eyes darting back and forth. He was obviously worried about his meeting with Caesar. Cleopatra tried to help by reminding her father of his great past. She spoke to him of the trip up the Nile he had taken many years ago, knowing he loved to talk about his adventures.

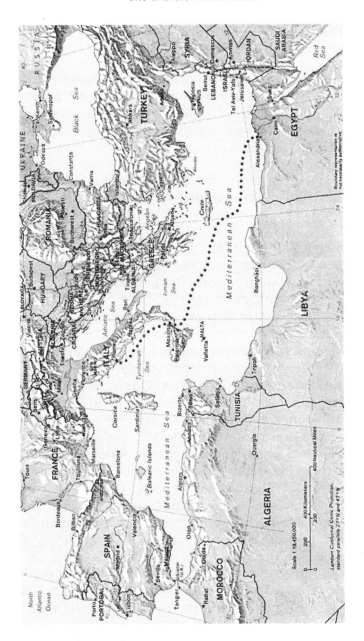

Cleopatra's voyage to Rome

She asked what his favorite memories were of his twenty-three years as king of Egypt.

He spoke of parties and feasts. She asked if he wanted to visit such wonders of the world as the Colossus of Rhodes or the Hanging Gardens of Babylon, hoping to hear him talk of the future and not the past. He yawned.

"He has no more imagination than Berenice," Cleopatra had often confided to me during the long voyage.

Ptolemy had often told Cleopatra that she was his favorite, but her affection for him was often tested. She was still young, but she had studied royals from the past to follow their examples. The Queen of Sheba so desired knowledge that she rode by caravan all the way to Jerusalem to meet King Solomon, considered the wisest man on earth. Queen Esther of Persia had saved her Jewish people from slaughter by bravely standing before King Ahasuerus. Queen Nefertiti was one of Cleopatra's idols, perhaps one of the most powerful women ever to have ruled. She reigned over Egypt in the fourteenth century B.C. She gave birth to six daughters. One of her daughters, Ankhesenamun, was portrayed in a modern-day movie, "The Mummy," as the lover of Pharaoh Amenhotep IV. She quickly rose to power at the age of fifteen. So, as she was nearly that age herself, surely it was not too soon for Cleopatra to prepare to be a queen.

As the beacons marking the harbor mouth came into view, Cleopatra had a rare moment of doubt. She stood close to me, both of us looking over the ship's rail. The drums were beating louder and faster now, pushing the oarsmen to their limit. The king liked to make a show of strength for the onlookers on shore.

Cleopatra grabbed the bicep of my right arm with both hands, still looking straight ahead. "Puzo, I'm scared," she whispered. Now, the future queen sounded like any other fourteen-year-old. "I'm not ready to face the fearless Romans. My tranquility has fled."

I flexed my muscles, loosening her grip. "You are more ready than you know, princess," I was able to confidently assure her, based on my knowledge of this historic meeting. I couldn't help taking it to the next level. "You will be the future ruler of Egypt; this I know."

She squeezed my bicep again. "Oh, Puzo, promise me you will be by my side every moment."

I was loving the simulation. The great future ruler of Egypt asking me to stay beside her every moment. I would say that this is every history teacher's dream, but it would be more accurate to say every man's dream. I responded in my best hero voice. "Every moment, princess. Every moment."

A breeze from land brought the welcome smell of trees and flowers. A pod of dolphins had joined us, leaping alongside our ship, keeping pace as if escorting us into port. Cleopatra let go of my arm and pointed. "Look, dolphin!" she cried. Her childish excitement reminded me of a little girl on a car ride to grandma's, seeing cows for the first time. "Thank you, Neptune. Thank you, great god of the sea."

Ptolemy was being fussed over by his entourage in preparation for his meeting with Caesar. After weeks of travel, we were down to the last ten miles up the Tiber River. We encountered many rude sailors along the way, spouting their filthy mouths at the two young women aboard. Cleopatra was fit to be tied. I suggested she take Neva below whenever we passed busy wharves or other vessels. After we passed the lighthouse of Ostia, I began to see the luxurious villas lining the shore. These were summer homes for the wealthy to escape the heat and the summer stench in the heart of Rome.

The banks of the Tiber were lined with lush vineyards and forests. But as we got closer to the city, the stench of garbage and sewage overwhelmed us. Cleopatra kept her scented veil pressed to her nose to mask the foul odors. Ptolemy seemed immune to the odors; he gazed at the sights and even occasionally waved to locals on the shore who pointed to our ship.

The river looked more like brown oil than clean water; it was filled with disgusting floating trash. Bloody rags, onions, broken pieces of furniture mixed with visible bits of human waste. Was this river their garbage disposal? The city's sewer? I hoped the stench would pass quickly, but soon learned it was to be the smell of all of Rome. From the windows of riverside houses, I saw servants dumping trash right into the water, to be carried out to sea.

Do these people no longer smell this wretched odor? For a moment I wished I was back on the ocean with a salty breeze. Or back in Alexandria, walking with Neva along the pristine Nile. But I knew the event that was about to take place, and I wouldn't miss this opportunity for the world. When we reached the walls of Rome, busy wharves along the Campus Martius were filled with merchant ships, unloading or loading their cargo. Our royal vessel would have to tie up here and transfer our belongings to carts and donkeys. King Ptolemy and Cleopatra were carried the remaining two miles in plush litters, muscled by eight strong slaves. The bumpy road made for slow travel, but I must admit that it was nice to be on solid ground after so many days at sea.

When we arrived at our destination, we were greeted by dignitaries in the customary white togas, and a handful of fat gentlemen with more than their share of chins. We were taken to a decent villa with a beautiful atrium, surrounded by colonnades in the Roman style, but it was located on the stinking river. Servants followed Cleopatra closely, waving peacock feathers to keep the flies away. Even the flowering fruit trees, fish ponds and fountains couldn't make up for the smell. Marble busts, far more delicately finished than the ones in Alexandria, were everywhere. I followed Cleopatra and Neva as they toured the villa, making sure to keep one hand on my sword at all times.

Cleopatra had confessed she feared this was a trap, and step one of the Romans' takeover of Egypt. I would do everything I could to protect the princess. Once our fat, toga-clad and somewhat unimpressive welcoming committee left, Cleopatra locked arms with Neva. "Let's bathe. I fear this stench will never wash off."

In a private suite, the bath was much like home, with hot water from a tap, provided by an underground fire. There was an assortment of pleasant perfumes and oils. I was to stand, alert, on the other side of a ten-foot-long concrete wall. From my post, I could hear almost every word echo off the stone wall that surrounded the oval tub. The girlish laughter made me smile. Cleopatra and Neva were the best of friends. They both clearly understood and accepted their roles. Sometimes they would lower their voices to a whisper to keep me from hearing.

Those were the giggles that made me want to peek around the wall.

When the bath was over and Cleopatra had been dried and perfumed, she joined her father on a balcony. King Ptolemy had one of his servants bring him a big glass of wine and a chair. He pulled out his flute and played an off-pitch tune over and over, trying to get it right. He made a high pitch chuckle with every mistake. "Wait, wait, let me try again," he would say to his guards, who showed no reaction. As far as their emotions were concerned, they might have been made of stone. Cleopatra took this opportunity to excuse herself, letting her father know she had planned some reading time with Neva. Two glasses of wine later, he wiped off his flute's mouthpiece. He tied it clumsily to his robe and waved for his servants to take him to bed. This was a routine they were very used to. Cleopatra and Neva stopped talking when the babbling king shuffled down a hallway to his bedchamber. His two most loyal servants escorted the wobbly Ptolemy and pulled a heavy door shut behind them. The silence allowed Neva to tell a bedtime story to the princess.

The next morning an elaborate caravan arrived at the villa to collect King Ptolemy and the princess, presumably to meet Caesar. The Hebrew slaves who carried the caravan had come from Jerusalem, captured by Pompey years earlier. They spoke to one another longingly about hope. Hope that their God would soon free them from captivity. Perhaps they didn't expect that an Egyptian princess from Alexandria, or her bodyguard, would be able to understand them.

Rome was surrounded by a thick stone wall that had been built over three hundred years before. The city was cramped, full of multi-story buildings, one apartment built on top of the other. In each house, several families lived above the ground-floor shops. There seemed to be no rhyme or reason to which businesses were next to one another. Graffiti stained every wall. Some were written in Latin, some in Greek. As we approached the famous Amphitheater, I saw names of gladiators; even the famous Spartacus. However, much of the writing was simple vulgarity. I was able to understand much of the graffiti just by looking at the expression on Cleopatra's face. I couldn't help thinking that the Romans had spent entirely too much time conquering others when they should have spent a bit more time sweeping their own front step.

It was now day two and we still had not met Julius Caesar. We thought he would be on the wharf ready to receive us, but rumor said he was up north building catapults and battering rams, preparing to conquer more of Gaul or possibly Britannia. People here were purposely vague but more likely unaware. We did have the displeasure of meeting Pompey the Great. He had prepared a banquet for the royal visitors. Cleopatra and Neva fussed over the princess's outfit. I was surprised to see her come out in a fresh white toga with a sheer silk sash tucked next to her skin. Her toenails were painted a powder blue. Delicate gold chains with tiny bells adorned her ankles. She wore a crown of henna blossoms over her hair, which was brushed straight to her shoulders. Her eyelids were a matching powder blue. She acknowledged my sincere nod of approval, then turned to Neva. "I want to appear royal but not cheap—like Berenice." Neva held up a mirror to give Cleopatra a final look; Neva's confident smile of approval was enough to keep the princess's gaze at herself to a minimum.

Tiny oil lamps set on the ground led the way to Pompey's banquet room. We passed large fire pits. Several pigs, ducks and assorted wild fowl were all being turned on spits. The banquet hall was a grand room that opened onto beautiful gardens, momentarily mixing the smell of roasting meat and wildflowers. The tables were arranged in a huge horseshoe shape, so all could enjoy the lavish entertainment. The pillows and fabrics piled on the diners' couches were similar to those in Alexandria, possibly because Egypt did so much trading with Rome. Only moments after Cleopatra and King Ptolemy settled into their table, a servant girl brought an elaborate display of assorted songbirds as an appetizer, along with asparagus tips and spotted quail eggs cooked in their shells. Red grapes were piled high all along the table. Moments later, huge slices of hot pork were served, and dishes of figs and olives were added to the feast. I saw Cleopatra look around the room for a sign that it was all right to start eating. She wasn't sure who all these dignitaries were. Certainly, there were senators and governors of nearby provinces. The king had already stabbed the large cut of pork, tearing off a huge bite with a growl of delight.

"Father!" Cleopatra whispered.

King Ptolemy looked up, chewing on his greasy mouthful of meat, a large hunk of pig still on his fork. He tilted his head, indicating to Cleopatra that others were doing the same.

"Let us watch our manners," she said quietly, delicately beginning to cut up one of her asparagus spears.

All three of us were startled when soldiers in red-plumed helmets marched into the room with trumpets. After a loud fanfare, General Pompey himself strolled into the room. When Cleopatra turned her head to see him, her pearl earrings swayed; I couldn't help thinking of plush dice on the mirror of a '64 Chevy after a quick stop. He wore a traditional white toga but also had a red velvet cape draped over his shoulder, and thick armbands as if he were Alexander the Great. He touched the handle of his sword and looked around the room, obviously searching for his guests from Alexandria.

When his piercing eyes found Cleopatra, she straightened up, holding her head high. I could see the pride in her attitude, and if she was nervous, she kept it to herself. I nonchalantly flexed my right hand and lowered it to the hilt of my sword. The ball on my wrist chain clinked against the sword, and Cleopatra knew I was at the ready.

Pompey obviously commanded the respect of the entire room. I saw Cleopatra pinch her father's leg, indicating for him to put down his knife and his goblet, as did the rest of the room. "Well, then," Pompey shouted, clapping his hands over his head. Dancing girls appeared, dressed in billowing, transparent silk, their tiny finger cymbals swaying to tambourines and African drums. A family of pygmies joined in, entertaining the room with their colorful outfits and painted faces, doing endless somersaults.

Utensils were once again lifted, and echoing chatter quickly filled the room. As the meal continued, Pompey made his way over to our table with a snide grin. When Ptolemy rose to greet him, Pompey clasped both of the king's hands and began to speak fast and loud for all the room to hear. The king did not understand a word of Latin. Cleopatra and I did. "King Ptolomy," the general said. "So, we finally meet, you

139

ape-faced buffoon. Indeed, you are half baked. A decrepit drunk with a nose like a plum. Did our trumpets wake you from your nap?" The room hummed with snickers as he let go of his guest's hands and turned to Cleopatra.

She held her arms tightly to her belly so as not to give the rude general any indication that touching her was an option.

"Ahhh, little child," he said as he looked Cleopatra up and down. "Aren't you a sweet piece of ass?"

Muffled laughter showed that both dignitaries and soldiers were enjoying Pompey's cleverness. I tightened my grip on my sword. I knew from history what was about to go down, and I hoped that history was correct.

Cleopatra eyed the room. I watched this fourteen-year old girl turn into a woman right before my eyes. "Sir," she began in Latin, "I am Cleopatra, Princess of the Nile, third daughter of the king, and pharaoh of Egypt. The man you have so cruelly insulted is my father." Her voice trembled at first and then grew firm.

Pompey's grin turned to embarrassment as she continued. Dignitaries and soldiers fell silent. King Ptolemy's red face and slumped body began to puff up, and a smile came to his face. He didn't understand his daughter's Latin words, but he certainly understood their tone.

"General Pompey," she continued, "We come before you humbly to ask your help, but not as fools. If this evening is sport for you and your baboons, to mock the royal family of Egypt with whom your country has traded precious items for years, just say so. We will return to Alexandria immediately and burden you no longer."

My hand was flexing, and Pompey noticed my tight grip on my sword. He softened his gaze and assumed a more humble expression as he looked back at Cleopatra. "No, indeed your highness," he said in a voice low enough for only the three of us to hear. "You are no fool." He raised his voice again and addressed the room. "Come. Let us sup."

As the night continued, the king drank too much and brought out his flute, much to Cleopatra's dismay. Pompey and Ptolemy exchanged loud belches as a compliment to the good food and drink. When the slaves finally snuffed out the torches signaling that the feast was at an end, Cleopatra sighed loudly, relieved that the night had ended without further embarrassment.

When she returned to the guest villa, she told Neva of Pompey's foolish attempt to insult them. She thanked Neva for helping her master the Latin that Olympus had diligently taught her back in Egypt.

I was so exhilarated by the whole experience, I didn't give much thought to what was going on back in the real world. Had I known, I wouldn't have been so happy. Only later would I learn that back at their makeshift travel port, Vlad and Andy were starting to panic. They had been unable to bring me back to reality. I had been dug in for fourteen straight hours. Ann had finally left at 11 p.m., instructing her to techs to "Stay with him" and "Keep trying to ease him back.

"Be careful," she warned them. "We don't need another incident."

Earlier I had wondered if there was a problem with older simulations like the one I was in. And there was a problem. It was in the details. Before inserting their own voices into the program, as they had with the George Washington and Mozart travels, the techs just had to wait for the drugs to wear off. Three times out of four, that was enough to end a simulation. Sometimes a little shake would bring a traveler back. Through trial and error—serious error—they had coined a term for their "little issue." They referred to it as a "travel tick." That implied that the traveler was dug in like a tick. If you pull too hard on a tick, you leave its head behind. If you try too hard to force a traveler back to the present, you risk leaving his mind behind. Two travelers had never returned. Both had gone home, laid down in bed and closed their eyes. That was almost a year ago. Their eyes are still closed. They are fed intravenously. It's very likely that they think they are still traveling, possibly stuck in their last simulation. Possibly off on an adventure of their own.

Following those incidents, the lawsuits started and Ann went underground. Ann was brilliant, no doubt, but also missing a few key traits, like empathy and sincerity. She was unabashedly ambitious and felt that the end always justified the means.

When Ann walked back in at eight the next morning, Vlad was sleeping near the fridge. Andrew was sitting at his multi-screen work area, shaking his head. His eyes locked with Ann's. She was waiting for something from him. Finally, he spoke. "I can't wake him." He rocked nervously in his office chair, his mask pulled down around his neck. "I even shook him. Nothing."

Vlad woke up from his chair nap as if he had never been sleeping. "We got a travel tick," he blurted, wiping the sleep from his eyes.

Andrew snapped back, "Stop saying that."

Ann came to where I was lying and eased the headphones off my head. I'm told that I looked in her direction, but right through her, then spoke. "I can't hear you." My head twisted as if leaning one ear towards whoever I was addressing in my dream world. "I can't hear!"

Andrew spoke up, "Heart rate back up to 140. You're gonna spook him!"

Ann didn't listen. "Hey, cowboy, we need for you to come back to reality." I began moving my head left and right, dragging the heavy goggles along for the ride. Ann continued addressing me. "Mr. Peregrine, we need for you to come back. Come back to Ohio."

Somewhere in ancient Rome, I twisted in confusion. The voice I was hearing did not match my Roman setting. "Who is calling me? Why can't I see you?"

Ann continued in a soft, reassuring, voice. "It's Ann from..." She hesitated. "From the dental office." She shrugged at Vlad and Andrew; they were anything but a dental office. "You've been in a simulation voyage for too long. We need to bring you back."

Andrew butted in again. "One-sixty and climbing... No, wait... Coming down. 155... 150."

My head relaxed and Ann continued. "I'm going to take off your simulation goggles. Do you understand me?"

I hesitated and then nodded my head ever so slightly.

When Ann lifted the heavy goggles from my face, I blinked twice and tightly closed my eyes. I took a deep breath and then eased my eyes open. "She's not the queen yet. We have to take the crown back."

Andrew smiled and whispered just a little too loud, "That's a bad-ass simulation, even if I say so myself."

Vlad nodded and smiled.

Ann snarled at them both.

"Velcome back, cowboy," Vlad said. "I t'ought ve lost you."

Ann was busily instructing Andrew to run post travel-tests and telling Vlad to check all of my vitals. She headed back out the secret door muttering to herself, "I'm too old for this shit."

# Chapter 9 - Neva From the Shadows

After thirty minutes of testing, I was starting to get anxious. "I'm fine; stop poking me. And get this IV out of my arm."

Vlad looked at Andrew and chuckled. "You heard da guy."

Andrew tapped a button on his keyboard and Vlad peeled the white tape off my wrist. After he pulled the IV out of my arm, he motioned for me to hold the gauze pad over the puncture. Moments later he motioned for me to lift my hand; in a moment, a small Band-Aid covered the spot. They forced me to walk around the office a few times and perform agility tests as if I'd just been pulled over for drunk driving. I found myself thinking, "I wish I still had Puzo's body. I would show them agility that would amaze them."

Vlad started wiping down the simulator chair. "Vell, who do you vant to meet next, Mr. Traveler?"

I straightened and re-tucked my shirt. "I think I can afford one more travel before I meet my maker."

Ann had just walked back in the door. The two techs looked at each other and then at her. She nodded her head slightly. Both men quickly looked down; it looked like they wanted to keep me from noticing their subtle communications.

"What?" I said, eyeing up all three, looking for any other signals among them.

Vlad kept his head down, but looked up to meet Ann's eyes.

"Tell me!" I insisted.

"No!" Ann snapped. "We're not going down this road again."

Andrew lowered the white mask from his mouth, uncovering a thick, dark mustache and a triangular soul patch under his bottom lip. "Ann, we have made adjustments. We can do this."

I looked at Ann for a response.

"This is how we got in trouble last time: playing God."

Vlad joined in. "Ve are not playing God. Simulations are based on calculated responses, based on knowledge ve have about our chosen historical figure—"

Ann interrupted. "But Jesus is someone different in each religion... to each person! It's impossible for us to simulate his version of a visit with Jesus!"

The unmasked tech stretched his neck, lowering the mask even more. "That's true," Andrew said, "but we can let you visit Heaven."

Ann took a deep breath.

Andrew waited to see if Ann was going to stop him. He continued. "You would have to fill out detailed questionnaires telling us about your favorite memories. We coax these memories and beliefs out and mix them with any one of our three outstanding simulations. Vlad and I have worked tirelessly to create settings of Heaven based on centuries of research. We already know your communication echoes and brain preference patterns."

He'd just lost me with his jargon, and my expression must have said as much.

Ann stared right through me, almost daring me to inquire further.

And so I did. "What are the problems with this voyage? Why is everyone so freaked out?" I looked at Ann and then Vlad. Both were tight lipped.

Finally, Andrew spoke up. "Because not everyone wants to return from Heaven." Again, a long silence.

"What are you saying?"

Ann was strangely quiet, letting Vlad and Andrew do the talking.

"Ve had a client dat decided not to come back." Vlad put his palms up and shrugged. "Not our fault ve create a place so nice."

I stared blankly at the ground with a finger and a thumb nervously pulling at my bottom lip. I was trying to imagine the incident. It sounded rather pleasant for the traveler. Especially if he had nothing but a painful death to look forward to here in the real world. Once again, the issue seemed to be on the tech side. "I want to go to Heaven."

Three hours later, I would be sent home with a head full from my latest travel, and excitement about a new adventure. I decided not to look at the handbook that they'd given me until Friday, so I could give my students my full attention from the most recent travel to Egypt and Rome.

The Heaven guide had been given to me in the strictest of confidence. No copies allowed; the book must be returned the day of the travel. I chuckled and thought to myself, "You won't find that on a travel guide. Trips to Heaven: Book now while space is available!"

Andrew would need an additional week to prepare, so my next travel wouldn't be for two weeks. They also let me know that the Heaven simulation would cost me $12k. Pretty much everything I had left to my name.

I never checked in at the hotel. There was no need. I had just spent the night in Rome. The two-hour drive home flew by. I rarely changed lanes unless the robotic voice of my GPS gave me the command. I was mindlessly driving, more in Rome than Ohio. I nearly ran out of gas, thankful that my old beater had a warning feature that dinged when the needle rested firmly on E. While filling up the car, I got a text from my principal. It wasn't the first one.

He had texted Friday night trying to verify that I was still good for an auditorium performance this coming Thursday. He'd tried to call once on Saturday and two more times early this morning. His latest text read, "You OK?"

I returned the text: "Ready for Thursday! Spent the weekend with Cleopatra, Caesar, Ptolemy and Pompey. Can't wait to share."

Just two minutes later, the principal replied. "Ummm, OK. Anything you need from me?"

I was going crazy, my head full of alter ago from my secret life. I couldn't wait to share. "Just give me a room full of students," I texted.

Half way home my right leg was throbbing. "Damn sciatica." My right arm ached, too. I took a shallow breath wishing I still had big arms, steel abs and the stamina of a sled dog.

When I finally opened the door to my condo, the smell of a dirty litter box overwhelmed me. I couldn't help smiling, though, comparing it to the stench of Rome. Baxter was sleeping on one of the dining room chairs. The house was completely silent until the refrigerator started a familiar hum. Everything was right where I'd left it two days ago. Or was it two weeks? Baxter lifted his head, jumped from the chair and circled my feet. He did his familiar "I'm out of food" dance. I scooped a big cup of food from its Tupperware container and filled the cat's bowl. The water bowl was also empty. "Bad dad," I admonished myself. Robotically, I rinsed the crusty water bowl, still lost in my head. "What's to become of Baxter when I'm gone?" The water had finally gotten hot enough to get my attention. I adjusted it back to a tolerable temperature and finished washing Baxter's bowl. As soon as I placed it on the ground, Baxter began to lap it up—and continued for quite some time. I knew I needed to come up with a plan for the cat.

Sitting at the kitchen table listening to Baxter lap up his water, I began to wobble. I was exhausted. I peeled the tiny bandage from my wrist, noticing how skinny and blotchy my arms had become. I'd urinated at Ann's lab— office, whatever it is, before I left but now I had to pee again. That duty done, I washed my hands and brushed my teeth. It was just past 2 p.m. but I was ready for bed.

That night, I dreamed about Vlad and Andrew. I saw myself sitting in the simulator. Andrew was like a mad man, typing away, creating scenery changes on his screen that were also simulated in my head. Vlad was egging him on to make the trip more exciting. I was back in the Amphitheater, fighting the same two barbarians as when I was in the actual simulation. I was simultaneously in the simulation and yet able to watch as Vlad and Andrew organized my adventure. As I made headway with my two barbaric challengers, Vlad kept encouraging Andrew to "add a lion!" and then, "add a second lion!" It had become a game to them. In my dream, Vlad had become uncharacteristically cruel.

"He's a dead man anyway." Vlad reached over Andrew's shoulder and pressed a button to release a third lion. Lions number one and two devoured my two challengers and lion number three was cautiously stalking me. I tightened my grip on my shield and held my sword up like a baseball bat, ready to swing away. As the lion got closer, I whipped the sword back and forth, sending the lion circling left. We did a slow dance number, both now circling to the left. The lion was well armed, its four huge paws equipped with multiple daggers on each one. The first two lions, which had made such quick work of the first two gladiators, were satisfied at first, each with a gladiator of its own to chew on. Then Vlad pointed at the monitor again, instructing Andrew, "up the odds in the lions' favor."

"Click, click, click," and all eyes were suddenly on me. The three lions all circled left taking turns roaring, each louder than the last. Number three, with the darkest mane, made the first move, double-pumping a swipe with a paw the size of a baseball mitt. I whipped my sword but came up empty. Out of the corner of my eye I saw one of the other lions make a move. I swung my shield with all my might... propelling myself right out of bed.

I hit the floor with a thud, knees first, then onto all fours before coming to a stop against my dresser. I was wide eyed, huffing and puffing. Baxter was frozen, claws digging into the comforter, his slanted cat eyes now wide and round. We stared at each other. I was glad he wasn't a lion. Baxter seemed glad that I was no longer thrashing around. The cat's tense muscles eased up and he melted back into the comforter. I couldn't help being pissed off at Vlad. I had to wonder about this. "Why did I imagine him to be so reckless with my life?"

I spent the next two days reading up on Caesar. I remembered that Caesar had helped King Ptolemy and Cleopatra regain the crown, but since I came out of that latest travel early, I needed a refresher if I was going to cover it with the students.

I prepared a thumb drive with photos and diagrams, sketches of Cleopatra and Caesar, maps and views of Rome and Alexandria. I wanted to be prepared. I wanted to take my students to Rome, 45 B.C.

Come Thursday, I wasn't feeling so well. I lay in bed, thoughts all a jumble. It's hard to describe cancer. Some days are better than others. You know that angry, frustrating feeling you get when your car starts to falter? You know it's going to stop working at the most inopportune time. Now replace that anger and frustration with fear. No, don't replace it. Add it. Then throw in uncertainty, nausea, sadness, bitterness, regret and confusion. The things you thought were important—just aren't. My thoughts were getting pretty morbid. "I don't know what I would be doing if I hadn't stumbled across Ann, if I didn't have my students. To see them engaged has changed my life. It has given me purpose. It's a cruel irony. Why do we wait for a death sentence to live?"

I continued studying like a fool. I read up on Cleopatra's trip back to Alexandria with Caesar. Reading was different now. Now that I'd been to Rome. Now that I'd met Cleopatra, Pompey and Ptolemy. As I read, I could see the events taking place. I stared right through the pages of the book when Caesar's men torched the Alexandrian fleet. I knew the fire would get out of hand and spread to one of the greatest and famed libraries of its time. I wasn't sure how long I stayed on that page, but it was wet from tears. The two-inch wet spot caused an undulating effect on the thin paper page. I flipped the page to inspect the wetness from the other side and got lost in another voyage. I closed the book. I was ready. It was time to become Puzo.

I tapped in "Hercules costume" on my phone and laughed. I didn't have to go any farther than Walmart to get a fairly decent costume. But I didn't want fairly decent. Click, click, click, eBay, Halloween costumes, high-end costume shops. I found half a dozen versions. I searched until I found the version closest to what I'd worn in Alexandria. Well, to the version that Andrew had for me to wear. I found Spartan costumes, Greek warrior, togas, and even Mark

Antony himself. I couldn't help it. I had to see her again. I typed "Cleopatra" into the search area of the costume site. A dozen costume versions popped up. "I think Andrew used this same site." I distinctly remembered two of the exotic outfits and the beaded hairstyle. I just stared at the model posing in the costumes. She was stunning, from the gold headband that held her beaded hair in place to the sandals that wrapped up her smooth calves like two golden snakes. The picture on the internet made her look older, sexier than the fourteen-year-old I remembered. I felt dirty as I eyed up one picture after another, trying to find yet another one of the outfits she'd worn in the simulation. And, finally, there it was, the one she wore to the dinner when she put the bearded executioner, Pompey, in his place. She was beautiful. In today's society, lusting for a young lady of fourteen will get you put into jail. But in 45 B.C., older men took teenage wives all the time. And royalty was often married off shortly after reaching double digits.

The outfit put the model's slender body on display. The shiny leather dress was strapless and clung to her as if it was shrink-wrapped. Around her neck she wore what might best be described as a Christmas tree skirt. Sorry, bad description. You know, the cloth you wrap around the base of the tree to decorate the floor below. The thing she was wearing was decorated with beads and jewels of many colors. Stunning, but tasteful. Her young shoulders were bare and her modest cleavage hard to ignore. Gold snake armbands circled otherwise naked biceps. Just below her elbows and down to her wrists she wore sleeves of fine, sheer black silk. A thick golden belt accentuated her already thin waist. From the golden belt dangled a matching drop. To me, it looked a bit like a fat necktie. But it certainly looked good on her. The skirt was short, exposing young, strong, smooth legs. It was hard not to get lost in the golden wrappings that went from her knees to her open toes. I clicked the "back" button and got back to Hercules. I had the costume delivered overnight. It was a nice feeling not having to worry about money. I was pretty sure my money would outlive me, based on my last prognosis. I could still hear the doctor's voice: "Get your life in order."

That night I dreamed again. And I dreamed big. It was only five hours in bed but two more weeks in Alexandria. I no longer seemed to need the goggles, the headphones, Andrew's computer or the magic serum, or whatever the hell that was. If I slept, I traveled.

When my costume showed up at 6 p.m. the next day, I was ecstatic. After the twenty-five minutes it took to figure out what order to put things on, I stood in front of the biggest mirror in my condo. I laughed at myself, a silent chuckle. I was in the outfit, but hardly Puzo the Great. I promised myself I would get fully into character by noon Thursday, even if I had to imagine myself with forty more pounds of muscles.

In my dreams that night, I died. A painless me paced the bedroom, occasionally looking at the motionless me lying on the bed. I wondered if I was dead or dying. If I was actually dead, why was I still here in the room? Shouldn't I be on my way to Heaven, or Hell? Was there a Heaven or Hell? Life after death? Or nothing?

I checked to see if the "still" me was breathing. Nothing. I checked for a pulse. Nothing. "Wake up," I yelled to the motionless me while vigorously shaking him/me. He/I jerked to an upright position, simultaneously gulping a long breath like someone who'd been trapped underwater, thankful to reach the surface. I sat there, sweat beading on my forehead, my body wet and clammy. My heart pounding like the drums on King Ptolemy's ship. I took a few deep breaths and looked out the bedroom window. My condo backs up to a wooded sanctuary. I watched two squirrels effortlessly scurry up a tall tree. One more deep breath and I melted back onto the bed. The sheets were wet and cold from sweat. I lay there exhausted. For a moment, I was glad to be alive. I looked out the window again. I watched the two squirrels disappear above the limited view of my window. Then, for just a moment... I wished I was dead. I wanted it to be over. I was afraid of how it might end. I closed my eyes hard and shook the feeling, refusing to think past my planned afternoon teaching my Cleveland students about Cleopatra and all of her acquaintances.

I filled the tub with hot water. There's something so relaxing about a hot bath. I would get in when the tub was half full. If I got used to the hot water early, I could make it even hotter as it filled. I always let the water fill to almost overflowing. Today I was tempted to just let it go. I shut it off with my foot as it was about to crest. The motion of my leg re-entering the water sent a tub-size tsunami back and forth, splashing onto the floor until the water settled back down. I liked to put my head underwater with just my nose peeking up for air. You would think the water would silence everything, but it didn't. Not if you listened. The sound of the water sucking down the overflow drain was much louder underwater. The bathroom fan was also louder. If the fan was off, and after the water drained below the runoff level, I could hear the neighbor's dog barking. I lifted my head and let the water roll from my ears. I couldn't hear the dog. I re-submerged and the barking was once again audible. I was suddenly aware that there were so many souls who were crying.

These cries were only heard by the few who really listened.

I opened my eyes, still under water. The popcorn ceiling, distorted by the one inch of liquid, reacted to my every blink. The bright light, centered in the ceiling, brought me back to my voyage to Rome. Back to my sunrise bath in the Mediterranean Sea with Neva watching me from the shadows. I wished she was here. No. I wished I was there.

The doorbell rang, ending my daydream. I didn't get visitors, except for Amazon. This was no doubt the final accessory. In my robe, hair still dripping, I tore open the box. Yes. My wrist ball-chain and my side dagger.

I dressed in full garb one more time, reliving my fight with the two nameless gladiators. I practiced with my new wrist ball-chain until I was able to quickly un-latch the ball and simulate tossing it at an unsuspecting combatant. I whipped the two-foot chain in a figure-eight motion a few times before accidentally whacking my forearm bone. I decided to save my attempt at theatrics for the event.

I changed back into my regular clothes which, by the way, I now hated. I promised myself a whole new crisp but tasteful wardrobe for my last few months. For now, though, I decided I would be Clark Kent for a few more days, sporting my usual mild-mannered style.

# Chapter 10 – On Stage

Thursday morning, I parked in the rear, near the gymnasium, hoping to enter unnoticed. As I put the car in park, my phone pinged. "You on schedule?" It was Mr. Bailey, the principal, again.

"Already here," I texted back.

"Waiting for you in auditorium," he replied.

I had my costume packed into my biggest suitcase. Everything fit except for my sword. When Mr. Bailey saw me, he smiled. His smile told me he was genuinely happy to see me. His interest in my baggage made it even more obvious that he was anxious to see the show. "Follow me!" he motioned. "What's in the suitcase?... No, don't tell me!"

I couldn't help but smile at his sincere excitement. He motioned for me to hand over the big suitcase. I obliged. He muscled it up the five steps that led backstage. I followed him through the curtains, now holding only my sword. For just a moment I was Puzo, making my way through the palace corridors. He opened a door marked *Dressing Room*. "All yours!" He said, sweeping his right arm to display a fairly elaborate area for a high school. Now that I think about it, I remember that he'd had one of the school's two gymnasiums converted into an auditorium two years ago. It made sense now. I remember hearing he had a background in theater. I didn't venture into this part of the school too often.

"What can I do?" he asked with enough enthusiasm that I was a bit confused.

I fished deep into my pocket and pulled out the thumb drive. It reminded me of Andrew holding up the drive that held the Cleopatra simulation. "Wait. I also brought my laptop." I unzipped a compartment on the face of the big Samsonite suitcase and pulled out the computer.

Mr. Bailey continued, "You will have a twenty-foot tall and forty-foot wide white screen behind you. I could play a movie behind you if you wanted me to. I wanted to plan with you all weekend. Where were you?"

I smiled and slowly unzipped the suitcase's main compartment. "I told you, Rome."

The principal squinted at me with a puzzled little shake of his head.

His excitement had me feeling a bit dramatic. I held the unzipped case opened just enough to get Mr. Bailey to tilt his head to see inside. I flipped the case wide open.

He looked at me for permission to touch the contents. "Hercules?"

It took a little wind out of my sails having to explain how Puzo was almost as famous as Hercules. Explaining how Puzo was Cleopatra's bodyguard prompted a nod of respect and I moved on to my next instruction. "Just hook up my laptop to your...your... projector, or whatever you use."

The principal smiled and chuckled. "Give it here." He looked at his watch and back at me. "Forty-five minutes."

I re-zipped my suitcase. "I'm starting to sweat," I confessed. "Wait, do I get a clicker or something to change the picture?"

"If you want..." He hesitated. "But I will be able to see all your frames from my screen. I can free up your hands if you trust me to match the picture to your story."

I gave him a look. I wasn't so sure about this. "How is your history?"

Mr. Bailey smiled. "In general, not so good, but I have spent a lot of time in Italy. I know Rome." He hesitated again. "I think I can match up a picture to a story."

Halfway through getting dressed, I was sweating and shaking. I needed to forget about fear, like I had with George Washington. I finished getting dressed. I strapped my weapon to my wrist. I tucked my dagger into my belt. When I slid the sword into its sheath, I became Puzo.

When I opened the dressing room door, I heard voices, many voices. The principal was making an announcement, asking people to slide in to make room for some of the people standing.

I closed my eyes and went back to my other life. I wished the students could have all been there with me. I wished they could experience her beauty in person. Her ability to communicate so eloquently with both rulers and peasants. I imagined Neva brushing and beading her hair. We smiled at each other. I wondered if she suspected that she and I would get married only a year from now, with Cleopatra's blessing, while on an adventure up the Nile. I opened my eyes just in time to see the lights dim. It was show time.

The first twenty-by-forty-foot picture was a view from the center of the Roman Colosseum. Yes, of course, I know that particular arena hadn't yet been built in Caesar's time. But I was confident nobody would care, if they even knew. The muscular back of a gladiator, scarred from battle, stood over a beaten victim. A lion strained on a leash just out of reach from the victor. An angry crowd yelled with thumbs pointing down.

I walked out with all the poise of a brave gladiator. I stared at the giant photo of the Colosseum, my head first shaking at the sheer brutality, and then nodding with pride at my abilities in this same barbaric field. Then I turned to face the crowd, feeling like Caesar himself.

I scanned the full auditorium. First I took in the seats in front of me. Everyone began clapping and cheering. A small group near the front stood. I recognized them from my last period class. My troublemakers. A chain reaction started, and my opening was delayed for a standing ovation before a word was spoken. I scanned the auditorium. It was bigger than I expected. I had to shield my eyes from the bright stage lights overhead. Two thousand people must have been packed into the auditorium, on their feet, looking at me. Where did they all come from? I motioned for everyone to sit down as if I were a king ready to address my people.

"This was my life." I paused. "This was my playground." I pointed to the man about to lose his life. "See his eyes? This is what death looks like." My voice was deep and powerful and echoed with command off the walls. "This was entertainment." I shook my head in disgust. "This was not a video game. There was no restart button or do-over. It was kill or be killed." I put my hands onto my hips and bellowed. "I am the great Puzo. I trained with Hercules until I was sold to the Pharaoh of Egypt, King Ptolemy. Who here knows who King Ptolemy's daughter was?"

Someone yelled from the darkness. "Cleopatra!"

I pointed in the direction of the voice. "Yes, and it was a twelve-year old Cleopatra who also received me as a gift from her father Ptolemy. She received me as a gift. You know. For entertainment. Like a smartphone."

Everyone in the audience was hanging on my every word.

I half expected to wake up from yet another dream. "But I didn't sing or dance. I killed other gladiators or lions or tigers. At least until Cleopatra insisted that I become her personal bodyguard." The next slide was a nearly twenty-foot-tall picture simulating a young Cleopatra. I stared at the picture for a long time. Two thousand people sat in silence. A first at our high school. "I was in love with her best friend and most trusted servant, Neva." I fiddled with the ball on my wrist weapon. "It was her eyes, I said, wiping a tear from my own. "We will come back to Neva, but first I have to tell you about Cleopatra's sisters."

As I painted the picture of life within the castle, it became obvious to my audience that not all danger came from opposing kingdoms. I could tell that the students were impressed when I told them Cleopatra knew half a dozen languages by the age of twelve. "Cleopatra was her father's favorite. This child of thirteen, fourteen years old was already being molded to take over for her father, Ptolemy. The king had ruled for decades, but his last handful of years were spent drunk on wine."

One of the students yelled, "Yeah!"

The principal's head spun to see who was interrupting.

I smiled and motioned for him to relax. "Yeah, the king liked his wine. Most nights ended with him sleeping in his own vomit. His trusted guards and slaves would clean him up and put him to bed. His daughters watched him slowly deteriorate and began posturing for his title, ruler of Alexandria."

For the next half-hour, I talked about the king's daughters.

"His oldest daughter, Tryphaena was in her early twenties. Stunning, like Cleopatra. She scared the hell out of me, even with my gladiator body." I took the opportunity to flex. Laughter filled the room. "She would cut off your head or poison you for not addressing her properly. If she thought you got in her way for consideration to become the next ruler, you'd best not turn your back on her.

"The king's next daughter, Berenice, was eighteen going on twelve. She spent most of her days playing dress-up. She had more servants than she knew what to do with. Makeup, hair, jewelry, baths, oils, mirrors. She needed constant entertaining from jesters, midgets, talented musicians and her pets. She had a cute pet monkey called Baboon. At least, she did until Cleopatra's pet leopard killed it. This incident may have been responsible for changing the course of history.

"But before we get into that, let me tell you about Cleopatra. She was quite different than her two older sisters. She was thirteen going on eighteen. She was well-mannered, and walked and spoke with royal intent. She was her father's favorite, and her older sisters knew it. Cleopatra had a special gift for picking up the mixed language that the villagers spoke. She was known to dress like a commoner and to sneak out of the palace to see what life was like for the villagers.

"This helped her to better understand Egypt. In her eyes, this knowledge made her the best choice for future ruler. Her father felt the same way, much to Tryphaena's dismay. Cleopatra studied the female rulers of history and often asked herself, "What would Nefertiti do?" When Tryphaena tried to kill her father, the king, Cleopatra set things into motion that would change history. Tryphaena's first attempt was thought to be sneaking a poisonous snake—a puff adder—into the king's bedroom. When the snake killed the king's lifelong friend and favorite servant instead, it was thought that it could have been an unfortunate accident. But two days later, when the king's taster sipped his wine, went into convulsions and died, the king knew an assassination plot was being attempted. He took a dozen of his most trusted men and went into hiding.

"Tryphaena sent her most trusted guards after the king to finish the job. When Cleopatra's leopard killed her sister Berenice's pet monkey Baboon, Tryphaena used the event to turn Berenice against Cleopatra. When Tryphaena tried to poison Cleopatra with tainted figs, Cleopatra knew it was time to join her father in exile. Through secret communication with their mutual friend Olympus, Cleopatra was able to meet her father at the harbor just before dawn. We barely escaped Tryphaena's surprise raid, having left our wing of the palace only minutes before she sent guards to do us in.

"You are looking at 'Puzo the Great.'" I flexed my arms and turned my rather pathetic, frail body for the crowd to observe. "Two hundred twenty-five pounds of muscle, with washboard abs and arms this big around. It was Cleopatra, her best friend and faithful servant Neva and me." Silence still filled the auditorium. "I fell in love with Neva on our two-week trip to Rome."

I sighed as I thought about Neva and paused for a long moment. I'm afraid I was lost in a sad smile.

I looked over the crowd. The students, my fellow teachers, everyone—all silently waited for my next words. "If I hadn't had to come back here, we might have been on our honeymoon." I chuckled and shook my head, trying to refocus. Heads twisted towards one another in confusion.

"I never saw Caesar," I confessed, now pacing the stage. "He had some fat grunts in togas meet us when we landed outside of Rome." I jerked my head up to the crowd. "I'm sorry, that's inappropriate." My eyes focused back on the floor and I began pacing again. "They put us up in a nice place... well, except for the stench of the Tiber River." I looked up again. "The locals would dump their garbage right out their windows into the river. And a huge sewer that drained the whole city ran straight into the river, too. It was pretty disgusting." I shook my head and crinkled my nose; just talking about it brought the stench back.

"We eventually met Pompey the Great!" I put my hands on my hip and puffed my chest, trying to mimic how Pompey had carried himself. I spoke in the deepest voice I could manage. "They called me the bearded executioner, but not to my face." I told the story of how Pompey had tried to humiliate the king and Cleopatra, and how her knowledge of languages put the pompous Roman in his place. "I stood behind Cleopatra with my hand on my sword."

Now I spoke in my best imitation of a young girl's voice. "'I am Cleopatra, Princess of the Nile, third daughter of the king and pharaoh of Egypt. The man you have so cruelly insulted is my father.'" I thought I did pretty well making my voice tremble at first and then grow firm, just like I'd heard her speak. "Pompey's grin turned to a grimace; the soldiers were silenced. After I quoted her indignant speech, I made an immediate character change back to Puzo, gripping and releasing the handle of my sword. "I would defend Cleopatra with my life. But I'm not gonna kid ya, I did not want to fight with Pompey."

Then I had to go with the story as it occurred after my simulation was interrupted. "It would be almost two years before Caesar returned and prepared an army sufficient to retake Alexandria. Not from Tryphaena, but from her younger sister Berenice. Shortly after our departure from Alexandria, two years before, one of King Ptolemy's spy rings kidnapped and killed his self-appointed successor, Tryphaena. That night, while his successful spies were celebrating their victory a bit too much, they were found in a drunken sleep and killed. This temporarily left Berenice next in line as ruler in Alexandria. Not much is said about Berenice in the history books."

"The king and Cleopatra were treated well in Rome for the most part, but we were basically prisoners until Caesar set a new objective: his army and ships would go to Alexandria. In the back of Cleopatra's mind, and no doubt Ptolemy's, too, was the possibility that Caesar would take Egypt for himself. It was a very, very rich province with enough plunder to reward his high-ranking followers and enough grain to feed his ever-growing armies. "Unfortunately, before we got back to Alexandria, I was brought back here to 2017." I chuckled unapologetically, confusing the crowd. I waited for the murmuring to die down.

"Yes, I was disappointed," I said. Now for the important part. "We have become spoiled and lazy. We take so much for granted. I know that you all know that I have been diagnosed with Stage 4 cancer. Knowing your days are numbered changes your life. You want to make sure that you're remembered for something, hopefully something good. I'm here to tell you that *your* days are numbered. Some of you will likely die in a car crash while texting. Some in a house fire, others by a gun carried by someone with a grievance. None of us are getting out of this alive." I stopped to take in, and blow out, a big breath.

"What will you do before you die?" I pointed into the crowd. "You, write that book… about whatever the hell you want. You," I pointed to a different section. "Learn to play an instrument." I was picking out random people in the crowd. "Learn to dance. Work on an invention. Develop a theory. Learn to speak other languages. Like Cleopatra!" I paused to let this sink in, then lowered my voice. "Tell the people who have influenced you just how much they mean to you. Learn to say, 'I love you.'" I went silent for another moment. I dropped my shield and unlatched my belt, sending my sword to the stage floor.

"Dare to make a difference, even if it's just to your aunt, your kid sister or your dog. I am thankful for this opportunity to stand before you. I am humbled by your graciousness in listening to me ramble. Please, don't wait for a death sentence to live." And there I stood on the stage, half teacher, half bodyguard. I bowed to the crowd.

The kids from my seventh-period class were first to stand, clapping and hooting. The rest of the auditorium erupted. I stood with my hand on my heart. It was all I could manage to gently nod my head in appreciation.

# Chapter 11 – Master Puppeteer

When I arrived for my so-called, trip to Heaven, Ann greeted me with sharper scrutiny than in previous visits. "Did you talk to anyone about what we are doing here?" I wasn't even in the door yet. Ann tugged on my shirt to hasten my entry and quickly locked the door. She stayed just inside the door with her face pressed against the glass. I took in her tiny features. Her hair was jet black and wrapped tightly in a bun. Even taking the bun into consideration, I guessed her to be about five feet tall and not a pound over ninety-five. "Are you sure you weren't followed?" Her actions had made me nervous and kept me watching her. After a long minute, she turned to face me. She flicked her fingers, indicating it was time to hand her the $12,000 I'd brought, as instructed, in a plastic grocery bag. "And the manual?" she insisted. "I'm sorry, I left it in the car." She huffed angrily. "Give me your keys. I'll have Vlad get it when you're in simulation."

I tried to get Ann to look me in the eyes, but she avoided my stare. "Ann." I waited until she looked at me. "No one knows I'm here. What's the matter? You're acting weird. Weirder than usual."

Ann finally met my eyes. Her cheek bones were high and pronounced, her eyebrows perfectly plucked. She had a very serious look. I noticed that she highlighted her eyelids with white and I was momentarily lost in an obscure thought. Why white? I never understood white eye shadow.

Ann lashed out. "This neighborhood! Twelve thousand dollars, in cash! We could get shot for two hundred." She glanced out the door one last time and then scurried to the back, beckoning me to do the same.

As we entered through the secret supply room, Vlad greeted me with an enthusiastic, "Hey cowboy, how's it going?"

His voice didn't quite match his body; this always made me smile. He was tall and fit and always wore a nice silky button-up shirt that showed off his well-developed pecs and thin waist. But, his head seemed a bit small for his body and his tightly cropped hair made his head look even smaller. I half expected him to sound like Mike Tyson. I finally answered, "Feeling pretty good, Vlad." I wanted to personalize the conversation, but realized I knew very little about my... doctors? Dream makers? Captors? I didn't even know how to categorize them.

Today, Andrew wasn't wearing his surgical mask or sitting behind the control desk. I had to do a double-take to be sure it was Andrew. "How are you guys doin'?" I asked, more polite than curious.

Andrew was first to respond. "You ready to travel, cowboy?" Andrew sounded funny referring to me as "cowboy." You could just tell it wasn't his lingo. Andrew was the opposite of Vlad. In need of a haircut, pudgy face and an extra twenty or thirty pounds of softness. No doubt from endless hours with his ass motionless in a chair, programming.

I smiled and blinked and let out a sigh. I was content. I had been looking forward to this travel all week.  I was nodding an inaudible but agreeable response.

Andrew was back in his cockpit again. He pushed up his glasses. "You are in for a real treat today!" I was glad he didn't force the word "cowboy" again.

Ann was already directing me to the chair. "Let's get your vitals going." I was barely in the chair when Ann cuffed my arm to take my blood pressure from the right, and Vlad was prepping my left for an IV.

Andrew continued. "This is going to be a longer voyage than anything you've experienced in the past. In fact, this will seem like your new life—if you just relax and enjoy." He put his left hand on his heart and then held his right hand up as if swearing on a Bible. "I won't let anything bad happen to you." He continued, looking back down at his keyboard. "One day might feel like one month, or even one year."

I thought out loud, "I can't think of a better way to cheat the system." My nerves were just starting to act up and my mind was racing. I started to babble, mostly to myself. "If I get a simulated thirty days out of every real day, I would get my life extended... I looked at my fingers to do the calculations. After all, I taught history, not math. "That would get me another five or six simulated years."

Ann ripped back on the Velcro of the blood pressure cuff, interrupting my thought process. "BP one-ten over sixty-five." She eased my head back to the headrest and gently stroked twice above my eyebrows to get the hair off my forehead. "Let's not get ahead of ourselves, cowboy."

Ann, Vlad and Andrew were tossing body stats at one another in preparation for the travel. I had tuned out the conversation until I heard Andrew say, "Ready for hibernation state." I would have let that go, too, if Ann and Vlad hadn't both looked at Andrew like he was a barber who had just said, "Oops."

"What does he mean, 'hibernation state'?" I asked. I'm afraid my nervousness came out with a little squeak in my voice.

Ann reached for the headphones and replied, "Same shit, new term. You relax and enjoy your trip to Heaven. Say hi to old friends, relive old memories. Go wherever you want to go." She nodded for Vlad to put the simulation goggles onto me and then she eased the plush headphones over my ears. Everything was dark and silent. Typically, I would have received my IV rush by now. But today, something felt different. Ann was clearly edgy. The whole process felt more rushed than usual. I had a moment of panic but then felt the cold, familiar rush of the magic concoction burn my left wrist and quickly race up my arm. I had another brief moment of doubt. "Did I just get taken for $12,000?" The tingle made its way to my head and instantly put all worries to rest.

I couldn't see or hear the worrisome conversation going on around me. Ann looked at Andrew. "Really, Andrew. 'Hibernation state?' Never talk like that until the headphones are on." Ann was shaking her head in disappointment.

Andrew got tight-lipped. He knew he would hear about this slip-up again and again.

"And you're sure you got all the glitches out of this loop?"

Andrew looked at Ann with a bobbing head. "Yes, it can loop endlessly and yet not be the same trip twice." Ann had a way about her that made even highly qualified professionals second-guess themselves. Each of these men were literally twice her size, but dared not cross her. Andrew wasn't used to being looked at with anything short of amazement. After all, he was one of the most brilliant simulators in the United States, maybe the world. And Ann paid him well for his talent, his secrecy and his silence. "I will be guiding him," he assured her, "but he will ultimately be choosing the direction of the simulation." Ann was studying the fluctuating stats on the simulator chair's monitor. Andrew continued. "I take him to scenarios and he fills in the blanks. Like a dream. If he gets off track, or starts to freak out, I can interject myself into the dream to guide him. It's like a video game but I can–"

Ann interrupted. "Yeah, yeah, I get it. Just make sure he doesn't wake up."

A bright light emanated through my eyelids. I squinted and peeked through my eyelashes. A blazing sun comfortably toasted my face. I blinked and smiled, remembering how much I've enjoyed these voyages. I suddenly became aware of the distant cries of seagulls. I held my breath, shut my eyes tight, and listened harder. I heard waves crashing and then more birds, more exotic than just gulls. A soft breeze delivered a delightful salty aroma and the rustling of palms. A distant seagull screeched. Now I felt my body swaying gently back and forth.

"It's beautiful, isn't it honey?" The soft voice surprised me. I realized I was snuggled into a soft hammock with Sally Davic. She'd been my college girlfriend for two semesters. We'd had a little fight, and each waited for the other's apology... that never came. We hadn't spoken in thirty years, but I had to confess that I secretly followed her on Facebook. The hammock seemed to sway all by itself. Sally began to toy with the small patch of hair on my bare chest. I felt nothing but bare skin against me. Could she be...? I hadn't even looked at her yet, but I knew it was her. A voice I hadn't heard in over thirty years.

I popped open my eyes. The sky was clear blue with white clouds constantly moving into new shapes, something like a lava lamp, another memory from the '70s.

Sally spoke again. "Do you want to go for a walk along the beach?" As she spoke, I could feel her warm breath on my ear. She eased her hand through my hair and kissed my ear. "Hey, you in there?"

I was inhaling her wonderful fragrance. But then I had a moment of clarity and mumbled, "Andrew?" aloud. Then I let myself get lost in the simulation. Sally almost tumbled out of the hammock trying to get up; I snagged her waist, feeling nothing but warm, bare skin, and pulled her close. "I got you." I told her that despite seeing her in person for the first time since college days, I felt as if we had spent a life together. A perfect, blessed life. Her hair was long, with soft reddish-blonde curls. I pulled her warm flesh even closer to mine. Her eyes were playful, and her body language was as hot as her body itself, clothed only in a scrap of fabric around her hips.

Then she said the words I had needed so badly to hear for so many years. "I've missed you." She spoke with her lips so close to mine that I found myself inhaling her breath, the smell of her lotioned body.

Her very DNA. "You make me so happy," she continued as she drew a figure-eight on my forehead, then down my nose and to my lips. Tracing my lips, she pressed her naked breasts to my chest. "C'mon," she whispered. "Let's go for a walk." We were in a private, horseshoe-shaped cove. I did a quick 360, noting a heavenly ocean in front of me, and tropical abundance all around. The salty breeze was subtle and perfect. The temperature was maybe seventy degrees with not a bit of humidity. Sally folded her fingers between mine and led me to the water's edge. Gentle waves broke onto our feet, darkening the fine light sand for just a moment until the ocean stingily sucked back the moisture. Sally was a perfect physical specimen, which spoke either to my shallowness or to Andrew's. I shook that thought out of my head and just admired her beauty.

She noticed me taking in her features and danced provocatively. With a pretty smile, she asked, "You like what you see?"

I chuckled and I'm sure my smile went from ear to ear. "Yes, you are more beautiful than ever."

Sally held out her hand as an invitation for me to take it. "C'mon, let me show you how things work here."

When I was finally able to take my eyes off of Sally, I resumed taking in my surroundings. The beach curved ahead, and crystal blue water met the sand with soft, steady caresses. Starfish and sand dollars advanced and retreated along with the waves. West Indian shells that reminded me of ice cream cones reflected in the sun. Pink and brown conch shells adorned the beach. It wasn't like most beaches, littered with busted shell fragments. To see perfect exotic specimens, all I had to do was look. Coastal horn snail shells and Buttercup Lucine. Wildly colored shells looked like fans from the Orient. Some looked soft and smooth as glass, with pastel colors melted into mosaics. Others were brilliantly tattooed, as if hand painted by mermaids who had all the time in the world. When I spotted a simple but perfectly formed conch shell, I had to smile again. I looked out to the ocean. But what ocean was I looking upon, I wondered? I looked back at Sally, who seemed content to watch me experience the beauty that engulfed me. Except for the damp shoreline, the sand was snow white and fine as powder. The bounty of shells ran in swaths and covered the beach as if pirates had floated along the shore, dumping one treasure chest after another.

Now I turned to the land side of this beautiful picture. Perfect palms danced to a warm, gentle breeze. At the sand's edge, endless wildflowers rolled up a long, gentle slope until they met blue sky. Not a house in sight. Not an overhead wire to be found. Nor even a way to get off the beach. Little birds playfully chased one another from exotic blooming bushes to flowering trees. The colors of the wildflowers were like fireworks. Their magical fragrances changed with every swirl of wind. One unruly section of wildflowers would give in to the wind as if stretching, and the rest would follow like a stadium crowd doing the wave.

My senses were on overload. I closed my eyes, trying to single out the sounds. The waves... the birds... Then I stopped and really listened. The waves were more than just one sound. There was the buildup of the approaching wave, the rolling crash onto the dampened, hardened sand and the sound of the retreat with an effervescence, like a newly opened can of soda pop. This all happened in a thousand staggered, repeating iterations, producing the most incredible harmonious sounds, fading into the distance. I opened my eyes to locate the birds that were providing a string backup to the waves' melody and harmonies. I was obsessed with birds. I watched gannets flying in formation; a petrel soared solo as if on patrol; a frigate bird eyed the fish below and dived with pinpoint accuracy. A single enormous albatross skimmed the water, occasionally sampling it with the tip of a wing like someone testing bath water.

I had to dial down my senses to engage again with Sally. Her sun-kissed skin was smooth and evenly toasted to a light golden brown. The breeze seemed to be acknowledging her hair; I imagined a godlike invisible spirit running his hands through her hair to make it move the way it did. Her eyes were green, and then blue, and then transformed into a green and blue kaleidoscope. She caressed my cheek and instinctively I closed my eyes. When I opened them, I was staring at her perfect breasts. Not the breasts of a teenager. The perfect breasts of a middle-aged woman. Full and round and natural. She eased my hands to her chest and held them there, lowering her head to get me to look back up at her eyes.

"Close your eyes," she said, softly but firmly.

I obeyed. She directed my hands to show me how she liked to be touched. I felt her nipples harden and she guided my fingers to feel the tiny bumps of her areolas. Then she placed my hands between her breasts and I could feel—and hear—her heartbeat. Next stop was her belly, still tight despite the years.

I couldn't help it. I had to look again. The hot sun made her skin glisten with a layer of sweat. Her thin waist blossomed into full, round hips. She brought my hands to her behind. She wore what would best be described as a Tarzan skirt. Admittedly a slutty Tarzan skirt, again speaking to my shallow version of what a heavenly lover should look like. She released my hands, freeing me to slide them under her tiny, primitive garment. I pulled her body to mine and we swayed to the beat of the majestic ocean. Looking up from the delights of her body, I saw a surprisingly devilish smile that assured me she was enjoying my touch, my curiosity, and my presence. The longest finger of my left hand played with a sweaty spot on the small of her back, just above the crack of her perfect ass. My right hand slid deep into the hair on the back of her neck. I unintentionally tightened my grip, forcing her head back.

She gasped, ever so slightly. "Kiss me," she whispered. We made out like acrobatic teenagers until we were both exhausted and laughing, drunk from the newfound awareness of complete satisfaction. She ran into the ocean looking back for me to follow. We played in the glistening waves for what seemed like hours. Sally made her way to shore and I, from behind, reveled in just watching her walk. We strolled along the beach picking up shells and helping the starfish complete their quests. We exchanged smiles and flirty conversation. I was drunk with contentment.

Once we got beyond our deserted cove, the beach thinned out. Beyond the sand rose rolling hills, covered with exotic vegetation. Rare birds that I'd only heard until now, fluttered and frolicked. They reminded me of wildly colored parrots but looked like nothing I'd ever seen on earth. I closed my eyes for another moment, to truly appreciate the symphony of the winged musicians. Off in the distance, the clouds seemed to form an elaborate train where the water met the sky—one box car after another leading up to the engine. Smoke billowed from the leading cloud, making it look like an old steam engine.

Sally squeezed my hand as we reached the end of the horseshoe-shaped private beach. She made me look back at our palm-filled paradise. "We can stay here as long as you want, just you and me. This is our cove."

I scanned the private paradise. The hammock was still visible, but just barely.

She turned me back to face the other direction. "But this is not the only cove."

I tilted my head; I must have looked like a curious dog.

"You can go to any of the coves ahead... But I can't go with you."

Now I was confused. I looked back at her. "I don't want to leave you." My voice cracked. "Why can't you come with me?" Sally's smile melted me, and I felt a tear roll down my face.

"You don't have to leave." She guided a windblown lock of her hair back into place. She eased me in for a passionate kiss. Her body was warm and soft and so comforting. When the seal of the kiss broke, I pulled her in for another. She placed one hand on each side of my face and pecked my lips one more time. "I'll be right here waiting for you." And then she turned away.

I watched Sally walk back to the water's edge. She spun around once to blow me a kiss and remind me with a silently mouthed, "I'll be right here."

# Chapter 12 – Bubbles on the Beach

When I turned back to the new expanse of beach, I saw someone in the distance. It was a man, walking my way. This cove was much smaller, not much more than a fifty-yard stretch of beach. I held my hand to my forehead to shield my eyes from the sun. As the man got closer, I was surprised to see that it was Andrew. He had simulated himself into my adventure.

"Well, what do you think so far?"

Now I was really confused.

Finally close enough, Andrew held out a fist looking for the obligatory but awkward man card, a return fist bump. "Did I capture Sally?" He put his arm around my shoulder and walked me in the direction of the next cove. "Your bio was excellent, Tim. I was able to develop six coves." Andrew paused, obviously looking for better words to explain. "Six areas of your life that you feel need addressing. First, you must know that I am a gamer. So this travel will have similar elements. I want you to be comfortable here, so I feel the need to explain how this works." Andrew looked me in the eye and nodded. "We on the same page, Tim?"

I nodded back—yes—but couldn't help turning back to see where Sally was.

"OK, just so you know, you can go back to be with Sally any time you want. Just walk back to that cove. And if you ever find yourself upset or with a question, you can find me here." Andrew gestured like Vanna White, showing off his little slice of paradise.

I nodded again. "What are in the other coves?"

Andrew smiled. "More of your thoughts, more of your dreams. More answers to your life's unanswered questions." Andrew's smile was almost unrecognizable since I'd never seen him smile in Ann's presence. Clearly, he was proud of what he'd programmed. This was his world. He eased me forward with a slight push on my shoulder.

I took a half a dozen small steps but then had to look back again.

Andrew offered a last bit of advice. "Be inquisitive. You are safe here."

I continued on across this narrow patch of beach. Once again, I became aware of the sounds of waves breaking on the sandy shore, and the chorus of wild birds. I began to relax. Ten steps before reaching the next cove, I turned to see if Andrew would offer any additional insight. The simulation played back exactly as it had a hundred steps back.

"Be inquisitive. You are safe here," he called again.

I turned back to the next cove. As it opened up, I was able to see other people. They were in different scenarios, but always in twos.

On my left was a small beach cafe with seating for maybe a dozen. Only one table was occupied. A couple seemed to be deep into conversation. I couldn't make out the conversation but based on body language, I was sure it was therapeutic. A young man was wiping tears from his face but laughing. A little farther up the beach, a tiny tiki hut had seating for eight yet only two sat at the bar. I was close enough that I should have been able to overhear their conversation, but I couldn't. It felt as if I wasn't supposed to listen in but was to understand that they were talking privately. On the open beach, another couple sat cross-legged in the sand. They were building a basic sand castle, but progress was very slow. The two exchanged murmurs and hand gestures that made me think they might be deaf. The sun was shining from far out in the water, casting long shadows back from the beach.

I stood on damp sand near the water, not sure what I was supposed to do. A cold rogue wave made its way farther up the beach than any of the others, easing me in the direction of this new cove. Once back onto dry sand, I turned towards the water, my hand shielding my eyes from the setting sun. I was starting to understand Andrews's subtle communication style. When I turned away to get a break from the glare, I noticed a single round table under a thatched umbrella-like roof. That's when I finally saw someone I thought I'd recognized. As I got closer, my suspicions were confirmed. It was my oldest, and once closest friend.

I was instantly filled with dread. I owed this young man an apology.

Vince stood up and beckoned me to come in for a hug. "C'mere!" Vince gave me a big bear hug and three pats on the back and moved back to take in my features. "Look at you, you look great!"

I took a moment to look at myself. I did look good, better than I'd looked in a long time. I laughed, remembering that I was in a simulation, where anything was possible.

Vince didn't seem to have an ounce of regret. He showed no signs of anger towards me.

"God, Vince, I am so sorry," I blurted. "You know, about the party and, uh..." I wondered how far back I should go with my apology. "Hell, sorry for everything, ya know? For being such a shitty friend."

A grass-skirtcd bombshell of a waitress cheerfully delivered two exotic rum drinks in decorated coconuts. I thought it was a bit cliché, the result of Andrew wishing he could forget that he was in a chair in a crummy strip mall somewhere in suburban Ohio. While Vince exchanged pleasantries with the waitress, I was transported back to my childhood.

This time, I didn't need Andrew's programming wizardry. My memories, unfortunately, were quite vivid enough.

When I was seven, Vince's family moved in a few houses down the street. They came from southern Italy. He was my age. Even though he barely spoke English, we immediately became best friends. Vince was my equal in almost every way. He was my size, my weight. Hell, we even looked alike, as my heritage was also southern European.

His father was very short, a borderline "little person," and very quiet.

One day a rubber ball seemed to fall from the sky, bouncing down his long concrete driveway. We kids had been very busy asking one another, "I don't know, what do you want to do?" The mystery ball must have fallen from heaven. You know... for our entertainment. Vince and I met eyes and the competition began. We chased that rubber ball, pushing each other, unconcerned what a fall on concrete would do. When he got to the ball first, I snatched it from his hands and turned my back. He wrapped his arms around me and bear hugged me until I couldn't breathe. We wrestled like embattled soldiers fighting for control of a gun.

Mr. Pasto quietly watched us fight.

When exhaustion finally set in, we started a verbal assault. "It's mine!"

"No, it's not. It's mine!"

Vince's father finally spoke up, calmly, in a deep voice for such a small man. "It's neither one of yours." I'll never forget what he said and did as I loosened my headlock on his son, who by now had stolen the ball back from me. He put his hand out and a red-faced boy with messed-up hair and a T-shirt half pulled over his head looked one last time at his prize before he reluctantly handed it over to his dad. "Who needs to spend money at the movies when I have you two monkeys to watch all day?" He carried the ball back up the driveway to his garage. He tossed the ball onto the roof and watched it lodge itself again in one of the gutters he had been cleaning. "Maybe this ball was up here for a good reason." He seemed to be talking to himself.

Both of us watched as this five-foot-tall man maneuvered a ladder three times his size, turning it sideways and tucking it back into its designated spot in his garage.

Vince looked at me, wiping a bloodied elbow. "What do you want to do now?"

I was busy trying to put my right shoe back on without untying it. "I don't know. What do you want to do?" It was that kind of friendship.

As the years passed, we were inseparable. We played football with the neighborhood kids on a patch of grass across the street that seemed to belong to no one. The out-of-bounds lines were a fence on one side and the sidewalk on the other. We thought nothing of tackling each other, as hard as possible, into the fence or onto the cement. By our early teens the neighborhood kids had evolved into a pack of wolves. Roles evolved and had to be reestablished whenever a new kid was invited to hang out or to join our games. We played baseball, kickball, kick the can, freeze tag, red light green light and every other game available to kids before cell phones were invented. If the girls looked like they were having too much fun playing hopscotch, we would interrupt their fun while we made fools of ourselves trying to impress them.

We were inseparable—until high school. Vince went to a technical school, South High. I went to North. Although he lived just around the corner, our paths now rarely crossed. I would occasionally be out with my friends and run into him with his new friends. His gang was into pot. I had just discovered beer. Our friends couldn't have been more different. I'll never forget the first time my friends saw him and his friends smoking pot at the beach. "Hey, burnouts," one of my buddies taunted them. Why don't you smoke that shit somewhere else?" I didn't say a word. Not "Hey, leave him alone" or "Hey, he's my friend" or "Hey! It's my buddy Vince." Nothing. I pretended I didn't even know him.

Vince kindly told my friend to "fuck off" and a fight ensued. I secretly wanted Vince to win but dared not speak up. It was a no-win situation for a teenager. Lose your best friend for good, or the people you see at school every day. Vince was holding his own against Steve until Ron hit him over the head with a half-full bottle of beer. Steve let out an approving "Ohhhhh" as Vince went to the ground. Two of Vince's friends stepped up shaking clenched fists, ready to defend the friend I had abandoned.

Before all hell broke loose, somebody's mother ran into view, yelling like a crazy woman. "Get out of here. This is private property. I've already called the police."

My friends disappeared, leaving me staring at two tall, thin and very stoned and angry true friends of Vince's. Vince finally sat up, holding his head. When he pulled his hand away, it was covered in blood. I looked at him, and then back at his two friends; they were taking turns looking at me and then the frantic mother, still shooing kids away with a broom cocked back like a baseball bat. I turned and ran.

I relived and regretted that day over and over. I had known Vince's phone number by heart since third grade. He lived a stone's throw away, and yet four more months passed before we would see each other again. It was Kim Amber's house party and it was a big one. Her parents had a big house up against the woods in Timberlake, a much more exclusive suburb than the one we lived in. Cars were parked on the grass, to the left and to the right of the unpaved driveway. There had to be seventy students, all at different stages of inebriation. Kids barely old enough to drive leaned against their cars with a beer in one hand and a cigarette in the other. Music blared from inside the house. I was feeling pretty buzzed having downed two Genesee Cream Ales on the car ride from Eastlake. Two guys from the wrestling team were locked up on the front lawn like horned stags fighting for the right to mate. The music from the house thumped; my boys and I walked towards the front door, nodding hellos, holding up our beers in juvenile celebration and general braggery. In the living room, three couples were dancing, each holding a beer bottle; apparently for stabilization. A couple on the couch was making out like they were the only ones in the room.

Kim was presiding in the kitchen where ten shot glasses were lined up side by side, pouring all ten shots without ever turning the bottle back upright. With a noisy cheer, glasses were raised, gulped, and slammed back onto the counter. Ken Frankle was sitting on the floor with his knees up and his head down. Ten minutes from now he would be sleeping in his own puke. Ten more shots had been lined up when Kim saw us enter her now crowded kitchen. She was already hammered and had to pass the upside-down bottle back and forth three times to fill the elusive shot glasses. When she noticed the bottle was empty, she tossed it into the sink. It shattered, sending glass shards onto the kitchen floor. Everyone laughed.

Kim separated one of the shots from the cluster on the counter. She held it up, spilling tequila onto her hand. When she tried to lick the spilled tequila, she spilled half the shot down her blouse. Somebody yelled, "Tequila!" and the shots were scooped up and forced down throats secretly repulsed by the liquor. My friend Randy let out a loud wolf howl from five feet away and tossed his shot glass into the sink. The others followed, and I knew it was going to be one of those memorable parties that would be talked about all next week. Little did I know, it would be talked about for much, much longer. Ken began to heave and spewed a lava-like substance between his legs. It splattered onto the kitchen floor, amid the spilled tequila and broken glass. I decided that it was time to find a new room.

I was the last into the kitchen, and therefore the first out. Clearly visible through oversized sliding glass doors, a fire blazed in the back yard. Sam pointed to the flames and we snaked our way through the crowded room toward the doors. The music was too loud to talk, but nods, handshakes and bottle taps acknowledged acquaintances. When I slid the glass doors open, the pounding music erupted into the back yard, turning the heads of the half-dozen people sitting around the fire. The smell of pot was immediately evident. Sam didn't waste any time ruffling feathers. "Who invited the potheads?"

Vince had been sitting with his back to us, but turned as he stood up. His eyes were slits and his body swayed. He held the stubby remains of a fat joint. I hoped that he would say something Christ-like that would magically unite our two groups. "Who invited the asshole?" didn't rise to that standard. Vince wobbled and sat back down, taking another hit off the tiny roach.

Sam puffed up his chest again. "Get that shit out of here." As four more of my friends piled through the door, my heart pounded. I sized up the two groups. My friends were hyped up on beer and tequila.

I'm not sure the stoner group had anything in common with one another except for the stinky roach between Vince's fingers. Vince stood again, flicked the roach at Sam's face and looked at me with wobbly disgust. "Hey, best friend. When did you start hanging out with such pussies?" There was venom in his voice.

Sam lunged forward, slamming two open hands against Vince's chest, sending him toppling into the fire pit. He landed on his ass, burning his hands as he struggled to get out of the flames before his clothes caught fire. The smell of burnt arm hair filled the air.

"What's your fuckin' problem?" Vince screamed. He held his burnt hands out as if waiting for rain. The two hotheads stood facing each other. The flames between them flickered, making shadows that would haunt my dreams for many years. Vince turned toward the house, but stopped in front of the door. He couldn't wipe his burnt hands and was unable to open the heavy sliding door. He was in obvious pain, and still I did nothing.

Sam hesitated for a moment, but if he wondered if he'd gone too far, he quickly dismissed the thought. "There you go, a burnt burnout," he taunted Vince. My so-called friends laughed at Vince's obvious pain. Someone inside slid the door open and Vince elbowed past Sam, shoved me out of the way and bolted back into the house.

I stayed in the back for another five seconds, but it may as well have been five hours. "You guys are assholes," I finally blurted as I headed for the door, hoping I wasn't too late to comfort Vince or, more likely, escort him to the hospital. He had nearly reached the front door when I called his name. He struggled to get out, wincing as he turned the doorknob. He ran between two parked cars and then turned to face me. "Some best friend you turned out to be."

That's when a Chevy Impala, with one headlight out, slammed into him. He was knocked down and run over. The car skidded to a stop on the thick grass, still on top of him. A drunken Randy Lacey stumbled out. "What did I hit?"

I was frozen. I heard someone yell, "Call 911! Call the police!" Vince's leg twitched from under the car, but I knew he was already dead. I hoped he was dead. I couldn't face him. And yet here I was, so many years later, ready to do just that.

* * *

Vince thanked the waitress and looked back at me. That whole recollection must have happened in a moment, but it felt every bit as detailed and enduring as any simulation Andrew had ever created. And now, though Andrew's programming genius, I was watching myself talking with Vince. That became background noise, as if I was looking in on someone else's muffled conversation. I watched as two longtime friends caught up. Their body language was full of laughter and sincere joy for one another's company. I pondered this. Was I looking at my future? Had Vince been in Heaven for all these years, meeting future residents? Who would come to visit me when their time was up? Is forgiveness one of the stages to get to Heaven, or is this Heaven?

Two simulated days later, Vince and I were exchanging sincere hugs and saying things like, "So nice to catch up," and "You'll be back this way, right?"

I continued up the beach, remembering that Andrew had said there were six stages or coves. I was ready to go to the next stage.

I walked back to the water's edge and closed my eyes. I was facing directly into the sun. I peeked at the waves breaking at my feet. I closed my eyes again and started to walk into the water. Extending my arms, exposing my palms at the radiant sun, I felt just a bit like Jesus. A wave of guilt seemed to leave my body like an evicted evil spirit. I waded into the ocean with my eyes closed, just listening. I half expected to be walking on water but stopped when it got as deep as my knees.

Seeing Vince had been great, but in this atmosphere, alone time recharged my battery. When I turned to face the shore, I was surprised at how far out I was. The bay was shallow for a good distance. The water was clear with a slight bluish green tint. The rolling waves now broke away from me. Off in the distance, I could see visitors, in pairs, meeting each other. Meeting with forgiveness, it appeared to me from their body language. Some looked awkward when they first met, others laughed, their problems and worries seeming to float off like helium balloons. I looked down the beach, wondering what awaited me. So far, I had met Sally, who promised she would be there waiting for me. And Vince and I had washed away all the juvenile garbage from our past. So far, so good. And so I walked.

I had no way of knowing then that back in the lab, Andrew was patting himself on the back for developing such a great simulation. "Stage one and two complete. He is 95 percent immersed, with only moments of real awareness. He is going to be a great candidate."

Ann's head was bobbing in approval. "Good. Keep him entertained. We need another resident."

Cove number three was just plain odd. I was once again alone on a beautiful beach. Bubbles were forming from under the sand and then released into the air. Some were the size of softballs, some the size of beach balls. They formed slowly on the sand and then slowly floated upward, wobbling all the while, their clear, rainbow-infused magic swirling around the sphere.

When I got close enough to touch one of the bubbles, I looked around for some sign of instruction or someone to tell me about these oddities. Sometimes it was just one bubble, other times a flurry. A big one formed ten steps from me. I watched as it tugged at the sand, like reverse gravity was trying to pull it to the skies. As it released, it wobbled and danced and started to float farther down the beach. Cautiously, I followed it. Just before it got out of reach, I stood on tip-toes and poked a finger at it. It popped. A soapy residue splashed my face and shoulders, making me blink my eyes shut.

Suddenly I was able to hear a conversation. "I hope Mr. Peregrine is OK. He turned out to be a really cool teacher." I opened my eyes and looked at some of the other bubbles forming on the sand. Some were way up the beach, some already too high to reach. Looking for more bubbles, I closed in like a kid guessing where the next lightning bug was going to show up. I had to be there when the bubble was first released from the sand. From that moment, I could see that I had only five or ten seconds before the bubble was out of reach. Some rose faster than others.

Nearby, a bubble broke loose from the sand. It was a small one, traveling fast. Pop.

"Yes, I miss him, but we haven't spoken in six years." The voice was my younger brother's.

"Surely these can't all be for me," I thought.

I popped another nearby bubble, hoping to hear my brother's voice again. Pop.

"Why do they always take the good ones?" I recognized this to be the voice of Mrs. Hingles, the English teacher. I scanned the beach, noticing that half a dozen bubbles were in the air at all times, and new ones were always forming.

I poked at another. "I think seventh period is my favorite class. Mr. Peregrine turned out to be a pretty cool dude." It was Billy's voice. Trouble-maker Billy Smith.

I smiled and chuckled. "Billy Smith, you might graduate after all."

I popped one bubble after another, surprised at all the folks who had taken the time to think of me. As the sun set, it became harder to see the bubbles. A big one floated right toward me as if it was tracking me. I'm not sure why I hesitated before I poked. "My son is a history teacher over at the high school. I am so proud of the way he turned out." It was my mother's voice. She had been gone for eight years.

Not a day went by that I hadn't thought about Mom. "Can she still see me?" I wondered.

I sat on the beach, my toes in the wet sand. The orange and yellows of the sky, along with the waves' steady beat, rocked me to sleep—or at least took me "off line." I had no way to tell how much time had passed. The sun began to show itself like a spy peeking over a newspaper. I yawned and stretched. When I turned to look behind me, I noticed the bubbles were still forming in the sand. It was as if the voices from earth filled them with helium and sent them, special delivery, to penetrate my own personal Heaven. "Had they continued all through the night?" I wondered. I spent the next hour selectively popping bubbles, feeling a bit like I was eavesdropping on what were meant to be private conversations. When I got tired of chasing them down, I watched as bubbles kept forming, finally content to let them wobble upward and out of reach. I was not forgotten or hated. I was loved and admired by so many. I sighed, feeling a bit foolish about having wallowed in self-pity the last few years. I pinched my bottom lip as I pondered my new perspective, and looked to the next cove.

# Chapter 13 – Lost in Fantasy

I walked a long, hot, stretch of beach and wished I had gone back to see Sally instead. I wondered why I was in such a hurry for the unknown. I took a moment to walk deep enough into the heavenly ocean to cool the tops of my feet that were starting to turn pink. A school of parrot fish detoured around my legs. I looked back down the beach, reminiscing about each cove, each stop. I was surprised to see that I had covered much more beach than I'd thought. Or was I just being made to believe that, to keep me moving forward? I waded out a bit deeper and sat in the crystal-clear water. My legs were in front of me, arms behind me, pressing into the sand for stability. Cresting waves washed around my chest. The consistent tug and push of the ocean's heartbeat had me gently swaying as if in an invisible rocking chair.

As I bobbed in the cool shallows, the sun's heat quickly dried and tightened my face. I pulled my hair back to further expose my forehead and tilted my face even higher towards the sky. A cool breeze seemed to conduct the heavenly orchestra. It twisted and tweaked nature's sounds. Flutes seemed to be warming up for a symphony; the distant seagulls were playing soft clarinets, and the dancing palms and other vegetation on shore filled in the rest of the woodwind section. The sounds and smells changed with every wave of the unseen conductor's baton. I sat there for hours, letting this imagined orchestra pull ideas out of my head. I saw myself meeting new people. I couldn't make out the conversations, but the body language was that of hope and happiness. People stood in line, waiting to see me. I watched myself scribble something on a blank page and close a book. Under a warm smile, a hand stretched out; I handed her a book as if it was made of gold. I looked to see how many others were in this line. It seemed to go on forever. I noticed some rustling about a dozen people back. A small thin man had grown impatient. He lowered his head and shoved the much bigger man in front of him. The line toppled like dominos towards me. The woman at the head of the line, unaware of the push impending behind her, reached out to hand me her book for me to sign.

At that moment, a crisp wave smacked me in the face, sending me tumbling onto my back, fighting for the surface and gasping for air. When I regained my composure, I cursed Andrew. I was sure this was his way of telling me to move on to the next element of his expertly crafted simulation. His pride and joy.

"Damn you, Andrew, for rushing me. Damn you for reminding me that this isn't real."

I stood up and splashed back to shore, nose burning from salt water, my ears clogged. I took a moment to bang on one side of my head until my right ear popped, letting the last of the ocean drain out. Instinctively, I looked for a camera of some kind that I could use to acknowledge Andrew. I wasn't sure if I wanted to give him a thumbs-up or the finger. Taking a deep breath, I decided to do neither. Instead, I used my right hand to comb the excess wetness from my hair. Again, I thought of heading back to Sally, but something told me Andrew wouldn't let that happen. "What will he do next to keep me following his quest? Will I step on a stingray? Get stung by a jellyfish?

Maybe a windstorm will come up and keep me from moving in the wrong direction."

I looked ahead, toward the next cove. But then I got a grip on myself. I laughed at my whiny thoughts and reminded myself that Andrew hadn't led me down any bad paths—yet. He had brought me to Sally. He gave me the chance to ask Vince for forgiveness. He'd let me know I wasn't some forgotten shadow of a man. "What does he have in mind for me next?" I couldn't have predicted or prevented any of the life-changing encounters this amazing software had or would put in my path. And now a firm breeze eased me into what I was confident was the right direction. Again, I had to grin, wondering if Andrew was smiling back as he worked me like some kind of avatar. "Onward," I said aloud, putting one foot in front of the other.

The sun was on its final descent of the evening, occasionally hiding behind low but swift-moving clouds. The walk was deceptively long. The bottoms of my feet felt raw, the tops now officially sunburnt. Fifty paces ahead, a protruding formation of black rock came to a point about forty feet into the water. It looked like the bow of a ship. Instead of running ashore, it appeared to be preparing for a maiden voyage, pointing out to sea. To get to the next cove, I would have to climb it, go into the water and wade around it, or wait for low tide. I made a rebellious attempt to climb over, but its edges were too smooth and too slippery. I had to wade well out into the water to get around this black stone wall. The cool water felt good on my feet. As I approached the bow of the ship, the rolling waves flexed and climbed past my knees and threatened to grab my testicles. I tightened my stomach muscles as the peak of each rolling wave chilled my groin. I felt my balls shrinking up in surrender. The waves began to push and pull, creating a dangerous undertow. The waves were now climbing up to my chest and I waded with my arms above the water, a bit like an orangutan. Trying to get around the ship's prow, I realized it had changed. The obstacle was now a monstrous rock covered with razor-sharp barnacles; I couldn't use it to stabilize myself. I panicked for just a moment, wondering if Andrew would actually let something bad happen to me. When I finally crested the farthest tip of the stone freighter, the waves pushed on my back, forcing one foot in front of the other towards shore on the rock's far side.

The sun was dropping faster than normal, like a decal on a car window being cranked down. "Apparently I wasn't supposed to get here before dark." With the safety of the sandy beach now in sight, I was able to lift my head and focus on land. The sounds of the night started up, just a bit too "on cue," making me think of Andrew yet again.

* * *

Not so coincidentally, Andrew was thinking about me, as I would find out later. "He refuses to fully commit," he grumbled, adjusting controls on his touchscreen monitors.

"Maybe you're not as good as they say," mumbled Ann, who was preparing to leave for the night. "I want you both to stay here tonight. This is the critical point and he is a perfect candidate."

Vlad had been unusually quiet this evening but finally spoke up. "I'm tellin' ya, ve got nothin' to vorry bout. Ve got a travel tick. He's not vaking up."

Andrew quietly rebutted him. "I'm not so sure."

* * *

I stomped the last few steps out of the ocean, noticeably chillier than it had been under the bright sunlight, glad to be back on shore. My teeth chattered and I hugged myself, noticing huge goosebumps on my pale legs. Far down the beach, a blazing fire danced against the distant palms. Crickets chirped and cicadas clicked. A variety of frogs played a short tune, but the unseen maestro slowly brought the volume down, replacing it with distant pops and cracks, as dried-out limbs from once healthy trees burned up for someone's heat. It wasn't clear who that someone was, as only fragments of flickering light illuminated a cluster of distant faces behind the fire.

As I closed in on the flames, I tried to make out my new surroundings. Long, dark bench seating surrounded a fire pit dug in the sand. Getting closer, I could see the benches were made from long, thick tree trunks, sliced down the middle. They rested, about two feet off the ground, on short stumps with a V cut into them. I was unable to make out any of the six dark figures, more shadowed than lit by the fire. It seemed the closer I got, the more the flames diminished. One of the five benches was empty and I sat there, knowing full well this was an intervention— and I was its target.

The flames erupted for just a moment as if some flammable dust had been tossed into the pit. When the fire subsided, I saw Vince sitting across from me. He stood and approached me. It may have been the flickering light, but it looked like his leg walked right through the stones that edged the fire pit. As if he were a ghost—or a glitch in a computer simulation—he stood in front of me, forcing me to look up. He shielded me from the fire and I suddenly felt a chill. My first thought was that I must have walked back the wrong way, returning to where I'd first encountered him. Vince extended his hands, palms up. He was looking so much like Jesus Christ, that it made me feel even colder. He spoke. "As I have forgiven you, so shall you forgive others." The flames flared up again, forcing me to momentarily shield my eyes. When the flash of heat and light disappeared, so did Vince.

I realized I was sitting across from what may as well have been mannequins. The flames flickered tossing shadows onto eye sockets, pointy noses and dark mouths, but revealing no movement on the blank faces. The only sound was the subtle crackling of the burning wood. The silence was unbearable.

Another burst of flames illuminated the face of a teenage boy. He pulled back the hood of his sweatshirt and smiled uncomfortably. "Do you remember me?" asked the shadow.

I was surprised that I knew the boy. He was Bobby Centry. He had lived down the street from me, many years ago. We had hung out occasionally in our early teens. Bobby and I once got caught playing in a construction site that was clearly off limits. We'd been playing army or tag or something in the developing subdivision's half-built houses. When I'd missed my 5:30 dinner, my father set out looking for me. He found us climbing out of an unfinished cellar just as the police were arriving. A neighbor had called to report us. When the police approached us, my father was in the middle of giving me a whoopin'. It was a pretty severe whoopin', with a two-foot-long piece of quarter-round he'd found on the job site, handy enough for my dad to pick up in the heat of the moment. Bobby fled, and escaped both my dad and the police. Back in those days, in my neighborhood, anyway, it was safer to face the police than your father.

I'd been forbidden to hang out with Bobby, and our friendship fizzled. If this was the incident I needed to forgive, it was easy. All was forgiven. "I had that beating coming," I confessed. "You got away clean. Good for you."

Bobby flinched and forced an uncomfortable smile. "No, I didn't. The police came to my house and told my parents. My old man gave me the belt every night for a week." He grimaced when he spoke of his father. "After that, he would look for reasons to beat me. I think he started to like beating me. After school, I had to come straight home. If I wasn't home by four, my mother would threaten with 'wait till I tell your father'. If I wasn't studying when he walked in the door at 5:30, I got the belt. If somehow I made him mad at dinner, I would get the belt at night instead of a good-night kiss. I was so mad at you."

I didn't know what to say. I crinkled up my forehead and ran a hand through my hair. "Damn, Bobby. I'm sorry about the beatings. But why were you mad at me?"

Bobby dropped his head. "Because your life didn't suck as bad as mine."

I shook my head. I felt sorry for never even thinking about what might have happened to Bobby.

Then he finished what he'd started to say. "And that's why I killed your dog."

At that, I straightened, furiously blinking my eyes. The blood seemed to drain from my body. "You what?!" I stood up. "That was you?" Another flare-up from the fire, and Vince was standing next to Bobby. Then a second flare-up and Vince was gone. The message was clear. It was my turn to forgive. I closed my eyes and took in a deep, smoky breath. My heart pounded and now my head throbbed, flush with blood. I took three intentional deep breaths, holding my hands on my chest. I let the anger drain out like an uncorked cooler full of water after all the ice had melted. Peace washed over my body. I took a final big breath to cleanse my mind and sat down.

"I forgive you, Bobby. I had no idea what you were going through."

That must have been enough. Bobby slipped back into the shadows.

Suddenly, I was very aware of the remaining shadows as the flames leaped up once again. What were they waiting for? Who were these shadows?

The now familiar flash drew my attention to one side. A tiny body glowed in the unsteady light. "Maybe it's another neighborhood rascal here to see if I have any forgiveness for him," I told myself. "Who are you? Take off your hood." I was hunched over on the bench, my elbows resting on my knees. "Are you going to say something?" I was in a hurry to get this cove's lesson—or lessons—behind me.

The silent youngster's head bowed. Delicate hands eased off the concealing hood. Her long blond hair tumbled out. Cathy Campbell. Sixth grade. This wasn't comfortable at all. I made myself laugh and dropped my head to my hands.

"You know you changed my life," I said. I raised my head to look her in her eyes, but she didn't meet my gaze, just stared straight ahead into the flames. "And not for the better," I added.

Twelve-year-old Cathy finally responded in a voice that was grown-up but still familiar. "It was sixth grade, and I still haven't forgotten. I am so sorry."

Cathy and I had both sat in the back of Mrs. Rutgers' class. One day, during quiet reading time, Cathy had let out a fart that vibrated off the classroom's wooden desk-chair combos. I knew it was her, but she'd pointed to me. Her face was bright red; she obviously was petrified that her life at Royalview Elementary School would be over should anyone find out that awful noise had been her. A girl. A girl farting in sixth grade had to rank right up there with a guy getting caught masturbating at the movies. As the wretched odor wafted ever outward, our classmates pointed and snickered. They called me "Stinky."

"I took the hit for you," I told her, "and you never even thanked me. For years I was called everything from 'The Gasman' to 'Shit Pants.' That nickname even surfaced in high school. By that point, the story had escalated to, 'He shit his pants in junior high.' That really made it hard to make new friends. It certainly didn't help my chances of getting a girlfriend, Cathy."

Her head hung in shame. "I know. I guess I figured, better you than me. I figured it was OK for a boy. I was so embarrassed. It was so selfish of me to let you take the blame." And then she said it. "Can you forgive me?"

Here I was, a grown man at the end of my life. I hadn't been called "Stinky" in decades. I laughed. "Of course. I guess it would have been even worse for a girl."

She smiled apologetically.

"All is forgiven," I assured her.

She smiled sheepishly. And then she was gone.

I was feeling noticeably lighter. I eased back momentarily, forgetting that the bench didn't have a back rest. The hard seat wasn't comfortable and I fidgeted, anxious about the remaining ghosts in my closet.

The flames grew rapidly as if someone had thrown a big Christmas tree branch on the fire. It died down just as fast, leaving me staring at a middle-aged couple. They sat next to each other but it seemed forced, like they'd been told they had to sit together. She poked his side with her elbow, indicating that he should say something. He looked back at her and began in a soft, crackling voice: "I don't know what to say, where to start."

These folks were strangers to me. They didn't look or sound familiar in any way.

Finally, the woman lifted her head and started to speak in a raspy smoker's voice. "We never even saw them. We were fighting about something." Her gaze went to the man sitting next to her. "We were drinking."

He nodded, eyes downcast, and added, "A lot."

Now I knew what was coming. I closed my eyes and tilted my head back while taking in a shallow breath. I massaged my exposed neck, wondering if I would be able to hear the rest of their apology, let alone forgive them. "Well," I said, angrily, "Go ahead, ask me for forgiveness." I stood and paced in front of my bench. "So I can tell you to kiss my ass."

The couple was silent while I ranted on.

"You ruined everything. They were on the way to my house for dinner. We were going to tell them they were going to be grandparents." My head shook back and forth. I grimaced. I clenched my fists, trying to keep myself under control. "When we got the news, we jumped into the car and raced to the hospital." My head drooped and I sat back down. I couldn't keep up the rage. My voice got quiet as if I was talking to myself. "We forgot about the ham in the oven. That night, I lost my parents and my house. Two weeks later my wife lost the baby." I felt myself shaking as I tried to keep my crying silent. "We stumbled through life for three months before she told me she was leaving me." I looked at the couple, not even trying to hide my disgust. "You really messed up my life."

The woman looked at her partner and I saw her wrap her pinky finger around his. "We messed up a lot of lives that day."

The man nodded in full agreement before finally speaking up. "I messed up everything." He looked at the woman. She was obviously his wife, or at least his lover. "Ya see, Linda didn't make it either. We were celebrating our engagement. We had just left our best friends in the whole world."

Linda squeezed his hand and pitched in. "We never should have opened that second bottle of wine. We–"

The man lifted his head apologetically as he jumped in. "It's my fault. I insisted I was fine to drive home." He stood, stiffening his jaw. "I deserve every day of the life sentence I received. Hell, I deserve two life sentences." He sat back down and spoke quietly. "And I certainly don't deserve your forgiveness."

My anger began to melt. I imagined the roles reversed. It could have just as easily been me. How many times had I been guilty of driving after a glass or two of wine? Even three or four?

Linda tenderly comforted her sobbing man.

I went over to the bench and sat next to the man who'd killed my parents. The man I held responsible for the loss of my child. For the disappearance of my wife. I put my arm around the man and pulled him close.

The stranger sobbed harder onto my shoulder. "I am so sorry. You have to believe me. I would give anything to have that day back."

I silently comforted the man for a good long time. When the stranger lifted his shirt to wipe his eyes and then blow his nose, I eased up on my embrace. The man turned his puffy face, his bloodshot eyes looking deeply into mine. "I am truly sorry."

It was my turn now. I drew in a deep breath and whispered, "You are truly forgiven."

And at that, the cove of forgiveness seemed to fade away. I found myself walking the beach again. Another dazzling sunset water-colored the sky. The intervention around the fire pit felt as if it had happened weeks or months ago. I had the strangest feeling I was missing time. A lot of time. I was turned around, not sure if I was coming from somewhere or headed somewhere. How long had I been walking? As the last of the sun dipped below the horizon, I drew near yet another cove. I quickened my steps; I hoped to get there before complete darkness. Faint shadows crossed my path with a polite "Excuse me," and the last of the light was gone.

I froze in my tracks. "Hello?" I listened to muffled voices conversing casually, as if somebody was out for a stroll.

"Hello, yourself," said a cheerful voice. "You must be new here."

I strained in a futile attempt to see her. "Yes, where am I?"

She giggled innocently. "This is where you meet people and get to know them without first judging them on their appearance."

I blinked my eyes, noting that there wasn't an ounce of difference between having them opened or closed—so I closed them. "How are we supposed to get around?"

She giggled again. That made me smile. "We help each other. Here, give me your hand." I extended my hand, which she gently grabbed with both of hers, then clasped with just one. "Follow me. I want to introduce you to friends of mine."

I followed her through soft sand. The ground seemed to get colder as the sand gave way to harder ground. When she stopped, I bumped into her. I could smell a slight body odor. I wasn't sure if it was mine or hers.

"OK, we're going to sit at a table with friends."

I shook my head in agreement—for all the good it did us in the dark.

The voice of a young man seemed to come from a few feet away. "Who do we have here?"

I waited to see if I would be introduced by the woman—or was she a girl—who had found me. I felt a bench in front of what turned out to be a picnic table and blindly maneuvered into the seat. When I realized that I'd never introduced myself to her, I chuckled silently. "My name is–"

I was quickly interrupted. "No names!" she declared. "We don't do names here. Not at this stage, anyway."

Sheepishly, I responded, "Then how do I tell you who I am?"

The girl giggled yet again and now three voices replied in harmony. "Surely you are more than a name."

I had nothing to say to that.

The newest voice offered up an explanation. "Your name tells us nothing about you. You didn't even pick your name. When I say, 'Who are you?', a proper answer might be, 'I am over-sensitive.' Or 'I am a bit of a bully.'"

The other familiar voice chimed in. "I am self-conscious about my looks."

A third voice, female, quietly added, "I'm very shy." After a long, dark silence, she followed up, "But I'm working on it."

The original voice repeated the original question. "So, who do we have here?"

The darkness was very patient while I thought. Finally, I blurted out, "I am bitter."

The girl, who I was now thinking of as "Giggles," chipperly replied, "Yes! That's it. Now you've got it."

I continued, "What is the mission here?" immediately wishing I could reword my question.

"The 'mission' here," as I imagined the voice's owner making air quotes with his fingers, "is to change or accept yourself."

The shy voice softly added, "Not as easy as you might think."

Giggles put in her two cents. "Some find it easier to change; others prefer to accept themselves as they are."

I tilted my chin up, proudly telling myself, "This is my travel. Somehow, I have chosen this path. I need to follow it bravely." I spoke to my new invisible friends. "I'm at a disadvantage. You all know each other, and I don't know anything about you." I waited for a response.

"That's not true," said the male voice. "I told you that I am over-sensitive and a bit of a bully."

I got a bit sarcastic as I corrected him. "That's not true. You said, 'A proper answer might be, "I am over-sensitive." Or "I am a bit of a bully." Silence filled the blackness.

The voice corrected the oversight. "I am over-sensitive and a bit of a bully."

I apologized. "Sorry. I can be a bit of an asshole sometimes."

Giggles... giggled. "Now you're catching on."

I heard some clanking and a squeak that I recognized as a wheelchair. I was sure it belonged to the male voice. "What do we do now?" I asked.

"I'll go," said Giggles. "Give me your hands." Outstretched hands fumbled in the dark until the circle was closed.

The group began to recite. "God grant me the serenity to accept the things I cannot change, the courage to change the things I can, and the wisdom to know the difference."

Giggles continued. "I laugh so I don't cry. I want to be a stronger person. I eat when I'm nervous. I eat when I'm depressed. I eat to reward myself. I eat to punish myself."

Mr. Wheelchair broke the silence that followed her brave admission. "OK, now try it again, the right way."

She giggled. "Oh, I'm sorry. That's right." She cleared her throat and started again. "In the past, I would eat when I was nervous. I would eat when I was depressed. I used to eat to reward myself. I used to eat to punish myself. I am not a victim of my past."

The blackness was silent, and then Wheelchair began. "In the past..." He took a deep breath and started again. "In the past, I hated people just for being healthy. In the past, I went out of my way to make jocks look stupid. In the past, I saw myself as less than a complete man. I am not a victim of my past."

Giggles giggled and quickly apologized. "Sorry, I can't help it."

The shy, presumably young, lady said, "I'll go next." The silence awaited her voice. "In the past, I felt like I was somehow less worthy of love. Like I was a bad person deep down at the core. My mother always made me feel—"

Wheelchair redirected her story. "Stick to the process. In the past..."

Her anxious breath made me feel like I'd heard a silent scream. "In the past, I was alone. In the past, I was misunderstood. In the past, I cut myself."

For ten long seconds, no one spoke.

"In the past, I wouldn't let people love me. I am not a victim of my past."

Mr. Wheelchair took the floor again.

"If we say, 'I am angry' or 'I am mean,' we take possession of the emotion. That is the moment that the emotion takes possession of you. You become a slave to the emotion. Understand, tall guy?"

I assumed he was referring to me, but decided not to respond.

"OK, let's try it again," said the voice from across the picnic table.

"I'll go," said Giggles. "In the past," she hesitated and took a breath for courage. "I assumed that everyone I met... described me as 'the fat girl.' Not 'the sweet girl' or 'the friendly girl.' Not 'the girl with crystal blue eyes or the trendy hair.' 'The fat girl.'"

Wheelchair spoke up. "How did that make you feel?"

Giggles was no longer giggling. She sniffed, and I didn't need vision to know she was wiping her tears. "It hurts." She choked and snorted out her response, "It hurts a lot."

Wheelchair continued. "What would you like to tell these people?"

She sniffled and gasped for air, obviously wiping her eyes and nose on whatever she was wearing. "I want them to know I'm funny and friendly." She sucked in three short sobs and blew out, a big long release. "And I would make a great best friend!"

I didn't need any light to see Giggles now. Someone in the group finally started a slow clap and the others joined in. She inhaled deeply and released what sounded like a lifetime of anxiety into the air.

"Anybody have anything to say to our brave friend?"

Little Miss Quiet and Shy was first to respond in her dainty voice. "I love you just the way you are. I don't care if you have one eye right in the middle of your forehead."

Giggles laughed. I heard shuffling and recognized the muffled noises as cross-table hugging. Giggles sniffed and firmly stated, "I'm done. That felt good."

"How about you, quiet one?"

"Me?" the shy, timid-voiced young lady squeaked.

"Yes. And speak so we can hear you," Wheelchair said in a voice that was more likely to send her into a corner.

"I was always different." Only the occasional squeak from the wheelchair interrupted her sentences as she slowly formed them. "I should have been born a girl." She waited for a gasp or a laugh that didn't come. "People are always saying, 'Is that a boy or a girl'? They don't even care if I can hear them. They act like I don't even have feelings."

I wondered if the others were just now figuring out, as I had, that she was a he, or was technically male, but knew herself as female. Which, of course, was the whole issue.

"I don't like boy things. I don't like getting dirty or spitting or fighting." His voice softened —no, I realized:

it was *her* voice. Isn't she entitled to be 'she' if she wants to be? "I like dressing up and doing my nails and wearing makeup. Why does that bother so many people? Why does that bother my parents?"

Giggles' stomach growled and she over-apologized. "Sorry. I'm so sorry. I can't help it."

Wheelchair interrupted. "What do you want to tell those people?" I mentally assigned the speaker the name Chris, since it could be male or female. Chris continued, almost inaudibly. "I was supposed to be a girl."

Wheelchair insisted, "Continue, but speak up."

Chris raised her voice almost too loud. "I was supposed to be a girl!" Then she settled back down. "I have the brain of a girl. Sometimes I feel like I'm wearing a man suit. When I change all the way to a girl... As she hesitated, I imagined her happily lost in thought. "...All the things I like to do will be acceptable."

Wheelchair prompted her, "How does that make you feel? What do you want to tell people who judge you?"

Chris snapped, "I want to tell them to eff off! I want to Taser them till they wet their pants! I want them to feel the same shame they've made me feel. I want them not to laugh at me." Her voice softened. "I want to be loved. I want someone to love me enough to teach me to love myself."

Giggles was sniffling again. "C'mere, you." The table shifted as Giggles got up to acknowledge Shy Guy—Shy Gal—Chris yet again. I was able to imagine a full-on, rocking, back-and-forth hug between the two strangers when I heard their soft murmurs of acceptance.

Wheelchair now took his turn without being prompted. "I want people to see me." Everyone waited for him to go on. "I don't want people to pretend I'm not there because I make them uncomfortable. I'm in a damn wheelchair. So what? Look at me! Ask me what happened. Ask me what it's like. Help me when I need help. Let me help you. Play games with me. Argue with me. Challenge me." His voice lowered but he wasn't finished. "Nod at me when you walk by. Even if you don't stop to talk, acknowledge me." He abruptly stopped talking. No one said anything for a long time. Wheelchair had fully shared his feelings. He didn't need our help.

It was still pitch black, but I closed my eyes anyway to summon up my own courage. "I'm scared." Silence. "I'm dying... And I'm scared." No one interrupted. "I did so many things wrong. I held grudges. I mean I really held grudges," I said, pointlessly shaking my head in the dark. "I punished people for having human feelings. If my wife looked at another man, I would get insanely jealous. I would pester her until I wasn't attractive to her anymore. Then I would try to hurt her by flirting with other women."

I had to stop; I had to remember what I'd just so easily blurted out to my unseeing new friends. I let out a single blast of a laugh. "Ha! I don't know why I'm afraid to die. I died five years ago when I lost my parents, my wife and my child." I rested my elbow on the table and dropped my head into my hand. "This is my farewell trip to myself. I'm not going back."

After no one spoke for ten long seconds, Wheelchair broke the silence. "You ready to go on to stage two?"

I'm afraid the sarcasm got the better of me again. "You mean this gets even more fun?"

Wheelchair gave a rare laugh. "OK, tall guy, this time you go first. Since it's easier to fix others than it is to fix ourselves, you get the opportunity to tell us what to do to get over our hang-ups. Get it?"

I nodded again, as if anybody could see me, and followed up with a more appropriate answer. "Yes, I got it." I turned in the direction of each voice, trying to decide who to start with. "Let's start with you, 'Giggles.'"

Hearing the nickname I'd assigned her for the first time, she giggled right on cue.

"I find you to be positively adorable."

She said, "That's so sweet."

Wheelchair shushed her and I went on. "I assume you're pretty heavy, based on what you've shared." Trying hard to sound sincere, I said, "Anyone who can't see your beauty is blind. Anyone who needs to cut you down to feel better is shallow and not worthy of your sunshiny personality and your giggles of pure happiness." Saying all that wasn't easy; my sigh might have sounded stressful. "However, you should learn when and why food became your master. I read something that helped me. I used to say it to myself the moment I started thinking about food. 'Every meal is...a short-term investment in how I feel and perform, a mid-term investment in how I look, and a long-term investment in my freedom from disease.'"

Her soft voice acknowledged this for the group. "I like that."

And then I concluded, "But you have to do it for you, not for anyone else." I stopped for a moment. "I'm done."

"I don't think so, tall guy," Wheelchair said. "Now that I know you have the balls to be honest, I want some of that."

I looked in the direction of the voice, trying to see him. The blackness made me bold. "You have a bravado about you. Something about your persona says, 'Respect me.' How long have you been in that wheelchair?" I waited for my answer.

"Eighth grade."

More silence. Maybe they were wondering if I would speak next, or if Wheelchair had more to share.

"I was playing at the neighborhood creek," he said. "I tried to climb the waterfall. Almost made it." This time he stopped talking for good.

"You sound like an adult now," I said, "so I'm going to assume that you're in it for the rest of your life."

"Yep."

"Then you'd best make friends with it. Soup it up. Nerd it out. Learn to dance in it. But you have to lose the chip on your shoulder. You have to decide if your wheelchair is half empty... or half full. Shit, I don't know what I'm talking about. I don't know why you guys asked for my input."

Wheelchair was ready for this. "No, you did good. I mean, I've heard all that shit before, but I'll need to hear it again and again. Sometimes ya just get down... you know?" Murmurs of understanding came from around the table.

"My turn," came a sensitive, anxious voice.

I was momentarily stifled, but so was everyone else. "What? Me again?" I asked.

Wheelchair laughed. "Hell, yeah, tall guy. You're doing great."

"Shy guy," I began. I corrected myself. "Shy *girl*. May I call you 'Chris'? To me, you're Chris."

She apparently gave this a moment of thought before acknowledging me. "Chris will work."

I nodded to the darkness. "You be you. The world is full of boring people all trying to fit into three or four standard molds. Fly your flag proud... but take a karate class or something just in case you ever have to get physical."

I was ready to stop there, but shy guy Chris chuckled and said, "More."

And so I pushed on. "Relationships are tough and I'm probably not the guy to give you advice in this category. I can't imagine how difficult and how interesting and exciting your love life will be when you decide to live in your own skin and meet people who make your heart pound. I am excited for you. You're going to be OK."

We talked all through the night. We came to understand one another better than most lifelong friends or even family members did. At the first sign of light, Wheelchair backed himself away from the table. I was barely able to make out his silhouette. "Hey, I got to go," he said. "My name is Danny. My friends call me Crank."

"My name is Tim. My friends call me... Tim." I could feel Danny smile. "See you around, Crank." When his shadow faded off I looked around the table. "Hey, Giggles, how come I get the feeling you're leaving too?" I could see she was a big, beautiful woman.

She giggled and reached her arms out to invite me in for a hug. "My name is Belinda. People call me Linnie." We hugged for a long time and I asked her if I could take her home with me.

She reminded me of something I'd said last night. "I thought you weren't going home?" She pulled me into her arms and squeezed me hard. She whispered, "Go home." When I finally let her go, she backed up into the darkness and vanished.

"Shy girl. I suppose you have a party to go to also?"

"Randi... Randi with an 'I.'" I could just barely see a beautiful smile in the first twilight. "Thank you," she said, and she, too, faded into the lingering shadows.

I watched the sunrise for the umpteenth time since I'd been on this shore. I wondered if I'd been put here to help those tortured souls or if they were here to open my eyes to the life struggles of others. Hearing the waves again made me realize what had been missing from last night's strange encounters. No birds, no crickets, no cicadas. And as if on cue, all the familiar sounds and smells returned to my new reality. Then, just as I had done every other morning I'd been here, I sat down at the water's edge with my eyes closed, facing directly into the rising sun.

Unrelated ideas crashed into one another in my head. For a moment, I was back in some nondescript Ohio suburb, in a rundown, boarded-up plaza, in a secret room, in a magic chair. I tried desperately to bring myself back to the beach, but my world was suddenly dark and silent. I was able to feel some kind of commotion around me as if I was being moved. If the previous night's darkness had taught me anything, it was to feel. I felt concern and anxiety and realized I was being reclined. I felt hands lifting me, moving me to another chair. No, it was a bed. And I was being wheeled somewhere new. A bump felt like a gurney was being used to open a door. I fought to hear something, anything. I was fully aware I was being relocated, but to where? Simulation goggles kept me blind; noise-canceling headphones kept me deaf. My mind raced. "Maybe I've crashed. Maybe I'm dying." I tried to get the thought out of my mind. I desperately wanted to go back to the beach.

Suddenly I stopped moving. I felt someone adjust my headphones and then... nothing. Stillness. Two minutes of silent blackness. Or was it two hours? It had gotten so hard to tell. I could feel my heart pounding. "I am dying. I must be."

But just then, the sound of waves breaking on the shore interrupted my madness. The sunshine was back, but a shadow blocked the sun from my closed eyes. Anxiously, I pried my eyelids open. Sally was staring at me, worry in her eyes, brushing sweaty hair from my forehead. "Baby, you were having a bad dream."

I gave her a heavy sigh. I was relieved to see Sally but disturbed to know that even she was lying to me. I had played along with every detail of the simulation but couldn't help having flashbacks. "What the hell is going on back at Ann Tranz Dental?" I wondered.

I was reminded of something Andrew had told me: "Days may seem like months."

"This may be my dying day," I convinced myself. "Possibly my last hours. Why am I trying to spend it anywhere but here in this absolutely beautiful place with Sally at my side?" I brought my gaze back to her. She stroked my cheek, gave me her beautiful smile and asked, "Where do you go? Sometimes you seem to forget that I'm here." I shook off any thought I had floating around my head about Cleveland and Ohio back roads and abandoned strip malls when I saw her mesmerizing eyes. I pulled her lovely body against mine. "How lucky am I to have you." I was grinning from ear to ear. "Let's go see if we can find a new shell today."

And I immersed myself in the simulation, deciding that "here," with the woman of my fantasies, had to be better than reality.

Over the next few simulated "months," Sally and I got to know each other very intimately. Not just sexually, although we did play out every fantasy I had ever imagined. More importantly, I felt confident that I had satisfied Sally's fantasies as well. Together, we built a simple but adequate shelter. We collected driftwood to keep our fire burning through the tropical nights. I peeled the leaves off long palm fronds and sharpened their spines for spearing fish. Sometimes we would fish together; other times I would go by myself. The water was full of beautiful, colorful fish. I hated to kill the fish and never did so except to survive.

Coming back with my catch, I was always greeted by Sally in her Tarzan skirt, topless and tanned, with a big, genuine smile, delighted to see me. On the days I went out on my own, Sally found a way to convert Mother Nature into a utensil or a beautiful bowl. One of the palm species produced a two-foot-long canoe-like vessel. And every day Sally would collect a fresh bowl of colorful flowers to liven up our simple shelter. We would spend days talking to each other, while we soaked and bent palm stems to make furniture. Wild bamboo was used for everything from a kitchen table to wind chimes. Alternating between soaking and steaming it over the fire, I was able to bend green bamboo. Once it dried out, it was strong and sturdy. Today I was showing off my latest bamboo creation. I had soaked and steamed and manipulated a hollow, two-foot-long joint of bamboo into a snorkel.

After dinner, I would write. I had found a large slab of black slate at the far end of the cove. Small slices of the rock that had sheared off made great serving platters. The flat main expanse of smooth stone reminded me of a big-screen TV. I picked up a shell and, using it like chalk, drew a large rectangle onto a section of the flat surface. I couldn't resist adding an antenna. I stepped back to admire this juvenile work and decided that it would be better served as an open book. I drew in a center spine for my three-foot-tall opened book, and then moved to the top left margin. In tiny letters I inscribed the words

"The Traveler." I began to tell my story, starting from the day I'd received my death notice.

# Chapter 14 – OK ... Not Heaven

I used one section of the huge rock to document my time on the beach. At first, it was just simple lines to track the number of days. Then I sketched a more elaborate calendar. Since I had no idea what day it was, I decided to create my own names. I started with Funday.

Funday, Buildday, Thinkday, Loveday, Supplyday, Inventday, Listenday.

I liked to theme our days. On one beautiful Loveday morning, Sally and I were swaying on our hammock, just taking in the beauty all around us. Our bodies were forced together by the hammock's design, not that we minded! Birds chirped and sang familiar, happy tunes. Clouds entertained us with changing forms, inviting us to guess their shapes as if we were on a game show. The sun pushed orange and yellow crayon smears toward the sky. An albatross glided effortlessly above us. We watched his shadow approach and then cross right above our bodies... and then the sky darkened. And the sounds subsided.

I was in total darkness. "Oh God, please, not another test or life lesson. I thought this was my safe cove." I felt my mouth moving, but I couldn't even hear myself. I screamed for Sally to wake me up, but she was no longer part of my silent, black world.

I waited for instructions, for light, for a sound that never came. Was this death? Had I finally died? I lay still for hours. Or minutes. Or days, for all I knew. It was maddening. "If I'm dead, why am I still aware? Please, don't let this be death." I screamed Sally's name again and again. Did I really scream, or did I just scream in my head? I called for Andrew.

"Andrew! Something is wrong. Somebody help me." Eventually, I became aware that I was in restraints. Now, complete panic set in. "Andrew, something is wrong." I screamed until I was exhausted, real tears itching my face under the goggles. "That's it. I have to get these headphones off. This is a glitch," I tried to convince myself. Prying and twisting my head as far as I could, I managed to get the headphones halfway off one side of my head. I stopped to listen. "Oh, God. No." The familiar sounds of breathing equipment. A respirator. I listened closer. It was more than one respirator; I could hear monitoring equipment beeping. Then I heard a moan. I froze, attempting to hear it again. There it was, another moan. "Hello, can anyone hear me?" Then I remembered the last thing Andrew had said to me before starting the simulation.

"Ready for hibernation state."

"Andrew, you son of a bitch!" I screamed. And then, anger giving way to despair, I sobbed, occasionally mumbling for "Somebody, anybody," to come help me.

I faded in and out of consciousness and awareness. The breathing machines hissed an awful repetitive rhythm. I found myself anticipating the next hiss of that dreadful tune. I tried to figure out how many others were with me in this hibernation state. With only the use of my partially blocked ear, I estimated there must be at least six others, maybe as many as ten. "What the hell is going on?" I must have just mumbled, but hoped somebody could hear me. "Am I some kind of Goddamn experiment to you?" I jerked violently, trying to free my hands or legs. I fought till I was exhausted... to no avail. But in all my thrashing I did manage to get the headphones nearly off. The sounds in the room made me wish I could put them back on. The steady hissing of the regulators and the beeping monitors were a constant reminder that I certainly wasn't in Heaven. And every so often, a random groan came from a male voice. He sounded pretty far away. I tried to get his attention. "Hey, the guy groaning. Can you hear me?"

That didn't get a response. I knew I had to try harder. I inhaled deep and let out a scream. I filled my lungs again and used every ounce of the air, dragging out every word. "Caaaan anyyyyyybodyyyyy heeeeear meeeeeee?" Exhausted, I fell asleep.

Ten minutes or maybe ten hours later, I was awakened by an unfamiliar sound. It was the squeak of a wheel. Like the wheel of a gurney. It sounded like another "patient" was being wheeled into this madness. I listened silently, fearing the worst if they were to find out I was awake and aware. The wheels stopped, and I thought about calling out. Then the wheels started up again and I froze. I heard a quiet voice; he seemed to be talking to himself. I tried to make out what he was saying. Moments later the faint squeak started up. "It's getting closer," I calculated, based on the noise. The squeaking stopped again. The man wasn't talking; he was singing. I imagined it might be a technician of some kind, checking in on his patients. I tried to work out a plot. "He must be wearing headphones. When he gets to me, I'll... I'll ..." I stopped, filled with frustration. "My fucking hands and legs and chest are shackled. I can't even grab him." The squeak started up again and then stopped at what I presumed was the patient—or the prisoner—closest to me. I flashed back to my time in the darkness with Wheelchair and Giggles and Shy Girl Chris. What had I learned there? I learned that words can be very powerful. They had to be. It was all I had. Once again, I heard the voice, singing under his breath. It was an Elvis Presley song. "Blue, blue... Blue svade shoes." The Russian accent was undeniable. It was Vlad.

I lay still but my mind raced through possible scenarios. I trusted Vlad. I trusted Vlad more than I trusted Andrew, and certainly more than I trusted Ann. I suddenly remembered the awful dream I'd had about Vlad turning the lions loose on me. The squeak of the rolling cart got even closer and then stopped. Now I wanted to know if Vlad was in the room alone. Was he checking in on his hostages, or administering something?

Just then, he spoke. "Uh oh, look vat you did to your earphones. Let me fix dat for you, cowboy."

All my planning went out the window. I just screamed, "NO!"

Vlad must have jumped back a mile because whatever was on his rolling cart was now on the floor. "Vat da hell!"

I finally found my words. "Vlad, something went wrong with the simulation! It stopped working days ago. I've been in darkness and silence, screaming for help. Why are you doing this to me?" I stopped talking. I could hear Vlad's heavy breathing. I could feel his eyes staring at me. Was he wondering how to respond? "Vlad? I know it's you." The ventilators continued their conversation, but Vlad remained silent. I begged. "Please, Vlad, I won't tell anybody what's going on here." Still nothing. "I promise. Please, Vlad, take off these goggles and talk to me."

Finally he spoke. "You are gunna get me into some serious trouble, cowboy." That sounded like he was going to oblige, so I stayed silent. I heard Vlad roll the cart, now upright again, off to the side. He lifted the dislodged headphones entirely off my head and all the room's ambient sounds doubled and deepened.

"And the goggles. Please, Vlad." Vlad pulled the bulky VR apparatus away from my face and eased them over my forehead as easily as if they were swimmer's goggles. As bad as I wanted to see, I still had to shut my eyes. The brightness was blinding. I peeked through tear-filled slits, slowly widening my view with each blink.

Vlad towered over me. Through the blur, I could see his expression was both confused and apologetic. "Dis is bad. Dis is real bad."

"Vlad, take off these straps."

Vlad answered in a soft, analytical tone. "But you are supposed to be here for two more veeks."

I raised my voice. "Take off these Goddamn restraints. Right now!"

A switch seemed to click in Vlad's head and he began to undo the buckles. "Ann is not going to be happy," he said, very matter of fact.

As soon as Vlad had the final restraint off, I held out my hand, a silent request for Vlad to help me sit up.

"How you feeling, cowboy?" Vlad said with a weird smile.

"Fuck you, Vlad. What the hell are you doing here?" Now I could see what I'd already surmised: a roomful of zombies in a vegetative state. "I knew you guys were up to something, but not this. I thought you just robbed dying people of their savings."

Vlad held out a hand. His meaning was clear: I should zip it. "Ve are curing cancer, cowboy."

I wasn't expecting that. I tilted my head like a puzzled dog.

Vlad continued. "Yep, dats vhat ve're up to." He paused for just a moment. "And you, my friend, are currently cancer free," he said, gently poking my chest.

"Bullshit." I scrunched my face into my sternest "I don't believe it" glare.

Vlad raised his eyebrows and shrugged. "Tis true. Ve needed to keep patients still for longer period while flushing their system. Ve vash away the cancer."

Now the scrunch on my face was more about doubt than certainty. "But here? Why not in a hospital?" But I already knew the answer.

"Look. Ve already know how to do it. Ve chust haf to show proof first. Lots of proof. Or ve get jail cell instead of Nobel Prize. Ve have to keep you still for two months vile ve fix you." Vlad gave me a cocky grin. "Vat you tink about dat?"

I massaged my wrists and looked around this sad room. "Is that how long I've been here? Two months?"

Vlad unhooked a clipboard from the foot of my gurney. "Six veeks, two days."

I looked back at the room, full of my fellow travelers. "All these people have cancer?"

Vlad nodded. "All of dem."

I touched my face and stroked six weeks' worth of beard. "And you can cure all of them."

Vlad answered with one word. "Mostly."

"What does that mean?" I motioned for him to help me stand, but Vlad held his palm to my chest.

"Not so fast, cowboy. You hafn't stood up for six veeks. It's like 'frigerator. The fluids got to flow to the right parts if it's been on its side too long." Vlad looked at his watch. "Andrew is going to be wondering vat is taking me so long. And ve haf to tell Ann."

That made me raise my voice. "Hold on! You've held me prisoner for six weeks. You owe me a little better explanation."

Vlad fiddled nervously with his upper lip. "Look, ve know Ann can be a little... he searched for the right word, "a little intense. But she is brilliant. She is da vun who figured dis out."

I looked down at my palms and flashed back to my meeting with Vince. I closed my hands and folded them over my chest. "Figured what out? What did she do to me? What is she doing to them?"

Just then Andrew opened the door to the room. "Vlad, what the hell is taking–" When he saw me sitting up, he froze. "Shit, what's going on? Why is he awake? I haven't run the reentry simulation."

Vlad looked at me and then back at Andrew. "Don' ask me. Yur da computer guy."

I eased myself off the gurney, holding on to the side for stability. "Vlad was just about to tell me what the hell you guys are doing here. What is all this?"

Andrew took a long look at the replacement IV bags, still on the floor after Vlad's cart overturned. "Ann is going to be pissed," Andrew said, shaking his head.

"I'm pissed!" I told him, sternly.

"Why are you pissed?" Andrew bounced back. "Didn't you tell him that he's in full remission?"

Vlad shook his head. "Yeah, I told him. He vants to know how."

Andrew looked at his watch. "Ann is meeting with another traveler in one hour."

That was it. I exploded, "Somebody tell me what's going on before I start yanking plugs."

Vlad held an arm out towards Andrew, indicating it was time for him to take the floor.

Andrew obliged. "You know when you go to a dentist... Well," he clarified, "a dentist in a nice neighborhood."

I nodded.

"They give you movie goggles to distract you from the work being done. Same thing here. But we send you on elaborate travels, dream vacations, while we flush your body of cancer."

I didn't wait to ask my next question. "Why the initial one-day trips?"

Andrew bent down to pick up an IV bag. "We learn a lot about you on these one-day simulations. I mean a lot! And to be real honest, we need the money. This isn't cheap to do. So the more travels we can send you on before the big one, the more likely the success."

"And the more money you make," I had to add.

Andrew fired right back. "It's not about the money, asshole. We are curing fucking cancer here. We cured your cancer. For free, I might add."

I sat back onto the gurney. "Free? I have given you a total of, what? Almost forty thousand dollars."

"Ahh," Andrew said, "but that was for simulations. You came to us. It's not like we kidnapped you. You got what you paid for. And a new lease on life."

About that last part, I couldn't disagree. In fact, I caught myself involuntarily nodding in agreement. But I still had plenty of questions. "How are you doing this? What do you know that the Cleveland Clinic doesn't?"

Andrew pulled a chair from one of the room's makeshift work stations, which was nothing more than a folding table and a cheap rolling chair. "We attack the cancer on multiple levels." He looked down at the floor for a long moment and then back at me. "To put it in layman's terms, we run a very customized blend of biologic response modifiers through the bloodstream. Ann uses a much gentler blend that oxygenates and strengthens existing red blood cells and stops the bad cells from growing and dividing. It works slower than chemotherapy but doesn't do all the damage chemo does. Our serum also contains gallium, which means we can monitor tumors and inflammation throughout your travels. Ann's serum actually works best when the bad cells are most active. While they're trying to divide and multiply, they're at their weakest. They get separated from the healthy cells and washed out of the body in small amounts. That's the reason for the six to ten weeks of stillness. The process has to be maintained until all active cancerous cells are washed out."

I hadn't come close to running out of questions, but Andrew looked at his watch and held up a finger. He wanted me to be patient. "There's more. The Heaven trip. It's mandatory. You have to learn to forgive others. Even stupid or mean people. You have to learn to forgive yourself. You have to learn not to judge people who are different from you, that don't look like you or have the same beliefs as you. If you can't do that, the cancer comes back."

Vlad pointed a finger at Andrew.

"Why are you pointing at me?"

Vlad pointed again, this time arching his finger to indicate, "Behind you." Andrew turned to see Ann standing in the doorway.

Her eyes bounced all around the room.

Vlad lowered his head towards the floor in front of him but rolled his eyes up enough to look for a response from Ann.

Finally, she spoke in an urgent tone. "Did you do the reentry simulation last night?"

Andrew just shook his head no.

Vlad finally spoke. "He vas avake ven I came in to change bags."

"You're going to have to do the reentry simulation, Mr. Peregrine," Ann insisted.

I gave her my most menacing smile and shook my head. "No way. I'm done being your monkey."

Ann approached me and tapped her nails on the gurney. Then she held up a finger, trying to get my eyes to follow it left and right. "Look, you can't just walk out of here."

I laughed. "That's exactly what I'm going to do."

Ann started again. "You can't just walk out of here after six weeks. You have to have your story straight."

I stood up, pushing her annoying index finger aside. "I don't need to have any story straight. You're the one breaking about fifty laws."

Ann rubbed her forehead as if she had a migraine. "Tim, please listen. We are doing ground-breaking work here. We have figured out how to cure cancer. We need six more weeks to prove our conclusions. You don't want to be the guy who gets in the way of curing cancer now, do you?"

I folded my arms. "What is this reentry simulation?"

She pulled a penlight out of her lab jacket and closed in on my eyes. "May I?"

I sat back, keeping the scowl on my face but allowing her access.

Ann spoke softly while shining the light into my eyes. "The reentry simulation is an absolutely beautiful trip to Buriram, Thailand to meet with Buddhist priests. You're going to need a compelling story to tell your friends, family and co-workers about where you were. The simulations, as you now know, are as real as it gets. You can say you were treated by these Buddhist priests and you are amazed that you have shown signs of complete remission. Give me six months to properly submit my findings and cover my tracks here. Please understand, I needed to do these tests."

I scratched my uncomfortably furry neck, pushing my jaw out to indicate I wouldn't be conned again. "I'm not taking your Thailand trip. I simply don't trust you to bring me back." Damn, that beard was itchy. I kept scratching my neck. "I'll read your script, or watch a movie. But you're not putting me under again."

Ann pulled my hand from my neck. "Stop scratching."

I couldn't help laughing. "You're a funny lady."

She tugged at the loose skin on my forearm, checking it for elasticity.

"Stop touching me!" I insisted.

"We need for you to spend the night."

I scanned the room full of zombies. "No fuckin' way."

Ann smiled. "Not in here. You can come back to my house. It's really important that we don't screw this up." She turned to her silent staff. "Vlad, please take complete vitals and start him on rice and crackers. Andrew, I want to see you in my office. We need to figure out what happened to the simulation and fix it before everybody starts waking up. And do you have written notes on Thailand that I can study with Mr. Peregrine?"

An hour later, I had been cleared for the twenty-minute trip to Ann's house.

# Chapter 15 – And I Began to Write

Ann let me know that eight others like me had been released, cancer free, with the same story of a trip to Thailand. So far, all the patients had been chosen based on having little or no family. But with the success of the trials, so came the need for more than one cover story. As Ann's secret facility filled with comatose patients, she was unaware that FBI agents were closing in on her. She had hoped her choices to this point would not draw attention as a few lonely cancer patients disappeared from the streets. But she was wrong about some of those patients. Like me.

Back in Cleveland, my disappearance had not gone unnoticed. The police had interviewed my neighbors, the principal and even my students. As stories of Ann's success began to leak, it was evident to her that she would have to move soon.

At one point, police came to her door in response to a homeless man who insisted that wild experiments were taking place there. Ann welcomed the officer in, making sure Vlad and Andrew heard her giving him a tour of her dental office. They had rehearsed for just such an event. By the time she and the cop reached the third exam room, Andrew was gowned and masked, pretending to do some kind of work on Vlad's teeth. Ann confided to the policeman that she did pro bono dental work for the homeless. "Under anesthesia, I'm sure they imagine all kinds of things."

"Em, hmm," the cop mumbled, still looking around. "What about the adjoining spaces?"

Ann wrinkled her face, her best impression of total bewilderment. "What about them?"

"No secret hideout where you have patients strapped down and blindfolded?"

This time Ann laughed. "The spaces next to me have been empty for years. The stinkin' landlord keeps promising to fix up this shithole but he hasn't even been in the United States for two years. Something about a visa issue. I send his money to Panama every month and he leaves me alone." The cop wandered around the place, looking up and down. He entered the medical storage room but after a few more moments of inspection he thanked Ann for her time— and for her services to the local vagrants.

The high school bought my Thailand story, hook, line and sinker, but, unknown to me, the FBI didn't. The feds had been called in when I first went missing. Turns out I was the fourth cancer patient to disappear from northeast Ohio over the last eight months, and not the last.

The FBI had already been in touch with my doctors and up to speed on my diagnosis. When I suddenly reappeared, cancer free, with a story similar to another recent "miracle cure from Thailand," the lead agent suspected there was more to the story.

When I asked for my job back, Mr. Bailey was ecstatic. When I didn't show up, and he couldn't find any sign of me for weeks, he thought I'd checked out for good. Maybe, he thought, on a last-hurrah tour of the world or on some crazy bucket-list escapade. He explained that he would need a few weeks to get the paperwork in order to reinstate me. Mr. Bailey asked me if I would consider another auditorium event. Reluctantly, I accepted, agreeing to tell the student body all about my trip to Thailand and my time with the monks.

My condominium was a strange place to be now that my cancer was gone. I reclaimed my cat from the neighbor and used my best pet voice to ask him for forgiveness. The moment I put Baxter down in the condo, he scurried under the bed. I changed the litterbox, filled the food and water bowls, even gave him a brand-new toy, stuffed with catnip. Apparently, Baxter needed to go to the forgiveness cove. I fussed around the house, bagging up old clothes and cleaning out drawers full of things I had saved for a someday that would never come. I cleaned this crap out, not because I was dying, but because it was time to live. I wiped away two months' worth of dust and ran the vacuum throughout my little home, completely freaking out Baxter. The background white noise of the vacuum and the brainless motion sparked thoughts of my last travel.

I especially thought about Sally. After all, she was a real person. Of course, the real Sally had no idea that she had been my fantasy girlfriend in my simulated Heaven. I pushed the vacuum's off button and listened to the motor wind down. I let go of the handle and laughed to myself. I made my way into the spare bedroom, my "office/workout room." This contained a simple desk with a modest computer and an elliptical machine. Neither piece of equipment had been used in a long time. I made myself another cup of coffee and settled in at my desk. I opened a spiral

notebook and headed the first page, "The Traveler."
And then I began to write.

I wrote deep into the night, documenting my life
from the time I'd received my diagnosis. When I filled
up the first spiral notebook, I started another. I had
eight blank notebooks left from a recent purchase of a
ten-pack and I filled four of them before falling asleep
in my chair. Five hours later I woke up and made
another cup of coffee. I did five minutes of stretching
and scarfed down a piece of toast slathered with
crunchy peanut butter. I wrote in detail about Ann,
Vlad and Andrew. I described her office and the secret
entrance to her laboratory.

I covered my trip to meet George and Martha
Washington. I relived every battle, every conversation.
I went on and on about little Wolfi Mozart and his
talented, ambitious family, about Cleopatra, King
Ptolemy and Pompey, and of course Puzo the Great.

Over the next three days, I obsessed over my
handwritten manuscript. It filled the eight spiral
notebooks and then another ten-pack. I scratched out
paragraphs, tore out pages, drew arrows and wrote
sideways in the margins. When I finished, I could
scarcely move my thumb and forefinger. My back was
stiff, and my eyes blurred. I slept for two days, waking
only to use the bathroom and snack on peanut butter
toast and celery dipped in peanut butter. On the third
day, I rose again… and finished my book. The day
after that, I gathered my eighteen spiral notebooks
and drove to see my editor.

Early in my teaching career, when I was working
in elementary schools, I had written short novellas for
my students. That's what had led me to find a regional
publishing house that specialized in educational

books. I'd had moderate success writing illustrated books about Mozart, Alexander Graham Bell, Thomas Edison, The Wright Brothers, and my latest one, about the adventures of real-life hero Davy Crockett. My sixth-grade classes had loved those books. The firm's editor-in-chief, Dave, liked my work, and I liked working with him. So I hoped he would see the value in this, even though it wasn't anything like what he'd published before.

But when I showed up at Dave's office, unannounced and disheveled, carrying an armful of spiral notebooks, I was treated with polite doubt. "Hi, Tim. You should have called. I'm with a client right now, but you can leave those right here."

I smiled. "No, I can't." I lowered my voice. "These are full of dirty little secrets." I grabbed Dave's loose sweater and pulled him uncomfortably close. "These are for your eyes only." When the editor tried to ease away from me, I pulled him in even more tightly. "Promise me!"

I knew my eyes were bloodshot; when he gave me a close look, he had to notice this, too. He placed his hand over mine. "OK, Tim, relax. Let me put them in my office."

I whispered to him—sounding, I'm sure, more than a bit crazy. "You have to read them tonight."

Dave's eyes told me he was worried about me. "OK, Tim. Let go of my sweater. I will read it tonight."

I had to be able to trust him. I slowly loosened my grip. "You promise?"

He repeated himself. "Yes, I will read it tonight."

At six o'clock the next morning my phone rang. I was in a deep sleep and didn't answer. At seven o'clock, the doorbell rang, followed by obsessive knocking. I woke, trying to orient myself to the moment. I stood but immediately fell back to a sitting position on the bed. I sprang up a second time and wobbled my way to the door.

Dave, the editor, scurried into the house with a brown paper bag under his arm. "Is this for real, Tim?"

That felt good. He had read it. "You want coffee?"

He waved away that distraction. "I have to know if this is just story time or if this is as real as you make it sound."

I motioned for him to sit down at the kitchen table while I fiddled with the coffee maker.

Dave pulled my spiral notebooks out of the bag and opened to the first page. "Did this really happen to you? Are you really cancer-free? Who else knows about this?"

I couldn't get in a word. I placed a cup of black coffee in front of him.

"You've been up all night reading, haven't you?"

Dave lifted the cup to his lips and inhaled, slowly sampling the first sip. "Yes, all night." He took a bigger swallow. "I finished it and hopped right in my car. What are you planning to do? We can't publish this... Can we?"

I pulled out the chair across from him. "Yes, we can. We have to. People are dying every day, and we have the cure."

# Chapter 16 – I am *The Traveler*

The following week, the principal, Mr. Bailey, let me know that my teaching status had been officially reinstated and I could start teaching my history classes whenever I was ready. He also let me know that he'd booked the auditorium for next Thursday so I could take the students on another adventure. My stage performances were the talk of the school, and started to get notoriety beyond the students and faculty.

Meanwhile, Dave reported that he had been engrossed in editing *The Traveler*. He'd gone so far as to hire a typist, on overtime, to transcribe my hand-written scrawl. Five days after first receiving them, he returned to my house with the original eighteen spiral notebooks and a thumb drive with the completed, edited version of *The Traveler*. With my approval, he agreed to take it to print.

The day of the school event arrived and, as before, the auditorium was packed. What I didn't know was that, in addition to the enthusiastic students and teachers, a pair of FBI agents were in the audience. I got a great response from my performance, this time teaching my audience about Thailand and prayer with Buddhist monks. I didn't say that I had pulled much of my information from the web. I could have done better, I thought. I stumbled in a couple of places, and wished I had trusted Ann enough to spend one more day in the simulation with the Buddhists that I'd pretended to have spent a month with. At the end of the show, I noticed two men following me as I greeted the crush of students. They were never more than a few steps away.

I was barely inside my house when I heard a knock. When I opened the door, the two men stood there with stony expressions, holding up badges. "Mr. Peregrine, we are with the FBI and we would like to ask you a few questions."

I could only stare at them, without saying a word. My thoughts ran wild and I'm pretty sure my blood pressure climbed.

"You can either invite us in or we can take you in for questioning."

I looked at the badges long enough to confirm that the two were, in fact, federal agents, and then my gaze quickly went back to the first man's lifeless black eyes. I eyed up the second man and tried to break the tension with a little laugh. "Is the FBI using robots now?"

Neither blinked. "What's it going to be, Mr. Peregrine? Here or downtown?"

I stepped back from the door and waved the men inside. I directed them to the living room sofa, suddenly aware that the spiral notebooks were in full view on the kitchen table. "So, I saw you at my event at school. What did you think?" I tried to break the tension without success.

Without a blink the agent on the left said, "We think you're lying about Thailand."

The suit and tie on the right reached into his pocket and pulled out a notepad and a pen.

Leftie did the talking. "We were called in to find you three weeks ago. When you reappeared last week, we tailed you, hoping you would go back to your little secret hideout."

I did my best to look confused. "I'm not sure what you're talking about; of course I went to Thailand. I can show you the airline ticket stub, if that will help. My passport was stamped, too." I did have a ticket to Thailand, compliments of Andrew's online talents, and authentic-looking stamps he had added to my passport.

Suit #2 flipped his pad to a new page. "We've confirmed that a ticket was purchased on the fourth of June for a trip to Thailand."

I nodded. "That's what I told you."

The suit flipped his pad shut and stared right through me. "But you never boarded that plane. You do know we track that kind of stuff these days."

I kept my mouth shut.

"Did you walk to Thailand, Mr. Peregrine?"

I didn't think that was very funny. I caught myself wringing my hands just as I noticed #2 was watching them, too.

He continued. "We've pulled your phone records and found you've made calls to a phone that we believe belonged to Ann Tranz. Your car was also spotted last month in an abandoned garage about a hundred miles from here. Since it wasn't reported stolen and you hadn't yet been reported as missing, the report didn't go anywhere. Not right away."

My mind raced for a new lie to cover my first one. "Look, I'm writing a book." I looked around the room, searching for a direction to take this opening gambit. "I made up the Buddhist story for my students." I still didn't know where I was going with this story.

"Look," Agent #2 broke in. "We know you didn't go to Thailand. We want to know where you were for the six weeks you were missing."

I wasn't very good at this, I realized. Once again, I was wringing my hands. "I was on the streets. I was facing death. I had given up. I would go to the West Side Catholic Church every day and pray. I still can't explain it."

The two agents looked at each other, obviously aware I was grasping at straws, making up any story I thought would be hard to prove false. "OK, Mr. Peregrine," #1 said, "We're going to tell you what we think happened and you can let us know if this rings true for you. You were contacted, coerced or kidnapped by Afina Annete Nalin. She goes by the name Ann. We've been after her for almost a year. She's wanted for questioning in the disappearances of sixteen people who've been diagnosed with late stages of cancer."

The expression on my face must have said everything.

Both agents nodded with that silly cop grin, acknowledging to each other that I'd confirmed their theory. "Look, we know she's saving people's lives," #2 said. "But they're not all happy endings. At least two of her patients never regained consciousness. There's a right way to do things" and he left the alternative unspoken. "We just want to talk to her."

I could see through his good-cop act; I knew he was lying. They wanted to arrest Ann and hand her over to bureaucrats who would tell her why she can't do what she's doing.

"Still want to stick to your church story, Mr. Peregrine?"

"Hey, do you know that over two thousand people die of cancer every day?" I hadn't planned to say this; it just came out. I must have sounded pretty crazy at that point. I looked from #1 to #2 and then back again. "That's more than one every minute. Another dozen people have died just while you've been sitting here, judging Ann."

The quieter agent—#1—stood and started looking around the house while #2 kept up the questions.

I couldn't watch them both, so I kept my eyes on the one in front of me.

"We've talked to your publisher," he told me. "He says you have a book here telling all about your little adventures over the last six weeks."

I didn't answer, but twisted my head to see where the other suit was going. "Hey, don't you need a warrant to search my house?"

He reached into his jacket pocket, pulled out a folded piece of paper and slapped it onto the counter.

My forehead was perspiring; I began to massage it.

The first agent was standing over the stack of nearly twenty spiral notebooks on the kitchen table. Motioning for #2 to check it out, #1 picked up the first notebook and read aloud: "The Traveler." He shuffled to the third notebook, thumbed to a middle page and read a few lines.

"'My heart pounded. Ann was telling me to relax and that she needed to take my vitals. She wrapped a blood pressure thingy around my arm and began to pump it up. For the first time, it was apparent that I was either about to take the trip of a lifetime or, more likely, about to be taken for $8,000 and put to sleep forever, here in the middle of nowhere.'"

"We've checked your bank records," agent #1 said while #2 began to bag up my notebooks. "There's no record of any daily transactions like food or gas. Just three $8,000 bumps and this $12,000 bump. What did you spend this money on?"

I felt defeated, but I wasn't quite ready to surrender. "I gave it away." I let a moment go by and added, "I think you should go now."

The two agents walked to the door with all eighteen of my spiral notebooks. "We're going to have to take this as evidence, Mr. Peregrine. So far it doesn't look like you've done anything that could get you into too much trouble." He waited a beat. "Unless we find out differently in these notes."

I sighed but remained silent.

"Look, we just want to catch this Doctor Ann. If we still need your help after reading these journals, you can expect to see us again real soon. In the meantime, don't go getting into trouble. Stay close to home. And don't try contacting Ann. That would piss me off. I would nail you for interfering with an investigation, aiding and abetting, conspiracy and anything else I can think of to make your new life miserable."

I closed the door and felt for the thumb drive in my pants pocket. I called Dave to ask about his encounter with the FBI.

"They must have been watching your house," he said. "I noticed them following me this morning. When I got to my office they stopped me in the parking lot. I told them I was your editor; they wanted to know what your book was about. I told them to buy a copy when it comes out. I swear, Tim, I didn't tell them anything."

I ran a hand through my hair and tried to massage my tense neck. "Do they know about the thumb drive?" I whispered this, suddenly wondering if my phone was tapped. "Send it to print! Tonight!"

"It's not that easy, Tim. I have to format it for paperback. And get press time lined up."

"So format it. Tonight! And schedule the printer, right now! Once the feds read my story, they're going to want to bury it."

By the next morning, I learned, Ann had been arrested. I wondered what would happen to the other patients who were having their versions of Heaven interrupted. I saw Ann and Andrew on TV, being escorted in handcuffs into a black FBI sedan. No sign of Vlad.

When news got out that I was one of the people who'd been "kidnapped," drugged and put into an induced coma, news crews began to show up at my house.

The first time I answered the door, a little blonde woman shoved a microphone in my face. "How long were you held captive?"

Another voice from behind her yelled out, "Did she really cure your cancer?"

By noon there were three TV news vans in the condo's parking lot and by the end of the week at least two hundred people were waiting out there, all wanting to know how Ann had cured me. The FBI had hoped to keep the story out of the news but failed miserably. On day five an envelope was shoved under my door. It was an invitation to go onto the Oprah show. I was offered $40,000 for my exclusive story on her 10 a.m. show the next Monday morning. I would have done it for free, but now that I wasn't about to die, I did need to replenish my bank account. Then thinking about what I might need to spend on lawyers, I countered with $60,000. It took just a couple of hours and the deal was signed. An exclusive interview with Oprah Winfrey.

Meanwhile, Dave quickly got a cover designed for my book. He got a few proof copies printed so I would have something to hold up to Oprah's viewers. As part of the negotiations, Oprah was to immediately get a copy of *The Traveler* so she could read it before the interview.

The Oprah interview was a shocker. Millions of people watched as I told them how Ann had figured out how to cure cancer. "We can't let her go to jail. If it wasn't for her courage and willingness to put her reputation on the line, her career... risk jail!" I wasn't speaking full sentences. I was too excited, jumping from one statement to another. "Ann doesn't have cancer. She is doing this for all of us. For all the people that have watched their loved ones dwindle away to nothing. We need to celebrate her courage, not punish it."

Oprah touched my hand. "What would you like to tell Ann and her staff?

"I'm sorry that I got you caught. You've given me a new life and in return, I've ruined yours and I've ended the lives of all the people who are going to die before all that over-monitored testing can be completed. I had Stage 4 cancer. I was told there was no hope; I was told to get my affairs in order. Ann may not be going about this by the book. But... two thousand people die of cancer every day. That's more than one every minute. Another forty people will die of cancer just during this half-hour segment." Oprah touched my hand again, this time smiling. "We have someone here that wants to meet you." I figured it would be one of the other cancer survivors. When Sally walked out on stage, I broke down. She was beautiful, just like in the simulation. She swallowed me up with a hug and I bawled on her shoulder.

Oprah held up my book. "'*The Traveler* by Tim Peregrine will be available any day now from Amazon and at your local bookstores." She kept the book up as the camera zoomed in. "We have thirty seconds left, Mr. Peregrine. Is there anything else you would like to say?" The camera zoomed off the book and panned to a close-up of Sally and me, now holding hands.

"Yes," I said, wiping my wet face with my sleeve. "I would like to ask people to rise up for Ann. She is a brilliant woman with a cure for cancer. This woman shouldn't be in jail. Every medical mind should be reaching out to share in her discovery. She deserves a Nobel Prize... not a jail cell. Please! Let's put cancer behind us."

\* \* \*

My book came out two weeks before Ann's trial was to begin. The book flew off the shelves. It was immediately a best seller.

As my story gained national and then international attention, it made news headlines everywhere: A team in Cleveland that took people right from the streets, people with cancer, and returned them cancer-free. The day the trial began, fourteen of those now cancer-free test subjects showed up in the courtroom. The prosecution focused on the two patients who had never regained consciousness.

Despite their best efforts to find unbiased jurors, the prosecutors had to contend with a jury that was obviously sympathetic to anyone trying to cure a deadly disease. They had to focus on the potential risks if they were to win over the jury.

As the trial went on, the defense brought the survivors to the witness stand, one at a time. As each one told their story, it became evident that we had all been willing participants, eager to escape the pain of a slow death from debilitating late-stage cancer. The trial became a spectacle, with big crowds forming outside the courthouse every day. Many carried signs: "SAINT ANN HAS THE CURE." "Ann's Kryptonite." "No Jail." "SAVE MY BOY." The public clamor swayed the jury—and did wonders for book sales. It seems everyone was watching the trial on TV. In an attempt to make a point, the prosecution attempted to bring in one of the comatose patients. As his motionless body was jostled from an ambulance, he awoke. His wife insisted that he be removed from the courthouse and brought right to the hospital. The trial was suspended for three days. Within that three-day period, the patient was stabilized, and his condition was verified: free of cancer. His wife immediately dropped the charges against Ann and sang her praises on national TV. "Ann gave me my husband back!"

Ann had been charged with an assortment of offenses from kidnapping to administering illegal drugs without consent. However, every patient agreed that they had consented to the treatments. We had agreed to pay large sums for our travels and had no regrets, even before we knew we were being cured of cancer. The prosecution finally dropped the charges at the request of the one remaining comatose patient's family. The Cleveland Clinic had offered to donate sixty million dollars to Ann's research and, in the meantime, give that one unlucky patient the best possible care and treatment at no charge, as long as was needed.

Ann accepted a requirement that she do ten years of community service. That meant she had to work an eight-hour shift, five days a week, at the Cleveland Clinic.

With Ann's help, over the next two years, the brilliant folks there sponsored and set up wing after wing to conduct clinical trials on late-stage cancer patients. Ann's procedure proved to be safe and painless, with a 97 percent success rate. Cancer, once diagnosed, was no longer a certain death sentence. Dedicated cancer treatment facilities sprang up all over the world. I wanted to call them "Travel Lodges" but the idea was shot down for fear of a lawsuit from Travel Lodge Hotel Chain. By year three, as the procedures were perfected, in-home treatment facilities were quickly marketed, permitting families to keep their loved ones at home during the four to six weeks the treatments required.

Andrew continued to develop his cutting-edge simulations and became a billionaire.

Vlad disappeared just before the raid. Ann told me that he'd made off with a hundred and ten thousand in cash that she'd kept in the lab. I mused over the fact that he had tried to take a short cut or quick fix to gain wealth as so many do in life. Rumor has it that he ended up in Chelyabinsk, his home town in Siberia, where he runs a Wild West-themed bar called the Cactus Club. Sometimes, I picture him leaning over the bar, serving drinks and chatting with his customers. I wonder what he calls them.

Sally and I are planning to get married. I have given up teaching, choosing a writer's life in its place. I often receive letters from my former students thanking me for impacting their lives with my creative teaching methods and calling me their hero for being a part of the cure for cancer. It always touches me, but I don't let it go to my head. I'm not up for another life lesson. I'm content with my new lease on life, my new purpose, and my Sally. Life is good.

Millions of copies of *The Traveler* have sold, and it is touted as the book that revealed this miraculous cure to the world. This is that book. And I am *The Traveler.*

# # #

THE END

Thank you for reading my book. If you enjoyed it, won't you please take a moment to leave me a review at your favorite retailer?

Thanks!
Rick Incorvia

Other books by Rick Incorvia:

*In Your Dreams*
*When I'm Gone*
*Reckless Ambition*
*The Gift*

Amazon.com

**Connect with the author**

**Website**: authorrickincorvia.com

**Blog**: authorrickincorvia.com/blog/

Interested in author insights, tips for new authors, prize drawings for readers, or what's going on in the head of author Rick Incorvia these days?
**Stay tuned by joining our list**: bit.ly/email-connect

*Read on ...*

# When I'm GONE

## Rick Incorvia

**When I'm Gone**
by Rick Incorvia


Chapter 1- Life After Death


What a great life we had. We were the best of partners. Hell, we had known each other since we were 15. We were married by 19 and bought our first house at 21. We discovered life together. We planned to grow old together. It killed me to see her so sad.

Now she spends her days sitting in front of my clunky old desktop computer. Sometimes she doesn't even turn it on. When she does, it's to respond to sad emails from people trying to comfort her. Unopened bills pile up on the far end of the desk. Today she is lost somewhere deep in her mind, doodling an endless spiral on a used envelope.

I met Maria at the sophomore dance in 1976. She was sitting alone in the hallway; her hands covered her puffy, tear-filled eyes and the sound of Nazareth's hit "Love Hurts" thumped in the background through the gymnasium walls. Bobby Randolph had just broken up with her for the third time that year. I had gone to the dance with my neighbor Lisa, but just to help her get Tim Ricker's attention.

Maria and I became the best of friends. We occasionally dated other people for short periods of time, but by 11th grade it was obvious that we were more than just friends. I made her laugh. I got her to do things she never thought she would. We dedicated the next 30 years to helping each other live, love, and laugh together. A moment of distraction while driving changed everything.

I spoke her name for the 20th time, knowing full well that she wouldn't hear me this time either. "Maria, I'm here." As I expected, there was no response from her, but this time the ears of our eight-year-old boxer perked to attention when I spoke. I had been trying to get Maria's attention for two days. Was it possible that the dog sensed me?

"Hey Murphy, can you hear me?"

Murphy sprang to an attentive sitting position and looked in my direction. She seemed to be able to see me, or at least hear me. "Hey girl, you can hear me, can't you"? Murphy barked a response that immediately initiated a reaction from my grieving wife. "Shh, go lie down," she said with a wave of her hand. Her sadness was unbearable.

I knelt down on one knee to acknowledge my loyal four-legged friend and she looked at me with scared eyes. I tried to embrace her with my new frail ghost of a body. Her head tilted in confusion as my hands drifted through her. I tried to scratch her chin like I used to, to no avail. However, I did notice the hair on her neck stood straight up.

I had worked hard over the last few days to develop minimal control over my new spirit body, but now I felt it draining. Murphy whined and lay down with a sigh. I felt weak and my vision started to blur. I attempted to hold onto the back of Maria's chair and I nearly fell over when my hand drifted right through it.

I was determined to communicate with another living being. I called out to my four-legged friend again, "Murphy." She stood and looked at me with a mixture of sadness, confusion, and exhaustion. I leaned into her and tried to stroke her back again. Her fur stood up as if a balloon had been rubbed on it, charging it with static. I knew she felt me. She probably would have been able to see me too, if she could have kept her eyes open. Her back legs wobbled, then buckled, and she quickly went to a sitting position. My balance shifted again and I tried to stop my fall by stabilizing myself on her back. I fell right onto her. I must have blacked out for a moment. When my eyes opened again, I was looking up from the ground. My vision had been reduced to black and white.

I stood quickly in an attempt to figure out what was happening to me. I looked at my reflection in the sliding glass door. I was now only two feet tall and I had a wet, black nose. Somehow, I had entered Murphy's body. This should have concerned me, but my first thought was that this was an opportunity to communicate with Maria. I attempted to say her name, but only a soft barrage of whining, barking noises came out. "Not now girl, go lie down," Maria responded, still twirling her pen absentmindedly.

My new sad doggie eyes looked at her, again with a soft whining sigh. Her small hand reached down. "I know, girl. I miss him too," she mumbled through bloodshot eyes and pouty lips.

Her touch felt so good. My eyes felt heavy with contentment and occasional blinks gave way to closed eyes. She kept scratching my head, but her mind was elsewhere. Whenever the scratching slowed down, I would nudge her hand to keep the connection.

My every instinct was to stay by her side. I was about to lie down at her feet when I heard a car approaching the long driveway. I was amazed that I was able to hear the car from so far away.

My ears lifted, and I rose to all fours and headed to the big sliding glass doors facing the front of the house. My thoughts said, "there is a car coming up the driveway," but the noise from my pushed-in boxer face just said, "woof." "Shh, that's enough," Maria responded, her tone assuring me that the visitor was not just expected, but welcome.

I watched Maria toss dishes from the sink into the dishwasher and wipe off the counter in the short time that it took her mother to come up the driveway and get out of her car. She came in the back door and set her oversized purse on the still wet, but now clean, counter. They exchanged a long, silent hug. Her mother finally eased Maria away and gently held her sad face in her chubby hands. A single tear made its way down Maria's face. "I know, honey, I know," whispered her mother.

I followed them everywhere, limited by my new canine form, wishing for a way to let them know I was still here. I barked and did my best loyal dog look to my mother-in-law. "I see you, Murphy," she muttered as she patted my bony head and quickly dismissed me.

My mother-in-law began to give Maria the same advice she had been given a hundred times in the last week. "I know it's hard, honey, but you have to keep yourself busy and start thinking about the future. He's not coming back." I yelped "I'm right here" in dog language.

"Mom, will you let Murphy out?" she huffed in a slightly angry voice.

A part of me was frustrated that they couldn't understand me, but another part of me, for some unknown reason, was excited to be going outside. I became aware of my stubby tail wagging out of control.

The moment the door opened, I bolted outside and discovered a whole new world of smells. The view was different from two feet off the ground. I immediately sniffed the fragrant grill. I knew nothing had been cooked on it in weeks, but it still smelled delicious. The view from dog level was of the dirty underside of the grill. The drip tray was overflowing and hardened burger fat had accumulated on the wheel base.

A fat yellow and black bee buzzed by on its way to the flower garden. The flowers weren't as colorful as I remembered, but they smelled magnificent. I took a moment to take in the once-familiar back yard from this new perspective. For a slight moment, I panicked, thinking I should stay close to Maria. Then I got distracted by a falling leaf heading my direction. I was on another planet. I was a four-legged smelling machine. It was as if I could spot something in the yard, point my nose in that direction, and actually smell the bush, the grass, the tree, or even the individual flowers.

I charged the falling leaf and jumped a good three feet off the ground. I caught the dancing leaf in my mouth and felt my muscular body gliding through the air, all the while adjusting in preparation of the landing. I nailed it. I spit out the leaf and stomped on it, then looked for another challenger.

A large monarch butterfly fluttered gracefully just above me. I stuck my nose in the air and inhaled with focus. Each flap of the tiny fairy's wings whipped up a slightly different mix of fragrances. I closed my eyes and exhaled slowly.

I heard tiny claws rustling quickly around one of the many trees in the back yard. I recognized the sound as squirrels chasing each other even before I saw them. I put my nose to the ground and began to sniff. I could tell when I crossed another animal's path. I picked up the trail of something fairly wild. I knew by the smell that it wasn't a cat or the neighbor's dog. If I had to guess, I would bet raccoon or opossum.

I followed the scent to the end of the property line. To continue, I would have had to dig under the fence. It was a thought, even an urge, but I fought it off and decided instead to test out my skills romping through the three-foot-tall grass near the back of the property. I was a beast. I tore through the patch of grass and burst into the open like a lion. My agility was like nothing I'd ever imagined. At full speed, I could dart left or right and nearly stop on a dime.

I did two laps around the yard at full speed before stopping to catch my breath and admire my accomplishments. I trotted down the stone driveway to the front yard. This area was normally forbidden to Murphy (but I wasn't Murphy); she was just a bit too intimidating to people passing by, since there was no fence to keep her in the yard. Truth be told, she was harmless. I was just starting to investigate the area under the front porch when I heard the back door open.

"Murphy! C'mon girl," called Maria in a soft voice from the back door. I peed quickly since this might be my only opportunity for a while, and headed back up the driveway toward the back yard. When Maria saw me, she gave me the evil eye for leaving the back yard.

I trotted through the back door enthusiastically, half-expecting a warm welcome and a scratch behind the ears. Instead, I noticed that Maria had a cell phone to her ear and barely acknowledged me as I entered the house.

Her mother had Maria making calls to the insurance company, the power company, and an assortment of other companies to help her wrap up loose ends. She was all business and I knew I wouldn't get a moment of Maria's time until her mother left.

I listened as her mother listed off tasks that I knew needed to be taken care of, but I still felt she was too cold and calculating, almost hurrying to get everything out of my name. I guess I was secretly hoping to hear them say what a great guy I was and how much I would be missed. I wasn't ready to admit that I was really gone.

I grew bored of their conversation and decided to lie down out of range of her mother's voice, as if that was possible. I laughed a dog's laugh on my way to the fairly dirty and smelly dog bed, thinking how rude it was that we didn't wash it as often as we had our own bed sheets. I instinctively circled the bed before settling down for my nap.

When I heard Maria's mother saying her goodbyes, I rose excitedly to escort her to the door. Maria hugged her and she was out the door. She didn't acknowledge me, or should I say Murphy. It was getting confusing.

I followed Maria around the house as she threw a load of clothes into the washing machine and then went into the bathroom. I considered peeing in the toilet and then flushing to get her attention, but I didn't think she was ready for that.

I followed her to the bedroom and watched her change into one of "my" oversized t-shirts. She stopped to smell the collar before pulling it down over her shoulders and past her waist. She pulled back the covers on her side of the king size bed, careful not to disturb the other half. Murphy was never allowed to sleep on the bed before, but I was hoping Maria would make an exception tonight.

I hopped up as gently as I could and crept toward her. My head was on her stomach before she even realized I was on the bed. She looked at me with surprise and said my name in a voice that was meant to sound disapproving, but it didn't fool me. I gave her my sweetest eyes and snuggled in closer.

"Hi Murphy," she said in her warmest voice. My tail began to wag and a sense of calm overtook my body when her right hand rested on my head. "I suppose you can stay here tonight, but don't tell Daddy." We had a silent moment, and then I felt her tummy start to vibrate. Her left hand tried to cover her face, which was crinkled in anguish. She quietly cried herself to sleep with her warm hand on my bony head.

I spent the night snuggled up to her, wishing I hadn't taken the last few years for granted.

Maria slept much later than I expected, but then again, I had always been the early bird. By six o'clock I had already checked out every part of the house that I could get to, sniffing and scratching all the while. My human brain seemed intact, but the animal instincts were getting stronger. By eight I was considering eating the disgusting dog food from the bowl that was way past due for a washing. At first the water tasted bad, but it was more of a mental thing. I got over it, but it sure took a long time to get my fill using just my tongue to lap it up.

By nine I was ready to risk waking Maria up. I needed to be her best friend. I wanted to feel her touch again or go on a car ride to the park, but I'd settle for a pat on the head.

I jumped back onto the bed and nudged her behind with my nose. She pushed me away, grumbling in an inaudible voice. I jumped off the bed and barked twice. It worked for Murphy every morning when she wanted to go outside to do her business.

"Okay, okay, I'm getting up. Hold your horses!" She peeled back the covers and threw her legs over the side of the bed. She sat on the edge of the bed a little too long, forcing me to let out another bark. "Okay, okay, hold on," she mumbled. She stumbled to the kitchen and turned the coffeemaker on. I was unintentionally right under her feet, waiting patiently for her to acknowledge me. She nearly tripped on me trying to retrieve yesterday's coffee cup from the other side of the sink.

"Murphy! Back off!" She hadn't been awake for two minutes and already she was pissed at me. "Give me a damn minute. You have food, you have water. What more do you want?"

I tried to tell her with my eyes that all I wanted was her love. "C'mon girl, let's go outside." I got so excited that I started to bounce like a deer in a field. It sounded like she was going to come out with me.

She grabbed a cup of coffee and followed me to the back door. When she opened it, I bolted out so excitedly that I made her spill her coffee. "Murphy," she yelled, "ya clumsy oaf!" Not a good start. As she checked her shirt for a coffee stain, she closed the door and disappeared back inside.

I dropped my head in disappointment for just a moment, but I was promptly distracted by the smell of a new creature. Even the fenced-in part of the yard was pretty big and it wasn't unusual for a rabbit or a cat to wander in.

As I eyed the shed in the corner of the yard, my back legs automatically gave way to a squat and I was urinating. The smell was pungent, but my concentration and urination were both interrupted by an annoying dragonfly that seemed determined to get my attention.

I watched him fly overhead, impressed that he was able to move like a skilled helicopter pilot. He came dangerously close to me. If I had arms and hands, I would have slapped him away. Instead, I froze as he closed in to my level. His big eyes came within inches of mine and I could hear his wings humming. Without warning he landed on my nose. I was a bit surprised and taken aback. We stared at each other. My eyes crossed as I looked first at his right eye and then his left.

With every passing second, I was more assured that the dragonfly had a message for me. He buzzed his wings at a slow rate and then suddenly stopped, settling on the tight arch of my boxer nose. I thought about swiping him off with my front leg that is apparently meant to act as an arm in some cases, but I didn't do anything. I couldn't. I was suddenly weak and tired, feeling the same draining of energy that I had when I entered Murphy's body. My back legs gave way first, but my front legs weren't far behind. I couldn't focus on anything other than the dragonfly's enormous bug eyes.

My life force was moving from my four-legged body to this tiny, big-eyed, winged creature. When my strength and awareness returned, I was looking Murphy in the eyes. She looked as confused as I felt.

With nothing more than thought, I began to vibrate my new wings and took to the sky. I felt so light; I was able to hover, fly forward or backward, or dart in any direction. Each eye functioned independently and gave me the ability to comprehend both visual worlds at once. My best friend, Murphy, watched me. I acknowledged her with what I thought was a smile.

My new body consumed me. I had always dreamed of flying, but as a human. I still had the ability to think as a human. I wanted to fly higher. It felt like some unbelievable dream or vacation of a lifetime and I liked it. I liked it a lot!

It took very little effort to master the flight manual of the dragonfly. Below me, I saw the wooded field I knew as my back yard. I signaled one last goodbye to Murphy and began to investigate my new world.

This new form certainly wasn't going to help me communicate with Maria. She was obsessed with dragonflies, but not in a good way. She would swat me out of the sky and pin me to a corkboard to examine me. For a brief moment, I welcomed the thought of her undivided attention, but I knew she would eventually grow tired of my Christ-like pose. I would end up unpinned and released back into the outdoors where ants would gobble up my dried-out carcass.

A soft rain began to fall, but I avoided the huge globs of water with minimal effort. Even in the rain my vision was amazing. A swarm of mosquitoes tried to avoid me on their search for shelter from the rain. I snatched one of them out of the sky with a stealthy movement and began to crunch his tiny body. I watched his friends quickly react to my predatory actions with my left eye and dodged another huge raindrop using my right eye. I was astonished at my visual ability and unsurpassed flight control. I decided to test out my new wings further.

I picked up speed, easily avoiding the now-steady bombing of raindrops. I could fly even faster than I had imagined, all the while documenting scenery from each eye independently. A distant flash of lightning caught my brilliant new eyes and I instinctively began to count the seconds while I waited for the ensuing boom of thunder. For the first time, I noticed that sound was not a part of this new life. I slowed down to scan the woods below for another opportunity to test my hearing. I hovered easily above the treetops, able to move in every direction and pick out potential shelters, food opportunities, and even distant predators that had also spotted me as their food source. I landed under a large leaf and listened for the sounds of the forest. I could start and stop my wings almost instantly and at an amazing flap rate. But still, I heard no sound.

My right eye caught a glimpse of a cardinal stealthily closing in on me from a few trees over and I instantly took flight deeper into the thick vegetation to discourage his pursuit.

The rain continued, but the raindrops seemed much larger and farther apart in this new life form. Steady streams of water rushed from the center vein of select leaves. These small waterfalls were visible from as many places as my two curious eyes could see.

I watched an armadillo scramble through the thick brush and was reminded that as a human, I could hear the creatures of the forest well before I spotted them with my eyes. I decided to follow this solitary creature, curious to find out just where he would disappear to. His progress was slow, and my mind wandered to the suddenly active woods. The rain had stopped as fast as it had started and the air was thick and moist.

Two bees emerged from the trunk of an old rotted tree and teamed up against me like bullies on the school playground. Their eyes were angry as they took turns hovering higher and lower in front of me. I wondered how their tiny wings could support those fat bodies. The bigger of the two bees got uncomfortably close. I've always been intimidated by bees, even when

I was a human and thousands of times their size. As equals, they were absolutely terrifying, with hundreds, even thousands of friends, ready to join their fight. I must have flown too close to their queen or entered the playground of their larvae. They chased me for a short distance, but they were no match for my new speed or agility.

Suddenly I emerged from the woods to see the most beautiful sight my new eyes had ever seen. Instead of trees and dirt, a glimmering pond reflected the now-blue sky and puffy white clouds. I flew to the center of the pond, felt the change in temperature, and saw moisture rising from the water.

I saw another dragonfly in the distance. She landed on a single blade of grass sticking out of the pond near the water's edge. She obviously spotted me with one of her darting eyes, but did not acknowledge me. She left the tall blade of grass and began to fly closer. It was captivating to see her dip her long tail into the pond as she flew. Maybe she was testing the water like humans do. Suddenly she landed right on the water! She looked at me with both eyes as if she knew I was a human wearing a dragonfly costume. I hovered closer and closer to the water. Although I couldn't hear, my exceptional vision enabled me to see the life under the water. I saw first one small fish, and then many fish, swimming about or hiding behind plants, avoiding aquatic bullies of their own.

As I got close enough to land, I was met by a celestial creature. It was my own reflection in the pond's surface. My wings were long, vibrating masterfully in unison unlike any flying machine ever created by humans. With a mere thought my iridescent wings instantly stopped beating and I settled on the pond. My wings were brilliantly colored and changed with every movement. A momentary buzz of wing power sent me skating across the pond like an Olympic skater. No, it was more than that. I was a god, walking on water.

I began to put on a show for the fish below and noticed that I quickly gained an audience. I wasn't sure if they were admiring my beauty and elegance, or sizing me up as a meal. I was amused by how they followed my every movement. If I darted right, all heads followed me. I darted left and then right again, and laughed a silent dragonfly laugh as I compared their reaction to cats watching a game of ping pong.

I recognized most of the fish as bluegills or catfish, but could not help but notice a fairly large, bright yellow and red koi. It looked like an oversized version of the many goldfish I had had as a child. This magnificent underwater creature moved slowly closer with all the cunning of an alligator. His eyes hypnotized me and I did not fly away, even as he got dangerously close. We seemed to have a mutual admiration for each other. I felt as if he wondered what it would be like to fly, as I was wondering what it would be like to swim with such ease and discover the secrets of the underwater world.

He came still closer, ever so slowly. If I could hear, I was sure he would be saying, "it's okay, I'm not going to hurt you." I sensed that I had found another soul that was also human once and wondered if all creatures were powered by the souls of the dead. I vibrated my wings for a moment, skating slowly closer, partially to keep his interest and partially to show him I was not afraid.

He was now close enough to end my short life as a dragonfly. He steadily rose to the surface to greet me. His lips came above the water and he sampled the forbidden air. He dipped back under for a breath of water and eased himself face to face with me. His humanlike curiosity had caught my attention. The urge to touch overcame us both. We locked onto each other's eyes and took a leap of faith.

The other fish stayed back and watched as if they, too, knew he was different. I clung to his upper lip with my two front legs. My consciousness as a dragonfly quickly faded. I felt as if I were dying. My perfect eyes went dark as my grip on his lip loosened. At first, I thought that I was simply being pulled under water.

My vision began to return, but it was very limited and blurry. As my focus returned, I could see the dragonfly was still sitting on top of the pond. I saw the dragonfly buzz a test flight of his wings and look at the new me as if to say, "thank you." I watched my old dragonfly host fly off. It was time to discover the beauty of the world of water....

# # #

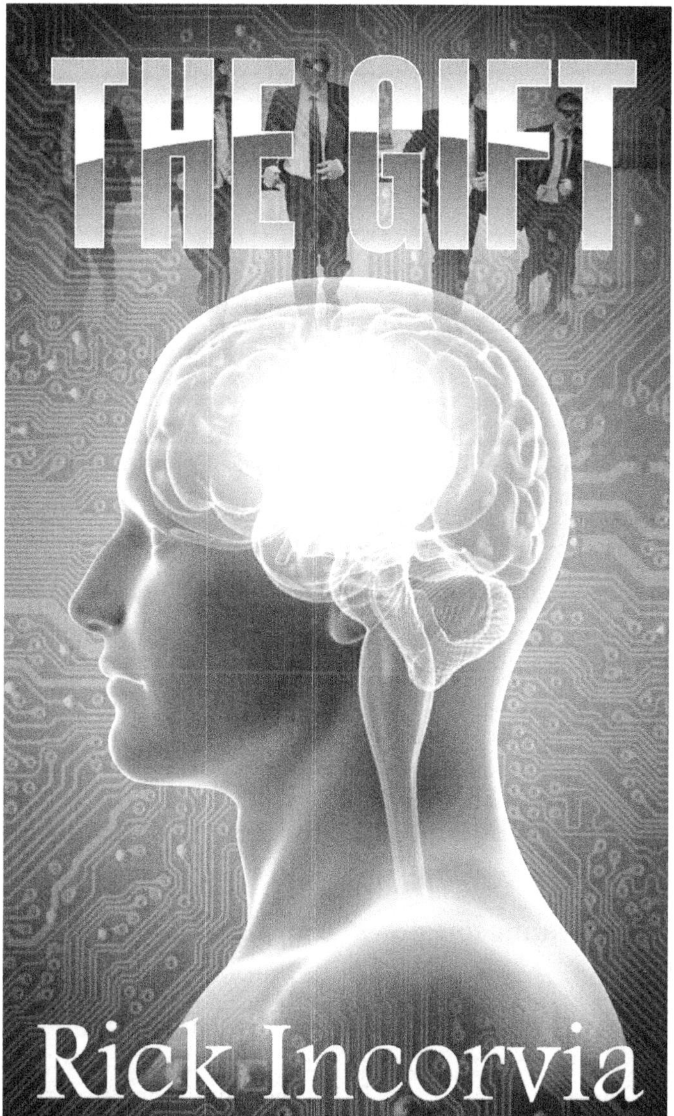
THE GIFT
Rick Incorvia

**The Gift**
by Rick Incorvia

# Chapter 1 - Gift or Curse

When Tim's 5 a.m. alarm buzzed softly, he expected the day to be like every other. He'd have a three-mile run, a healthy breakfast and a long hot shower before he headed in to work.

When the phone rang at 5:05, he knew something was wrong. His staff knew not to bother him before 8. That was his "private time."

"Hello, Tim speaking."

The line was silent long enough for him to consider hanging up. "Tim Kerbric?" a deep voice asked.

"Who wants to know?" Tim replied with a bit of attitude.

"This is Sergeant Jenkins at the Beacon City police department. I'm afraid we have some bad news." Again silence, as if he was waiting for Tim to ask a question. Tim waited patiently. "There's been an accident. Well, more like an incident."

Okay, now he had Tim's attention. "Well, are you going to tell me or make me guess?" Tim glowered as if the voice on the other end could see how irritated he was. "I'm sorry, Mr. Kerbric. I understand you were good friends with Hoyt Pendleton. May I ask when was the last time you saw him?"

"You certainly can ask, but you're not getting another word out of me until you tell me what the hell this is all about. You do know it's 5 o'clock in the morning." Tim hesitated, tightening his grip on the phone and wrinkling up his forehead. *Why won't this cop tell me what's up with Hoyt?* He was getting angrier by the moment. This was his best friend they were talking about. "Was he in an accident? Is he in some kind of trouble?"

"Actually, Mr. Kerbric, we were hoping he was with you. We got a call from his wife last night. She says a couple of professionals broke into the house and roughed her up a bit.

"Lisa? Lisa is hurt?" A surge of desperation rose in Tim's throat.

"She's fine. She says he might be with you. Something about Thursday night cards with the boys. She says you all play cards every Thursday. What time did Hoyt leave your place last night?"

"What? Wait," Tim stammered. "I haven't seen Hoyt in months."

The line remained silent.

"Said they were looking for something they called 'The Gift.' Any idea what they meant by 'The Gift'?"

"What? No!" None of this was making any sense. There was more to this story than he was hearing.

After a long moment of silence, Tim demanded, "Who is this?"

The officer muttered slowly, "Like I said, I am Sergeant Jenkins. I can't tell you any more over the phone, Mr. Kerbric, but I think it would be in your best interest to come to the station."

Tim hung up the phone. He tried to wipe the sleep from his face. He dragged his hands through his hair a few times and slipped yesterday's shirt over his head. He pulled a pair of blue jeans from his laundry basket and clumsily hopped on one foot, trying to slip the second foot into the pants leg. By the time he slipped his sockless feet into his black loafers his mind began to catch up with what he'd just heard. *It sounds like someone broke into Hoyt and Lisa's house and Hoyt is still missing.* He wondered if this had been just another fight over Hoyt's obsessive work ethic.

Tim suddenly remembered a call he'd gotten from Hoyt a few days ago. He had sounded out of breath and heavily caffeinated. "I did it, Tim," Hoyt puffed, "I fuckin' did it." Assuming that Hoyt had finally told Lisa he wanted a divorce, Tim had settled in for one of Hoyt's rants. "It's all about the blood flow. Who knew? I'll tell you who knew... I knew, that's who." Just out of the shower, Tim had responded robotically. "Of course you did, Hoyt. You're the smartest guy I know."

Tim had been about to tell Hoyt he'd call him back when Hoyt interrupted. "It's all about basic vitamins, minerals and properly timed frequencies." The guy was uninterruptible. "You have to come over!" Tim could barely hear Hoyt over the treadmill. *That damn treadmill.* Hoyt spent hours on that treadmill every day. He said it helped him think. Hoyt didn't give Tim time to answer. "I gotta go. Call me tomorrow. You're gonna love this."

On the way to the police station, Tim played the conversation over and over in his head. Thinking back, he began to realize that Hoyt had been especially intense lately. He knew Hoyt wasn't the cheating type. The more he thought about the phone call, he figured the lie about Thursday night cards was an excuse to spend time at the lab. Time to work on some kind of breakthrough.

And that got him thinking about another phone conversation, weeks earlier. Hoyt had called him. He'd confided that he was deep into mineral enhancements and absorption rates, which put him on the brink of developing a better mental awareness product. It was sure to put him into the big leagues, he'd insisted. It was hush-hush but was apparently a mix between science and technology. But just as he'd started to tell Tim about his breakthroughs, he'd stopped abruptly. Softly, almost in a whisper, he'd said he couldn't really talk about it yet.

At the station, two cops watched silently as Tim's eyes met Lisa's for the first time. "Oh, my God Lisa! What happened?"

Lisa was breathing hard, her eyes red. She couldn't keep her hands still. "Do you know where he is? I can't find him. I think he's in trouble." Tim hugged her and did his best to calm her.

The police quickly steered them apart into two separate interrogation rooms. "What am I doing in here?" Tim snapped. "Am I a suspect?"

Sergeant Jenkins didn't introduce himself, but Tim recognized him from his deep voice. "A suspect for what? Do you know what happened to Hoyt?" Tim tightened his lips and went silent for a moment. This was the voice from 5:05 a.m., just as annoying in person.

"Do I need my lawyer?"

The officer smiled and chuckled, "No, Mr. Kerbric, I just had to find a quiet place to talk. The station has been a zoo all night, like someone is passing out crazy pills." A fellow cop poked his head in and asked if he could see the sergeant for a minute. Jenkins shot the intruder the "Can't you see I'm busy" look and then slowly proceeded to stand as if it pained him to be on his feet. He was awkwardly tall and sported the typical police belly, no doubt from too much paperwork and too many donuts.

He left Tim alone in the room for nearly twenty minutes. When he finally came back he repeated his crazy pills line from earlier. When Tim had gotten Jenkins' call at 5:05 this morning, he had been aggravated. Now, he was all the way to pissed off. Sergeant Jenkins started talking again. "Look, we're hoping you have something that might help us find Hank."

"His name is Hoyt," snapped Tim, irritated that the officer was either not taking this seriously or just couldn't be bothered. Tim knew Hoyt had borrowed a large amount of "hard money" from some pretty shady guys to develop his "Enhancements" or whatever he was working on. But he had no intention of giving up this information before hearing everything that Lisa had to say.

* * *

Lisa was in the next room struggling through a similar experience. Two officers were in the unusually warm room with her. Officer Melbern was a pudgy older man, stuffed into a cheap wool suit. His five-foot three-inch fireplug of a body was circling the table like a shark. His breathing was labored and he took turns wiping the sweat from his right brow, then his left. Rubbing his palms onto the seat of his pants, he started his questioning. "When did you last see your husband?" When Lisa took too long to answer, he fired another question at her. "What were you two fighting about?"

Lisa backed up her head and blinked her eyes until they were wide open. "Don't even think about accusing me. I'm the one that called you."

Officer Anita Cleveland was a thin, fit woman in her mid-forties. The two officers looked at each other for just a moment and Officer Cleveland spoke up in a soft but firm voice. "These are standard questions that we have to ask the spouse. If not now, it always comes up later. Best if you just answer the questions."

Lisa sat up straight in her chair. "I don't like his attitude... Or the tone in his voice."

When Lisa calmed down, she told the officers that Hoyt had been missing for two days. "It wasn't unusual lately for him to spend the night at the lab. Yes, we'd been arguing some recently and I figured he was spending another night at the lab, obsessing over his latest discovery."

Officer Melbern jumped all over her response. "Another night? How often does your husband stay out all night?"

Lisa inhaled, ready for a heated response, but then recovered, closing her eyes and slowly letting her breath out through her nose.

Officer Cleveland, who up to now had mostly listened silently, started to jot down notes. This got Lisa nervous again. She sat back in her chair and folded her arms. After ten seconds of silence, Officer Cleveland spoke. Her voice was soft, reassuring. "Help us find him." Officer Melbern was standing between his partner and the one-way mirror, hands on his hips. Armpit sweat stained his jacket. Lisa had to close her eyes to stop taking in more details of this human train wreck. She struggled to collect her thoughts.

"I left him a message at the lab last night. It was about 10. I told him if he didn't come home, I was packing his stuff and putting it at the curb." Melbern and Cleveland listened without comment. "I must have fallen asleep around midnight. Later that night, I heard the door open and I figuring it was Hoyt trying to sneak in all quiet. I prepared myself for what you would call a little domestic quarrel" she said throwing a smug look at officer Melbern. "Then suddenly something bashed me on the head. I must have blacked out. When I started to come to, I could hear that someone was rummaging through every drawer in the house. And then I remember a guy yelling 'C'mon, let's go.' That's when somebody—it must have been a second guy—grabbed me by my hair. I couldn't see him, but he whispered in my ear, 'Where is "The Gift"?' I was too stunned and too scared to talk and that's when he hit me. It was a cell phone, I think."

She instinctively touched the gash over her right eye, indicating that it was the second of the two gashes she'd gotten. The officers who showed up to the scene had cleaned her up and put butterfly bandages over her wounds before taking her to the station.

"When was the last time you saw your husband?"

Lisa snapped, "I told you. Two days ago."

The annoying cop continued his harassing tone. "And remind me: what were you fighting about?"

Lisa flipped him a subtle middle finger and said, "Take me home." She could see the two were looking at each other and thinking: *domestic issue.*

As they left the interrogation room Officer Cleveland suggested that Lisa check into the hospital. Lisa insisted on waiting for Tim and sat, arms folded, across from Officer Cleveland's desk. Ten agonizing minutes passed.

\* \* \*

Tim walked around the corner, hoping Lisa was still at the station. Officer Cleveland stood to greet him. She asked if he would be willing to swing past the hospital with Lisa to have her checked over. Tim nodded his head, silently agreeing, and mumbled under his breath. "C'mon, let's get out of here."

Officer Melbern, who was one desk over, had to get his last words in. "Stick around. We may have more questions for you" Tim could tell these cops weren't even sure a crime had been committed. Just inside the exit doors, Tim and Lisa gave the right of way to two cops who were struggling with an angry and slurring man of enormous size.

Giving this trio a wide berth, Tim grabbed both of Lisa's arms to get her attention off the cops and back to him. "Have you been to the lab?" Tim winced as he studied her banged-up face.

"No, I haven't been to the lab." Lisa widened her bloodshot eyes and pointed to her face. "In case you haven't noticed, I am a victim and these guys are questioning me like I did something. I know Hoyt is in trouble. He hasn't answered his phone in two days." Lisa brought her voice down to a whisper. "What is 'The Gift'?"

Tim just shook his head. He looked dumbfounded. He remembered Hoyt's words from earlier in the week. *"I did it, Tim... I fuckin' did it."*

His expression must have changed enough for Lisa to notice. She raised her eyebrow. "What? You know something. Tell me!"

"He told me that he 'did it' but I wasn't really listening. I thought you two had a fight and he finally left."

Lisa pulled her head back like she always did before making a statement. "Wait, what? Why would you say that? We're doing fine." This didn't sound convincing. She looked to see if any of the roomful of cops had heard Tim say that. She whispered to him, "We fight, but then we make up. Sometimes, we make up all night long." He was pretty sure from her body language what that meant.

*Atta boy, Hoyt.* Tim knew he'd better keep that thought to himself.

He led Lisa outside so they could continue their conversation without being overheard.

Lisa started right back at Tim. "Tell me exactly what he said to you."

Tim walked a few steps and then stopped. "I don't remember exactly." He paused a moment. "He said, 'I fuckin' did it!'" Tim closed his eyes and mimed holding a phone to his left ear. "Wait; then he said something about vitamins and minerals. But he was way too excited for whatever it was to be about; a better vitamin C tablet or a new dissolvable capsule. It sounded like he'd made a big breakthrough. Shit, I should have listened to him. I should have come to the lab."

Tim and Caroline used to hang out with Hoyt and Lisa every weekend. About five years before, Caroline had been diagnosed with cancer—the bad kind, non-small-cell lung carcinoma. The next two years were tough, consumed with chemo, special diets and vitamins. Hoyt had Tim's wife on a barrage of immune system builders, but in the end, the cancer still won. Tim didn't blame Hoyt, but he was still mad at him for giving him hope. Tim had stopped believing in magic pills and had never quite been able to get so involved again with Hoyt's latest vitamin hype. Hoyt and Lisa had still tried to invite Tim to events, but Tim felt more and more like a third wheel and began burying himself in his work. And all that, he reflected guiltily, had kept him from paying much attention to Hoyt lately.

"I'm not going to the hospital," Lisa said. After insisting that Tim come back to the house with her, she began to shake her head back and forth ever so slightly. "All I did was bitch at him for working late. We would be fighting within thirty minutes of him coming home. He'd disappear into the workout room and run forever on that stupid treadmill."

"He has a treadmill at home, too?" Tim asked. "Oh, my God. Are you kidding me?"

"He puts on that damn hat with the headphones and runs for hours," she continued. "Then he showers and comes to bed looking for action. Honestly, sometimes I think he's in there watching porn."

Tim pulled at his bottom lip. "Do you know what he listens to?" he asked.

"He says Mozart. Says it helps him unwind. But last week, I think he was learning another language."

"Another language..." This left Tim speechless for a moment. "Why would you say that?"

Lisa was wringing her hands. "I thought he was cheating on me or listening to a dirty-talk 800 number. Why else would he suddenly be so sexual? One night last week, I thought he had someone in there with him. I heard him speaking Italian—I think it was Italian—and it was a conversation, not just repeating a few words, or some sentence he'd rehearsed. I got closer to the door and I could tell it was his voice, so I thought he was on the phone with someone. How could my husband know another language without me knowing? We've been married for twelve years. I finally knocked on the door and ask him who he was talking to. When he didn't answer me, I opened the door and peeked in. He was wearing his stupid stocking cap with headphones. When he saw me, he yanked a cord out of the cap. It was plugged into his cell phone."

"Wait, he was wearing a stocking cap with headphones?" Tim interrupted. "What, like big noise-canceling headphones? Or earbuds?"

"No, the headphones are built into the cap. He got them off the internet. Wouldn't stop talking about them. Are you going to let me finish?"

She waved off Tim's questions, indicating he should have a little patience. "I asked him who he was talking to. He said he wasn't talking to anyone and that I should respect his privacy when he was in his room. I asked him what language he was speaking, and he just told me he was developing apps for learning. He looked down at his phone and I could see that both of our voices were being recorded. He picked up the phone and clicked a few commands on the keypad. He was yelling, 'Now I have to start from the beginning.'"

"Lisa, is that cap still at your house?" She raised her shoulders and twisted her hands, palms up, to indicate she didn't know. "Obviously, you've tried to call him. Does his phone go to voicemail or just ring?" Tim was firing questions at Lisa faster than she could answer. He reached for his phone and tapped in the three-digit speed-dial to his office number. "Hi, Chris. Yeah. Uh-huh. Listen, I'm not going to make it in to work for the next few days. Can you tell people I'm on vacation? Make up something. Yes! Everything is fine. Oh, I just have some personal stuff to take care of. Okay. Uh-huh. See you Monday."

Tim had made the mental switch to investigator mode. He may have watched too many reruns of CSI but when he pulled up into the driveway, he expected to see cops bustling about gathering clues or at least the door taped off. "Have the police been here yet? Have they dusted for fingerprints?"

Lisa looked at him with one eye raised. "Really, Tim. Yes, they were here, but I was afraid to stay at the house and made them take me to the police station. It was the middle of the night!" Tim was puzzled and opened his mouth to ask another question, but Lisa interrupted.

"They said they would send a squad car to keep an eye on the house, but I don't think they're taking this seriously because nothing was stolen. The cops did come here once, almost a year ago, for that big fight we got into. It was stupid. I'm sure they think this is more of the same thing, like a domestic violence issue. They probably think we had a fight and I'm protecting him or something."

Tim had no comment. He waited, expecting to hear more.

"It's not... right?" Lisa tightened her lips and clenched her fists. Her eyes were like slits and her head moved slightly back and forth as if to say, "How dare you?" Tim wished he could take back the question.

Lisa fumbled with the key. Her hands were shaking. Tim put his hands over hers and eased the key from her. Push, twist and slowly open. He planned to go straight to Hoyt's combined study and workout room but stopped to study the scene just inside the house. A single dining room chair was knocked over. All the knickknacks from the fireplace mantel were scattered, and shattered, across the tile floor. Kitchen drawers hung open and a small potted plant lay dumped into the sink. A long wooden coffee table, snapped in half, lay in a V shape as if someone very large had landed on it. Tim followed the mess into his friends' bedroom. "Wow, they tore up your bedroom."

"Yes, and my office."

"Did they get to his office?" Tim blurted.

Lisa reminded him that she had been in and out of consciousness while the intruders were in the house. "Something spooked them. I don't know how long I was out. But they broke my Noreen coffee table on their way out. When I woke up the second time, they were gone. I sat in front of the door, to be sure they couldn't sneak back in, and I dialed 911. A cop was here in ten minutes, but the guys were long gone. He helped me clean up my face and I asked him to take me to the station to make an official statement. I was afraid to drive there myself." She looked away a few seconds. "But I was more afraid to stay here in case they came back."

Lisa followed Tim to Hoyt's office. The door was open. Lisa hesitated. "This door is never left open." Tim entered, anticipating a disaster like he'd found elsewhere in the house. To his surprise, everything was in order. He was pretty sure no one had made it to Hoyt's office. He scanned the room, seeing plenty of confirmation of what he already knew, which was that Hoyt had a place for everything. On the desk was a note pad with yesterday's date. Below the date was a numbered list. Hoyt numbered everything.

1. Transfer funds

2. Gun

3. Call Tim

Tim picked up the list and showed it to Lisa. The pad of thin, lined paper drooped in his hand as he scanned the room. A hamper near the door overflowed with smelly workout clothes. In the immaculately organized room, it stood out like a sore thumb. Lying on top of the clothes was the stocking cap. Hoyt's phone was still attached.

Tim looked at Lisa and then studied the cap. He eased it over his tightly cropped head and adjusted it so the built-in circular headphones were right over his ears. He flipped the phone over as if it might have a secret button to push. He looked at Lisa for a nod of approval and pushed the "power on" button. He was discouraged to see the lock screen pop up. He turned the phone so Lisa could see the screen. "Of course, Hoyt has a secret code," he said.

"It's 1397."

"Hoyt told you his code?" Tim said, incredulous.

"Of course not. I've been trying to get it from him for the last two months. Something is weird with him. He is so distant and then so loving." Then she registered Tim's puzzled look. "It's the four corners of the pad. I saw him do it last week."

Tim tapped the pad's four corners, 1397. The phone opened to a recording. When Tim pressed the "play" icon, Hoyt's voice was making audio notes, recapping his latest thoughts from the night's work.

"Memory retention and cognitive learning is increased exponentially if you properly prepare to receive knowledge, properly receive knowledge and then lock it in. I believe our brain was designed to retain almost everything we experience with our five senses. I believe that I have uncovered the secret to audible learning with nearly 100 percent retention."

Lisa was all of five-foot-three and on her tip toes, ear to ear with six-foot-two Tim, trying to hear what her missing husband was saying. "I can't hear!" Tim shushed her with a wave of his hand. Lisa responded with a pissed-off glare and stuck her ear back against his.

"June 30th, 2016 notes. Retention is multiplied when we maintain extremely high levels of some basic vitamins and minerals like ascorbic acid, choline bitartrate, resveratrol, blah, blah, blah." Hoyt was famous for using "blah, blah, blah" when he felt he was carrying on about too much detail. "And... and... here's the surprise kicker." On the recording, Hoyt paused for effect. "You must maintain a heart rate of at least 120 beats per minute or higher." He laughed. "No one has figured that out till now. I have recently introduced two hundred fifty milligrams of N-acetyl-cysteine, ten milligrams of pyrroloquinoline quinone and one hundred milligrams of high potency CoQ10 and have been able to run for much longer periods, maintaining a heart rate of 120 to 135 beats per minute for nearly two hours."

Tim paused the recording. "I think we found the 'gift' they're after."

Lisa shook her head as she looked at Tim, as if she couldn't take him seriously with the silly cap on his head. He pushed "play" again. Lisa yanked the speaker plug from the phone and Hoyt's voice came loud and clear directly from the phone, easy for them both to hear. Lisa looked at Tim, a smug twist to her lips. "Take off the hat, dumbass."

Hoyt's voice continued: "The initial challenge with learning while the heart rate is over 120 bpm was that you're moving. Reading while running is not easy, so..." More hesitation and the sound of papers rustling. "So I dipped back into some old subliminal research from the 1970s; a Dr. Zemoremi claimed that certain high-pitched tones prepare the brain to accept audible information and that a specific low tone locks the information into long-term memory. Of course, everyone thought the doc was crazy and his results were weak because he didn't add nutrition into the mix—or the high heart rate. But using his research from a forty-five-year old book, I have been able to dial in the optimal subliminal high tone that opens the brain to learning." After another moment of silence, Hoyt began to speak again. The background noise was different, and Hoyt was obviously recording from somewhere much quieter. "Today is September 20th, 2016. I am amused by my old recordings. I have come so far in the last few months. I can barely contain myself. I have to show this to someone. And I am just about to –"

The recording went silent, except for a distinct rustling that must have been Hoyt taking off the cap. Lisa stared at Tim as if to echo his unspoken question: *Is that it? Is it over?* After what seemed like endless silence, but actually must have been less than a minute, the recording continued. Hoyt spoke in a whisper. "I think someone is in the house." Tim could hear faint noises over Hoyt's shuffling and the movement of his phone. "Shit. Someone *is* in the house." The recording went silent again, for a long time. Tim took the opportunity to turn the volume all the way up. He clearly heard Hoyt open his office door. Lisa caught his eye and nodded; she'd heard it too. After another twenty seconds of background noise, a distant voice faintly but clearly called, "Hoyt, is that you?" Lisa's mouth fell open. She was listening to her own voice from last night. Hoyt's recorded voice softly whispered, "Shit." A bang and clatter meant he must have dropped the phone. Footsteps raced away down the hall, followed by a scuffle and a big thud.

"Oh, my God!" Lisa said. "Hoyt was home last night when those guys came in. They took him!" They both stared at the phone. *Is there more?* A final voice, indistinctly, said, "C'mon, let's go." The phone went silent, this time for keeps.

Lisa closed her eyes and began to tug at a thick lock of her blonde hair. "Oh, God, please let him be OK."

# # #

Made in the USA
Monee, IL
14 July 2022